SAINT NICK
STEALTH OPERATIONS SPECIALISTS
BOOK ONE

ELLE JAMES

TWISTED PAGE INC

Copyright © 2025 by Elle James

All rights reserved.

No part of this book may be reproduced in any form or by any electronic or mechanical means, including information storage and retrieval systems, without written permission from the author, except for the use of brief quotations in a book review.

Without in any way limiting the author's [and publisher's] exclusive rights under copyright, any use of this publication to "train" generative artificial intelligence (AI) technologies to generate text is expressly prohibited. The author reserves all rights to license uses of this work for generative AI training and development of machine learning language models.

ISBN EBOOK: 978-1-62695-675-9

ISBN PAPERBACK: 978-1-62695-676-6

ISBN HARDCOVER: 978-1-62695-677-3

Note: Previously published as Nick of Time by Harlequin Enterprises.

Dedicated to my readers who make my dreams come true by keeping me in the business I love dearly...WRITING! I love you all so much. Thank you for buying my books!
Elle James

AUTHOR'S NOTE

Stealth Operations Specialists Series
Saint Nick (#1)
Rogue (#2)
Crusher (#3)
Draco (#4)

Visit ellejames.com for more titles and release dates
Join her newsletter at
https://ellejames.com/contact/

SAINT NICK

STEALTH OPERATIONS
SPECIALISTS BOOK #1

New York Times & USA Today
Bestselling Author

ELLE JAMES

CHAPTER 1

Nerves prickled on the back of his neck as Nick St. Claire climbed the steps in the Brooklyn apartment building two at a time. The heavy smell of garlic and onion filled the air in front of apartment 12-C, masking any other scents. His stomach growled, but he kept moving down the hallway to 12-H. He hadn't eaten in twelve hours, but now wasn't the time to remember unnecessary details.

His boss and friend, Royce Fontaine, moved on silent feet behind him. As a Stealth Operations Specialist, trained in all forms of warfare, including military operations in urban terrain, Nick understood the necessity of speed and surprise.

This mission wasn't dictated by the government as it had in the past with the SOS agency. They were the new Sealth Operations Specialists, having disassociated from the US government.

With the new president hellbent on widening the divide between the extreme right and the extreme left and using the military to police cities run by the opposing parties, members of SOS resigned and joined forces with Brotherhood Protectors, led by former Navy SEAL, Hank Patterson.

Keeping the SOS team intact, they'd moved headquarters out of Washington to a little town north of San Antonio, Texas.

It would have been faster and easier to fly from DC to NYC than from San Antonio to NYC. Thankfully, SOS had access to Brotherhood Protectors' new private Lear jet which had picked up Nick and Royce at the San Antonio Airport and flown them to a small, general aviation airport in New Jersey. They'd been met with a private car and transported into New York City.

The late-night flight had been in response to an e-mail message from Royce's old Army buddy. "Need your help. Life or death. Come now."

Royce had dropped everything, including an important case regarding death threats against a U.S. senator. He'd grabbed Nick on his way out the door of the SOS offices in Beuer, Texas, shouting for Tazer, one of the very capable female SOS agents, to cover for him while he flew to New York.

When Nick arrived at the door to 12-H, splintered wood didn't bode well for what might be inside. He pulled the SIG Sauer from the shoulder holster beneath his leather jacket and nodded to Royce. Then he leaned his back against the wall and pushed the door open wider.

The room was a shambles. Every piece of furniture was turned over or ripped. Nothing stirred in the living space, but a noise from a back room alerted Nick that they weren't alone.

He slipped in first, followed by Royce. In a low crouch, Nick swept his gaze across the room searching for bogeys before he entered the hallway.

A weak moan echoed off the walls in the bathroom to the right.

The sound of glass shattering was followed by a metallic clanging from the room to the left.

Nick pointed at Royce and then to the bathroom. He then pointed at himself and the room with the clanging noise. Without waiting for his boss's response, Nick leaped over scattered clothing, books and tables and burst into a bedroom, weapon at the ready. Whoever had broken the window was probably down the fire escape by now.

"Not without backup, St. Claire!" Royce hissed behind him.

Nick ignored Royce, not stopping until he reached the window. He paused beside the broken glass, peering around the wooden frame, careful to limit his exposure to gunfire, not at all anxious to take a bullet. The clang of feet jumping down the fire escape stairs assured him that whoever was on them was in a hurry to be gone.

Using the barrel of his weapon, Nick swept the jagged window glass to the side and leaned out just in time to catch a glimpse of a broad-shouldered person dressed in black moving down the metal fire escape of the three-story apartment building. Nick swore. Almost to the ground, the guy would escape into the maze of dark city streets before Nick or Royce could do anything about it.

To hell with that. Nick climbed through the window and descended the steps two at a time. The noise of his shoes hitting the steel was deafening, but not so bad that he didn't hear the ominous popping sound of shots being fired or the ping of bullets ricocheting off the brick near his head. He kept moving. If he stopped, the shooter would have time to make good his aim.

A bullet glanced off the metal railing next to his leg. Another sprayed pieces of masonry over his head.

Nick didn't slow. Gun ready, he hit the ground feet first and performed a perfect airborne drop and roll, grateful for the thick leather jacket covering his elbows and back. He clambered to his feet and took off in a zigzagging run, bullets flying around him.

The man in black rounded a corner, disappearing out of sight.

Nick stuck to the shadows and ran the length of a

building to the same corner. He stopped, poked his head out and saw nothing.

Streetlights shone down on an empty avenue. The only movement was a lone car heading his way at a slow speed. Nick ducked back behind the building in case the car contained the assailant. When it pulled to the curb and shut down, an old man dressed in khaki slacks, a light blue sweater and orthopedic shoes climbed out and reached into the back for a bag of groceries. He carefully locked the door and headed into the building.

Nick stepped out into the street, tucking his weapon back in the holster under his arm. He kept his hand on the grip, ready for anything.

He walked quickly down the street searching for the man dressed in black. He didn't see him. Damn, he'd slipped away. Nothing Nick could do about it now but go see if Royce needed help.

Retracing his steps, Nick found his way back to the apartment and entered through the front door, climbing the steps to the third floor.

When Nick entered the destroyed apartment, Royce was on his cell phone to the local police giving enough details to get them started. When he'd completed the call, he ended the call and slipped it into his pocket. "Got away?"

"Yeah." Nick nodded. "He had a head start."

"The gunfire. Yours or his?"

"His." Nick didn't fire his weapon randomly, especially not in populated urban areas where stray bullets could take innocent lives. "Who was the moaner?"

Royce's jaw tightened. "Frank Richards."

"The guy we came to help?"

"Some help we were." Royce drew in a breath and let it out slowly, his lips forming a tight line. "We were a few minutes too late."

"Damn. Did he give you a clue as to who might have done it?"

His boss shook his head, a frown drawing his brows together. "He died without uttering another word. But I found this and a pen lying on the bathroom floor close by." Royce held up a small pad of paper with a page half ripped off. "I think whoever shot him took the message."

"Let me see that." Nick took the pad and tipped it back and forth until the light cast enough shadow over where the pen had dented the pages below the missing one. "What does it say?"

"North Pole, AX or AK. Help Santa."

Nick barked out a mirthless laugh. "The man was clearly delusional. Already in the throes of death."

"No. He wrote it before he was shot. There's no blood on the pad or the pen and his fingers had blood on them when he died. I think he means for us to help someone."

"There is a town in Alaska named North Pole. It's

close to Fairbanks. You suppose that's what he was talking about?"

"Maybe."

"Why there? Do you think Santa is a code word for something?"

"I don't know. What I do know is that whoever did this was after something, and I'd bet my reputation they didn't find it."

"And they weren't afraid to kill for it." Nick stared down at the man lying on the floor, his face pale and tinged gray. "You think our shooter will look in North Pole, Alaska next?"

"Perhaps." Royce's gaze fell to the man lying on the floor. He wore a New York Knicks sweatshirt and jeans.

"How do you know Richards?" Nick moved to the living area.

Royce followed, the pad in his hand. "I met Sergeant Major Richards when I was an active duty Navy SEAL. He was a member of the Army Special Forces assigned to participate as a subject matter expert in a joint task force training exercise. We had a few beers after the training and since then, I've always kept in touch. When I'd come up to New York, I made it a point to look him up."

A computer sat on a desk in the corner, with several bullet holes in the CPU.

"Look at this." Nick bent to examine it. "Any

reason why a shooter would target a man and his computer?"

"I'll have Swede look into it." Royce jerked the cord out of the wall and unhooked the CPU from the monitor. "In the meantime, I want you up in Alaska. If they were after something and didn't find it, there's a chance that's where they'll look."

Nick shivered just thinking about the cold. "Couldn't he have chosen Florida or Texas?"

"Whoever killed Frank might kill in Alaska." Royce pushed back his shoulders and stared toward the bathroom where his buddy lay. "I want you there ASAP. I'd go with you, but I've got another case on the hot plate. Soon as I can, I'll join you."

"What am I looking for?"

Royce glanced at the pad. "Start with Santa."

CHAPTER 2

"First name, please." The agent behind the counter stared at the computer, fingers poised for input.

"Mary."

"Last name."

Mary sucked in a deep breath and let it out. When you had a last name like hers, you did a lot more explaining than if you were christened with a name like Jones, Smith or Henderson. "Christmas."

Both clerks working the busy Fairbanks Airport car rental counter looked up at once, smiles on their faces. Even the good-looking guy in the black Stetson next to her shot a glance her way.

Why couldn't her parents have given her a different name? Did they know how hard it was growing up with a name like Mary Christmas?

Mary sighed. If her father hadn't been so supportive, full of energy and the spirit of Christmas, she might have been a lot less adjusted. But the truth was she was a member of the family who owned a store called Christmas Towne in North Pole, Alaska, and that was how things were. Or they were until her mother had died. Then it had been just her and her father to carry on the Christmas Towne legacy. Mary had tried hard to fill the void her mother left to the point she'd forgotten to have a life of her own.

"Here's your keys." The clerk waiting on the man next to her handed him a map. "Do you need directions, sir?"

"Yes, how do I get to North Pole from here?"

Mary cast another glance his way. Nice. Very nice. And going to North Pole. Too bad his hat would blow off the first second he stepped out into the Alaskan wind. And too bad she wasn't interested. Nice-looking men tended to lie and break girls' hearts. Or at least this girl's heart.

She'd almost refused to come home for Christmas this year, preferring to stay in the tiny apartment she'd rented in Seattle. If not for the desperate message from her father, insisting he needed to talk to her, she'd have skipped Christmas altogether. She hadn't even bought a tree for her apartment. The whole season, once a happy occasion to be enjoyed with family, was now a depressing time of the year. Christmas without her mother had never been the same. Without her father...well, she might as well skip Christmas altogether. Her dad had Jasmine now. He didn't need Mary anymore. Mary should be happy she had a stepmother, but the word *stepmother* made her grind her teeth.

Not that her *stepmother*, had done anything specifically to earn her distrust. There was just something about the woman that set Mary off. Somehow, she had maneuvered her way between Mary and her father from the first.

The devil in Mary's conscience nagged at her. Could it be because Mary couldn't get used to the idea of another woman in the house? Or was it because her father had known Jasmine before he'd ever met Mary's mother? Jasmine had been sure to share that information with Mary whenever they were in the same room, claiming she'd known him long before he settled in Alaska. A fact Mary's father had never shared with her.

"I'm sorry, ma'am. I don't seem to have a reservation for a Mary Christmas," the clerk said.

"I know. I flew space A. I didn't know I was coming until this morning."

"Because it's so close to Christmas, we've been booked solid. We don't have a single car left."

Mary's shoulders sagged and her heart sank into her boots. "You're kidding, right?"

"No, ma'am. I wish I wasn't." He glanced down the line of rental car counters. "Have you tried the other services here at the airport?"

"Yes, and they all said the same thing. You were my last hope."

"We just rented out the only car we had left to that gentleman." He nodded to the man wearing the ridiculous cowboy hat walking away with the last set of keys. "I'm sorry. Perhaps you could find a hotel shuttle to get you to a hotel for the night and see if someone turns in a vehicle in the morning."

"That's not an option. I'm not staying in Fairbanks." Her gaze locked on the man with the last rental car key. Hadn't he said he was heading for North Pole? If she hurried, maybe she could catch a ride with him. Once she was there, her father would make sure she had a vehicle to get around in.

Balancing her bag of presents in one hand, she turned her rolling suitcase and raced through the airport.

She caught up with the man just as he stepped out the door into the continuous twilight of an Alaskan December afternoon. "Sir!"

A bitter wind blew her words away, or the man was ignoring her. He didn't slow one bit until his cowboy hat flipped off his head and blew straight at Mary.

She let go of her suitcase handle and dove for the hat, catching it before it dropped into a pile of dirty snow. She held it out, pasting a smile on her face. She could have tripped on her own snow boots when the man turned his brown-eyed gaze onto her.

"Thank you."

"You're welcome." She bit back a smart remark about most people didn't wear cowboy hats in December in Alaska. She didn't know if he had a sense of humor and she definitely didn't want to make him mad when she planned on begging a ride from him. "Are you headed for North Pole?"

He plunked his hat on his head and didn't answer for the first five seconds. "Yes."

Good. He was headed her direction as she'd thought. Mary breathed in a gulp of the icy air. "I'm headed that way myself and you just happened to get the last rental car in the airport. Is there a chance you could give me a lift there?"

His frown deepened, making her think he'd respond with *fat chance*.

His mouth opened. "Yes."

"I'll pay you half of your daily rate for today." Mary stopped and stared at him. "You will?"

"I said yes." He continued toward the nearly empty rental car parking lot.

Mary scurried after him, wrapping her woolen scarf around the lower part of her face and pulling her hat more firmly about her ears. She'd forgotten how unforgiving the wind blew in Fairbanks.

When they'd settled in the front seat of the sedan, Mary tugged her glove off her right hand. "I'm Mary Christmas. And you are?"

Instead of taking her hand, he studied the controls and started the car. "Nick."

"Nick?" She closed her eyes so that he couldn't see her rolling them. "Do you have a last name?"

At first, she didn't think he was going to answer. He pushed the shift into reverse and brushed her arm when he braced his hand on the back of her seat. He was close enough that Mary could smell his aftershave, a potent woodsy, spicy scent. His brown eyes glowed in the light from the dash. "St. Claire."

Mary caught her breath and stared straight forward.

When Nick had the car in gear, he asked, "Do you know how to get to North Pole?"

"Yes, I lived there most of my life."

"Then you can navigate."

"Fair enough."

He handed her his cell phone.

"I won't need that. I could get there with my eyes closed." Mary gave him directions and leaned back in her seat, letting the heat warm her hands and cheeks.

A small smile curled the corners of Nick's lips. "Aren't you afraid to ride with strangers?"

"If we'd been in Seattle, I would never have imposed on you, but here in Alaska, it's probably a fair bet you're not a mass murderer."

"I thought people with questionable pasts moved to small towns in Alaska to escape their lives in the lower forty-eight."

Mary snorted. "They might think they can escape, but the population is so limited in smaller communities, everyone knows everyone else."

"Therefore, if a stranger comes to town, everyone will know him as a stranger?"

"Right." She smiled his way. "You'd definitely stick out as a stranger, especially this time of year. In the summer, not so much. Droves of tourists visit North Pole in their RVs and on tour buses, but they eventually leave. Not many people come in the darkness and freezing temperatures of winter." Her smile slipped. Some people left Alaska on business trips to warmer climates and greener pastures.

Her lips pulled into a straight line. She'd been so naïve. That was old news. She'd since moved to Seattle and two years had passed. Mary shook her head to clear the cobwebs and concentrated on the man beside her. "Why are you coming to North Pole? Looking for a place to escape?"

"Would you believe I have business with Santa?"

"Maybe." Mary stared hard at him. Something about the way he said the words didn't ring true, but she hadn't heard much from her father in the past few months. Since her father had found a life of his own and the new wife. Jasmine.

Nick glanced at her. "What's Santa's real name?"

The smile returned to Mary's face. "Santa Claus."

"No, really. What's his real name?"

"For as long as I can remember, he's always been

Santa Claus. I've asked him hundreds of times what his real name was, but he never told me. He signs his name as Santa and his Social Security card and driver's license all say Santa Claus."

Nick shook his head, a frown dipping between his brows. "I don't get it."

Mary shrugged and settled back against her seat, refusing to fall into the trap of trying to explain the whole North Pole, Alaska, and the Christmas Towne phenomenon. Some people didn't get it. The man next to her probably never would.

His loss.

Bradley, the two-timing-bigamist, never understood it either. He'd laughed at the whole concept. He'd probably been laughing at her all along as well. Look at the dumb bumpkin from the sticks of Alaska, too stupid to see through his lies.

The fifteen miles to North Pole flew by. Her heart banged against the inside of her chest when her hometown came into view. Colorful Christmas lights sparkled year-round on the houses and the candy cane lampposts. She never tired of bright colors. Living in Seattle, she missed the cheery lights even in the summertime. As the Christmas Towne store came into view, tears welled in her eyes. Red and white diagonal stripes graced the boxy entrance. Pictures of reindeer and Santa's sleigh stretched across the whitewashed exterior walls. She hadn't realized how much she'd missed home until she came back.

"This is my stop." She stared at the building trying to imagine the first impression of a stranger to what she considered home. It looked like a red and white fantasy castle in the middle of the Alaskan landscape. The house beside the store was painted brown and trimmed with fake gumdrops and candy canes, the two buildings could have been out of any child's most elaborate dream. The little cottage beside the store looked like a gingerbread house good enough to eat, covered in a fluffy foot of snow with drifts up to the windowsills.

A light still shone inside the store. Had her father kept the store open late for the Christmas season? Several cars and a North Pole police SUV stood out front. Christmas Towne had some of the best coffee in North Pole. Many people came all the way out from Fairbanks to eat dinner and buy gifts from the diner and store. They made it a shopping expedition complete with small children anxious to sit in Santa's lap and tell them all their wishes.

"If you'll park in front of the store, I'll introduce you to my fa—Santa." When he shifted the car into park, she grabbed for the handle and jumped out, anxious to ask her father what was so important she had to fly home at the drop of a hat. At the same time, she didn't want to let Nick get away without finding out what business he had with Santa.

Nick met her at the back of the car. popped the latch on the trunk and lifted her suitcase as if it weighed nothing. "I'd appreciate that introduction."

"A small price to pay for giving me a lift." She led the way to the glass doors and entered. Inside, it wasn't a mob of shoppers she ran into. Instead, she was met by North Pole Police Officer Trey Baskin and Chris Moss, one of Christmas Towne's employees, Betty Reedy, the Christmas Towne baker and her stepmother, Jasmine Claus.

They stared at her, their gazes shifting to the man beside her as though seeing her with a man was so unusual they were stunned into temporary silence. Mary sighed. So, it had been a while since she'd brought a man home to North Pole—two years to be exact. And this one wasn't even *her* man. "Trey Baskin, Chris Moss, Betty Reedy and Jasmine Claus, this is Nick St. Claire. He was good enough to give me a lift from the airport."

Chris Moss, the teenager her father had befriended and hired on as full-time staff, was first to stumble forward, his face creased in a worried frown. "Mary, I'm so glad you're here." The pale tinge to his young skin set off alarm bells in Mary's subconscious. Chris had been the most optimistic teen she'd ever known since her father took him under his wing.

Mary grabbed his hand and held tight, her

stomach doing full gainers in a sea of airport food and acid. "What's going on?"

"It's Mr. Claus." Sixteen-year-old Chris squeezed her hand, tears welling in his eyes. He opened his mouth to talk and closed it again.

Betty stepped forward, her happy face drawn and looking all of her fifty-five years. "Your father's missing."

CHAPTER 3

Nick schooled his face to show no shock. So, Santa was missing and Mary Christmas was his daughter. He really shouldn't be astonished that the petite blonde next to him was Santa's daughter. Not with a name like Mary Christmas and in a town called North Pole with streets like Santa Claus Lane and Snowman Lane. Why shouldn't Mary's father's real name be Santa Claus? And given that Nick was sent by a dead man to help Santa Claus, it all made sense in a weird, surreal way.

Whatever the case, he knew his job remained here. If the dead man in Brooklyn had wanted Royce to help Santa, Nick was the first line of defense to find the man and protect him from the fate of his buddy back East.

While Mary questioned the officer and the tearful Mrs. Claus, Nick studied the people gathered.

He started with the boy, Chris, with his shaggy brown hair hanging down past his collar and a skater look to him. Dark circles smudged the skin beneath his eyes and his gaze darted around the room in nervous jerks.

Betty Reedy, the woman with salt-and-pepper hair, slightly rounded figure and soft blue eyes wrung her hands, her mouth pressed into a grim line. She reached out and pulled Chris into the curve of her arms and whispered something into his ear.

Chris nodded, jammed his hands into his pockets and stared down at his shoes.

Mrs. Claus, with her Slavic accent, was the most unusual of the group milling about the front of the store. She stood no more than five feet tall and carried herself ramrod straight, making good every inch of height. She'd combed her sleek salt and pepper hair into a smooth chignon at the back of her head, exposing a long, thin neck.

Then there was the cop, doing his best to document the details of Santa's disappearance. Trey Baskin, in his police uniform, jotted information into his notebook, a frown pressing his brows into a V over his nose. He'd probably never handled anything more violent than a knifing in a bar fight.

And Mary Christmas stood among them shooting questions at each, her voice strained. She reached out and pushed a long strand of silky blond hair back away for her face, revealing a delicate ear studded with a single pearl earring.

The curve of her jaw and the smooth line of her neck captured Nick's attention more than they should have. When he realized he was staring at her, he turned away and wandered around the spacious shop. Decorated like an old-timey general store with rough wooden beams and wooden barrels filled with toys, the place was a treasure trove of delight for children and adults alike. In one corner was a workspace littered with wood pieces that, once assembled, would be a toy train set. An apron hung on the wall behind a stool. The whole setup looked like Santa's workshop where he demonstrated toy making.

In the center of the store stood a large chair resembling a throne, decorated with red, white and gold paint. A fuzzy red jacket trimmed in white fur hung on a peg beside it. Santa's chair where he entertained the hopes and dreams of hundreds of small children each year.

Nick snorted beneath his breath.

A camera and several lighting umbrellas stood among fake Christmas trees and giant candy canes. Get your picture taken with Santa...for a charge.

On closer inspection, Nick noted tiny cameras in each corner of the building. A fairly elaborate security system for a place so far north, but then maybe Santa had problems with the locals hiking through several feet of snow to steal Christmas gift items during the endless winter nights.

"Can I help you?" The voice behind him with its hint of a Slavic accent sounded as cool as the wind outside.

He turned toward the tiny, thin woman. She wore a deep red velvet dress trimmed with white fake fur at the wrists and neckline. Her brown eyes were red-rimmed, and her face was lined and pale.

Mary had introduced her as Jasmine Claus. Santa's wife? She didn't look anything like Mary. Was she a stepmother? Santa's new wife? "When did you discover Mr....Claus was missing?" Nick stumbled over the name, feeling more than just a little ridiculous. How long had it been since he'd stopped believing in Santa Claus? Had he ever believed in the fairytale? Growing up in foster care in Texas wasn't the best environment for misplaced beliefs.

The woman touched a tissue to the corner of her eye and sniffed. "What was your name again?"

"Nick St. Claire, a friend of Mr. Claus." Nick moved back toward the others standing in the center of the store.

Jasmine followed him. "My husband never mentioned you."

"It's been a long time."

"I've known Mr. Claus a long time. I have no memory of your name."

"We don't know each other well. How long did you say you knew Santa?"

"We've known each other since back when we were much younger."

"Really?" Nick lifted a nutcracker in the shape of a wooden soldier from a shelf and pretended to study the cracking mechanism. "I thought you were newlyweds."

"We are. I—we just recently found each other again."

Nick glanced up and caught Mary's gaze.

Her long blond hair framed a pale face and beautiful blue eyes glassy with tears.

He found himself drawn to her, crossing the floor to her side before he realized what he was doing. The tug of concern pulling at the muscles in his chest was foreign to Nick. He didn't know this woman.

Until yesterday, he didn't know a man named Santa Claus existed other than in the movies and fantasies of children. Why should he care about how the woman next to him felt about her missing father? His primary focus should have been on finding Santa Claus. The man and his daughter were nothing more than another assignment. Emotions weren't part of an SOS agent's authorized equipment list.

"This whole situation is crazy. Santa is probably fine. Perhaps he stayed at a friend's house or something. In the meantime, I have to let people know the scheduled deliveries might be delayed if we can't find my husband soon." Jasmine sniffed and dabbed at her eyes, moving toward the checkout counter. "If you have any more questions concerning my husband, ask Officer Baskin. I have calls to make, and I need to close the shop."

The front door to Christmas Towne slammed closed and everyone turned to see who entered.

A stout man with gray hair and brown-black eyes hurried through carrying a microphone in one hand. He was closely followed by a man hefting a camera on his shoulder with NEWS printed in bright blue, large block letters on its black plastic casing.

"Ah, Mary. I'm so glad you're here," the man with the microphone said.

A soft groan escaped Mary's mouth. "Please, not now, Silas."

He crossed the floor to stand in front of the petite blonde.

Too close for polite conversation. His stance appeared more threatening than casual.

Nick took a step forward before he could catch himself.

"As soon as I heard the news, I hurried over." Silas waved the cameraman closer

"With the media?" Mary closed her eyes, her lips moving as if she were counting to ten.

The man she'd called Silas raised his brows. "The public has a right to know the most famous man in North Pole is missing." He rubbed his hands together like a kid anxiously awaiting a new toy. "What we want to know is why? After thirty years of playing Santa, why has he disappeared? Could it be a mysterious criminal past caught up with him? Is Santa on the run from the law?"

Mary threw her arms in the air. "Good grief, Silas! My father is not on the run from the law. *He's* not the criminal. More likely he's the victim. Now get out of here before I have you thrown out."

Jasmine Claus stood a few feet away. Her lip curled in an amused smile. "Really, Silas, that's a pretty pathetic attempt to slander my husband. Santa is a good man. Everyone knows it." She crossed her arms over her chest and turned to the man in uniform. "Don't you agree, Officer Baskin?"

The officer nodded. "Silas, now's not the time to be a pain. Leave quietly, please."

"I have a right to know about a man who pretends to be Santa. Imagine all the children who've been fooled by a potential criminal. Parents will be up in arms." He shot a narrow look at Mary as she inhaled deeply. "Notice I said potential. I'm not accusing your father of anything. I'm just a concerned citizen."

"Silas Grentch, you're only concerned about getting your hands on the best moneymaking business in town. I thought you couldn't stoop lower, but you never fail to amaze me." Mary looked to Officer Baskin. "Can you make him leave?"

The officer smiled dangerously and stepped toward Silas.

"I'm leaving." Silas held up his hands and backed a step, one eye on the cameraman. "Are you getting this?"

"Out." Mary pointed her finger toward the door, her blue eyes flashing.

Nick almost laughed out loud at how quickly Silas Grentch scurried for the exit. "I'm leaving, but the truth will come out. Mark my words. It'll be a dark day in North Pole when Santa Claus is brought to justice."

The cameraman paused at the door with his camera pointing at Mary. "Miss Christmas, with Santa missing and Christmas getting close, what will happen with Operation Santa?"

Mary's eyes narrowed, her fingers curling into tight fists. "We'll find Santa before the planes leave. Children in the remote villages will see him."

The cameraman nodded, lowering his camera before he left.

After the door closed, silence reigned inside the cheerfully decorated Christmas store.

"I'm sorry you had to come home to Silas's shenanigans, Mary." Betty took Mary's hands and pulled her into a tight hug.

Nick witnessed the entire strange scene, his mind ticking through all the slurs and innuendos flung at the missing Santa and his family. One thing stood out like a shining beacon. These people knew Mary Christmas, and from the looks of it, they cared about her. His gaze slid to the new Mrs. Claus. Well, almost all of them cared. Jasmine Claus warranted some looking into.

Officer Baskin touched Mary's arm. "If you hear, see or even smell anything, please pass it along to me or one of North Pole's police officers. I'll start checking with Santa's friends in town."

A tear slipped down Mary's cheek. "Thanks, Trey."

Nick resisted the urge to reach out and brush the tear away, clearing his throat instead. "I'm new to town. Is there a hotel where I can get a room?"

The police officer dropped Mary's hands and zipped up his parka. "Try Christmas Towne Bed-and-Breakfast. It's just two blocks east of here. I've got to get onto this. The temperature is supposed to drop down to minus twenty tonight." Although the officer didn't add that a man couldn't survive in that kind of temperature, he didn't have to. As he left, a chilling wind gusted through the double doors.

Mary's gaze followed the officer, her skin even paler than a moment before.

Nick's gut tightened. "Do you have a place to stay?"

"When I left Seattle, I thought I'd stay with my father. I didn't make any other arrangements." She turned toward her stepmother.

"I'm sorry, Mary." Jasmine's mouth twisted into a weak smile. "I'd let you have your old room, but I didn't know you were coming, and I'm in the middle of a huge remodeling effort. Your room is stacked with boxes. The bed is dismantled and leaning against the wall. You could have the couch, but it too is stacked with boxes. You'd be better off getting a room at the B and B as well."

Mary stared at Mrs. Claus for a long moment, her shoulders stiffening, her mouth pulling into a thin line. "I see." Then she smiled and turned to Nick. "Thank you for the ride."

Not that he had any responsibility for the woman, but Nick couldn't leave her without transportation. "If you're going to the B and B, you might as well let me take you."

"It's only two blocks. I can manage on my own." She buttoned the front of her coat and tied the sash around her middle with a hard jerk. Then she turned to Mrs. Claus, her expression as serious as a firing squad. "If you had anything to do with my father's disappearance...you'll have me to answer to."

"Mary Christmas!" Jasmine Claus pressed a hand to her red velvet dress and tears welled in her eyes. "You don't realize how much I love your father. I'd do anything for him. I crossed oceans and continents for him. I love him more than life. How could you even imply such a thing? I want him back just as much as you do."

Mary didn't answer, but turned toward the door, grabbing the handle of her suitcase as she went. "Remodeling, my fanny," she muttered beneath her breath.

Nick's gaze zeroed in on the way Mary's eyes shone suspiciously, as if she were close to tears.

The teenager, Chris, held the door for her and stared hard into her eyes. "It'll be all right, Mary. Your father will be all right, and we'll find him."

She reached out and gripped his hand, as if glad for one person's support in this world gone crazy. "Thanks, Chris."

Nick followed her out into the blistering cold where he snagged her suitcase.

"I told you, I don't need your help anymore." Mary reached out to take the suitcase from him.

He backed away, refusing to let her have the bag. "Let me help."

"I can take care of myself."

His face softened. "Even two blocks is a long way with a windchill factor of minus thirty. Please, let me take you where you need to go."

As if to reinforce Nick's words, the cold wind blasted through Mary's thick wool coat and winter scarf.

Beyond exhaustion, Mary didn't argue. Instead, she climbed into the passenger seat while Nick stored her case in the trunk.

When he climbed in behind the wheel, she turned

to him. "I don't want you to think you're stuck with me. But thanks." She leaned her head against the headrest and closed her eyes. "I should have known something was wrong. I should have come home sooner. My dad is the only family I have left."

"Why should you have known?" Nick's hand paused on the shift.

"Yesterday I got a message on my answering machine from Dad. He said it was urgent that we talk. When I tried to call him back, I got Jasmine and she didn't know where he was. That's when I caught a flight from Seattle to Fairbanks."

"Did he say what he wanted to talk about?"

"No." Mary sighed. "My father is normally pretty laid back. He must be in big trouble, that's all I can think." She'd been talking to Nick as if he weren't an outsider, weren't a man she'd met only a couple of hours ago. Mary turned to him, her eyes narrowing. "Why are you in North Pole? You told Jasmine you knew my father. You told me you had business with him. I don't recall my father ever mentioning your name."

He pulled out of the parking lot, easing onto the snow-covered road. "He probably hasn't. We don't talk much."

"Obviously."

North Pole sported at least a foot of snowfall, giving credence to the town's winter wonderland atmosphere.

Mary gestured toward a large old house banked in snow. "This is the B and B."

After they secured rooms, they climbed the stairs and stood back-to-back at their respective rooms.

Nick turned to Mary. "I'd like to help you find your father."

She faced him, her brow furrowing. "Thanks, but you really don't need to get involved. You've already done enough getting me here." She turned her back to him and jammed her key into the lock on her bedroom door. She liked to think she could handle the situation on her own, but the fact her father was missing, and no one seemed to have a clue as to his whereabouts swept over her in an overwhelming wave. Her hand trembled on the metal key.

"At least meet me for breakfast somewhere besides here. I like more than a continental breakfast and I'm new to town." He paused as though waiting for her response.

Mary couldn't find her voice to say no. Her throat clogged with unshed tears.

"If it makes you feel better, we can go Dutch."

She glanced over her shoulder again, her lips forming the word *no*. But one look into deep brown, twinkling eyes and she couldn't resist. Much as she hated to admit, she needed help. Maybe by having breakfast with the man she could get to know him better before she committed to his offer. She swallowed hard and, before she could change her mind, she blurted, "How about the Christmas Towne Diner at eight o'clock? It's just across the street."

"Sounds good." He gave her half a smile. "Good night, Mary Christmas." Then he closed his door behind him, the deep resonance of his voice lingering in the hallway, warming Mary's insides.

Their rooms were located across the hall from each other and for some reason that idea disturbed Mary, not like an irritant, but like a full-body awareness. She was far too conscious of Nick's good looks, broad shoulders and brown-black eyes. Not to mention, the more she was in his company, the more she seemed to rely on him. And she didn't want to rely on anyone but herself. She'd relied on her father for so long, she'd forgotten to have a life for herself. The time she'd been in Seattle had slammed that observation home. She didn't know how to be alone, and she still didn't like it, but she was trying.

Mary spent the next hour calling everyone she knew in North Pole, asking if they'd seen her father. Those she managed to speak to replied with the same news. Not since yesterday.

Discouraged, she gathered her toiletries and made a run down the hallway for the bathroom. As she reached the door, it opened and Nick St. Claire stepped out. With a towel thrown around his hips and nothing else, he could melt the heaviest snowfall. Water dripped from his midnight-black hair. A particular droplet landed on his chest and tangled in the dark, crisp hairs.

Mary focused on that drop, her mouth going as dry as Arizona in August.

"It's all yours," he said.

Her mouth dropped open and she forced her gaze upward to his eyes.

Nick's grin made Mary's face burn. "The shower. It's all yours."

Snapping her mouth shut, Mary pressed her brows together. How could this stranger throw her into such a state of moronic confusion? "Of course." She stepped around him, bumping into his bare arm. The scent of soap and shampoo wafted across her senses.

As she reached the security of the bathroom and closed the door behind her, a soft chuckle echoed in the hallway. Mary snapped the lock over the doorway and leaned against the wooden panels. Surely, he didn't think his bare chest and broad shoulders had her confused. Did he?

Her face burned hotter. Damn, the man was trouble. She should never have agreed to meet him in the morning at the diner. As soon as she finished in the shower, she'd tell him she'd had something come up and that she couldn't have breakfast with him. Squeezing her eyes tight, she inhaled and exhaled, concentrating on banishing the image of a shirtless Nick from her memory.

As if!

She hurried through her shower, brushed her teeth and pulled on her fluffy bathrobe. Still practicing what she'd say to Nick, she stepped out of the bathroom, heading for the door across the corridor from hers.

A big man bulked out in a winter-white parka, ski mask and snowpants stood with his hand on the knob of her bedroom door. When he spotted Mary, he barreled down the hall and slammed his shoulder into her, exiting out the rear of the building.

Mary banged into the wall, her breath knocked out of her. Pain smashed into her shoulder blade and radiated through her back and she cried out.

Nick's door sprang open and he raced out into the hallway. "Mary! What happened?" He reached her in three long strides and grabbed her shoulders, his hands spreading warmth through the thick fleece of her bathrobe.

"I'm all right. Someone just ran into me and left through the back exit."

Noise from a room down the hallway caught their attention and they both turned. The sound came from her room.

Nick grabbed her hand and ran to his room, shoving her inside. He held out his hand. "Give me your key."

Wordlessly, she handed him the key from her pocket.

"Stay here," he commanded, and then he closed his door, leaving her alone inside.

Unable to stand by patiently by herself, not knowing what was going on, Mary eased the door open and peered out into the hallway.

Nick slipped the key into the doorknob as quietly as possible and stepped to the side of the door before he flung it open.

Crouching behind Nick's door, Mary could see straight into her room. The window stood wide open, a flurry of snowflakes and wind blew through the confined space, turning the warmth of the quaint little room with its handmade quilts into an icebox. Other than the antique furniture, the room stood empty.

Mary stepped out into the hallway, wrapping the robe around her, chills setting in. Someone had been in her room. The thought made her shake all over.

Nick brushed the snow off the sill and pulled the window closed, latching the lock in place. When he turned to see her, he frowned. "I thought I told you to stay put."

Her back straightened and she moved into her room with more purpose. "It's my room. My things are in here."

"Yeah, but it could have been dangerous."

Despite her desire not to show any weakness, a big shiver made her shake from her head to her feet. She pulled her robe tighter. "I could see there wasn't anyone in it." Her mouth firmed into a tight line. "Besides, you don't have to yell at me. You're not my boss or my father."

"I wasn't yelling," he yelled. His forehead creased into a deep frown before the hint of a grin wiped it away. "I'd rather you stayed in my room until we figure this out." He hooked her elbow and led her out into the hallway.

She only half resisted, not wanting to stay in her room by herself. Somehow it felt as if the entire B and B had been violated and was no longer a secure place. She let him lead her into his room, where he tossed on a sweater, his winter coat and snow boots.

"Where are you going?" she asked.

"To follow the footprints."

"By yourself?" She grabbed his arm, stopping him from zipping the jacket. "What if those guys are dangerous?"

Nick shook off her hand, slid the zipper up to his neck and ducked around her, grabbing a gun from the dresser by the door. "Just stay here."

The gun sent another wave of chills across her skin and Mary stood where Nick left her, wondering what the hell she'd gotten into by coming home to North Pole. And just who was this gun-toting mystery man named Nick St. Claire?

CHAPTER 4

A BLAST of arctic air hit Nick like a freight train. He staggered at the force and bent into it, pushing through three feet of snow to the side of the B and B where Mary's room was located. Disturbed snow only confirmed his concern. Someone had come through Mary's window while she'd been in the shower. And from the looks of the footprints leading away, he'd gone back out the same window. Which didn't explain the man in the hallway who'd run into Mary before exiting through the back door, a much more civilized approach than the window.

Nick trudged through the snow as fast as he could, following the footprints into the woods. Every so often, he looked over his shoulder to keep the light from the B and B in sight. The snow blew sideways in near-blizzard conditions. Although he'd like to catch the guy, he didn't relish getting lost in the storm. An engine roared to life in the distance and the noise diminished as if moving away. Sounded like a snowmobile. Another engine revved and followed the first. Had the two men been working together? And what did they want with Mary?

Figuring the men were out of his reach, Nick hurried back to the B and B to ensure that Santa's daughter was safe. He also wanted to inspect her room for any tampering or clues as to why someone would be there.

The blue-eyed woman met him at his bedroom door still wearing her robe. The towel had been removed from her hair, and wet tresses lay finger-combed into sleek, damp strands reaching all the way to her waist. Her rounded gaze darted from him to the exit and across the hall to her room, where her door stood open. "Who was it? Did you catch him? No, of course, you didn't or you'd have been gone a lot longer. You scared me to death." She slapped her open palm against his chest. "Running out of here like some cop on a mission. And what's with the gun?" She backed up a step and glared at the hand holding the weapon. "Why are you carrying it?"

He shrugged, stalling. "Doesn't everyone carry a gun in Alaska?"

"Rifles and shotguns when they're hunting or out on the trails, but not so much the handguns." Her eyes narrowed. "Just what are you doing here in

North Pole? You don't really know my father, do you?"

Busted. Now, how did he back out of this? "I don't suppose this could wait until morning?"

She crossed her arms over her chest. "No way, cowboy."

Nick sighed and cupped her elbow. "Come on. Let's check out your room, and I'll tell you what I know."

Mary resisted only a minute, her eyes still narrowed as if she didn't trust him any more than she trusted the men who'd invaded her room. The thought disappointed him, although why, he didn't know. In his line of business, he was always living a lie to infiltrate the situation.

"I'm watching you, Nick St. Claire, or whatever your real name is. And I'm trained in self-defense so don't try anything."

A smile tugged at Nick's lips. "So noted." Mary Christmas was no pushover. He bet she meant it about the self-defense training. He stepped into her room and stood perfectly still, staring at everything as it lay. As far as he could tell, there wasn't anything odd or out of place. Her suitcase leaned against one wall, the clothing she'd worn earlier littered the bed, and a minimal assortment of toiletries lay scattered across the dresser. "Can you tell whether anything has moved from where you originally set it?"

Mary's arms dropped to her sides as she inspected

the room. "Everything looks the same except the water on the floor from the melted snow." She opened the dresser drawers one by one. "No. Nothing in here is different from when I unpacked."

When Nick caught a glimpse of lacy black panties and a matching bra, his heartbeat stuttered. He could picture the beautiful Mary, dark lace resting against pale skin and nothing else. With a gulp, he turned his attention to the rest of the room. "What about the bed?" From one leap of the imagination to the next, he could have stuffed a sock in his mouth.

Her color high, Mary moved toward the queen-size mattress. "I don't remember turning back the covers." She touched a hand to the pillow.

Nick snagged her wrist, arresting her movement before she could lift the pillow. "Let me."

Shrugging off his grip, she stepped to the side enough to allow him close to the bed. "Are you worried someone planted a bomb under my pillow?" she asked, her indignant tone fading with each word.

"Not really, but better safe than sorry." He lifted the pillow.

Mary gasped.

A small box wrapped in shiny red wrapping paper lay against the crisp white sheets.

The fear Mary had felt only a moment earlier dissipated. "Dad."

"This box?" Nick frowned. "Do you think your father left it?"

"It has to be him." She reached out, grasped the gift and tore off the paper.

Nick grabbed the wrapping paper as it fell to the floor, lifting it with the tips of his fingers. He wrapped a tissue around the foil paper. "If it's all the same to you, I'd like to keep this."

She shrugged, staring down at the small white box resting in her hand. A smile lifted the corners of her lips for the first time since she'd learned of her father's disappearance, denting Nick's indifference like a head-on collision.

In a voice almost too soft to hear, she whispered, "We used to play a game called find the present when I was a child. He'd wrap a clue in the gift and hide it somewhere. When I found it, I had to guess what it meant and follow it to the next clue."

Mary lifted the lid of the box and pushed aside a fluff of tissue paper. Buried inside was a shiny silver key.

"Any idea what the key belongs to?"

"No." When she reached out, he caught her hand, wrapping his warm fingers around her cold ones.

"Wait, there might be fingerprints." He continued to hold her hand, his shoulder rubbing against hers.

"They'll be my father's." Mary pulled free of his fingers.

He maintained his hold. "Are you sure?"

"Yes, of course." She held up the tissue where words had been scrawled in pencil. "That's his writing as well." She squinted as she read the message. *"The past holds the secrets.* What do you suppose that means?"

"I don't know but let me have the key. Maybe we can lift a print off it." He snatched a tissue from the box on the dresser and carefully lifted the key from the box. "I'll be right back." Nick gave her a quick glance and then strode across the hall to his room, where he retrieved a fingerprint kit from his suitcase.

"I tell you, it's my father's handwriting. I'd know it anywhere." Mary followed him across the hall and closed the door behind them.

"Still, it doesn't hurt to check prints against the databases."

"My father is not a criminal." Mary crossed her arms over her chest, her chin jutting out at a stubborn angle. "Aren't those databases geared toward criminals?"

Nick would rather she stayed back in her own room, but given the circumstances, he didn't throw her out. Instead, he set his gun on the bed dresser and got down to the business of lifting the prints. He'd send them to their office back in Texas and see if they could find a match.

"I get it. You're not going to answer my question, are you?"

"Nope."

Mary wrapped her arms around the middle of her

cotton-candy-pink bathrobe. "Are you a cop or FBI agent?"

He glanced up for a brief moment, a flash of memory pulling his lips into a tight line. "Former FBI."

"So, you're CIA or something like that?"

His attention returned to the fingerprints. "Something like that."

She shook her head. "I'm standing here in my bathrobe talking to a stranger, and I don't even know if he's one of the good guys or the bad guys." Mary chewed on her bottom lip, her brows furrowing into a worried frown.

"I like to think I'm one of the good guys," he said, returning his concentration back to his task. "For the most part."

"Yeah, sure. And I guess it was a coincidence you showed up at the airport when I did, my father disappeared and someone broke into my room." Her hands fisted and she propped them on her slim hips. "How do I know you're one of the good guys? Do you have credentials to prove it?"

He completed his task before he stood. "I'm going to wash my hands, and then I'll tell you what I can."

"I get it, you're not going to tell me anything."

"Pretty much." He pushed past her, strode through the doorway and down the hall, where he washed his hands in the communal bathroom. All the while he picked through what he knew to come up with what he could tell her. He hoped it was enough to appease her. As a government SOS agent, he wasn't at liberty to divulge his true duties. By doing so, he placed his entire organization in jeopardy and he wouldn't do that, no matter how pretty the girl was. And Mary was a knockout.

However, since the government version of SOS had been disbanded, he wasn't tied to those rules anymore. It still felt strange to be working in more of vigilante form for now.

MARY PACED inside Nick's room. Despite her misgivings, she couldn't or wouldn't believe the man was one of the bad guys. So far, he'd been nothing but polite and helpful. Although she didn't believe he was on the wrong side, she knew he was holding back information and she meant to extract it, one way or another. That he'd avoided the truth made her angry. She stoked her anger, letting it build with each passing minute.

Her gaze landed on the gun he'd laid on the dresser, a thought forming in her head.

By the time Nick walked back into the room, Mary had braced herself, ready for anything. She held the gun he'd carried in both hands and pointed it at him. "Now, tell me what you know or I'll shoot you."

Nick smiled, shaking his head. "You won't shoot me."

His patronizing attitude only made her angrier. "If you know so much about me, what makes you think I won't?"

He closed the door behind him and then lunged for the weapon, yanking it from her grasp. "For one, it isn't loaded."

Deflated and feeling on less firm footing, Mary straightened her back and flicked her drying hair over her shoulder. "So, I wouldn't have shot you anyway. Just give me answers, not more lies."

"Have a seat."

Mary glanced around the room, realizing the only place she could sit was on the bed. His bed. Tingling awareness started in her chest, spread south into her belly and lower still. "No, thank you. I prefer to stand."

He nodded, his expression hardening into an impenetrable mask. "I came because a dead man in Brooklyn, New York, left a note to help Santa."

"A dead man?" The blood drained from Mary's face and a hand fluttered to her chest. "I never knew my father had friends in New York. I don't understand."

"Neither do I, but if the man took the time to send help to Santa in North Pole, I thought it important enough to check into. Given that your father is now missing, there might be credence to his request."

Mary sat on the bed and rested her head in her hands, willing a sudden attack of nausea to abate before she made a bigger fool of herself. When she finally had her stomach in check, she glanced up. "That still doesn't tell me who you are and why you were with a dead man in New York."

"Let's just say we received an urgent call from him but arrived too late. By the time we got there, he was already dead."

"We?"

A smile tipped the edges of his lips, the effect sending danger signals ricocheting through Mary's brain.

"Never mind the 'we.'"

"Argh!" She stomped her foot. "I don't like all the secrets. Can you at least tell me who the dead man was?"

"Frank Richards. Does the name ring any bells?"

Mary scratched through her memory. "I've never met a man by that name, nor has Dad mentioned it. My dad and I are very close."

"What about your stepmother?"

Her jaw tightened. "She's only been in the picture for the past couple months. Before that, my father and I had no secrets from each other."

"What do you know about his life before he moved here?"

"My dad's lived in North Pole ever since I was born."

"Where did he live before that?"

"I don't know, I never asked. I knew he'd been in the military, but he didn't like to talk about it." For someone who loved her father more than any man in her life, she didn't know him very well, did she? Her breath caught in her throat and she swallowed hard.

"What about your mother?"

"She was from Fairbanks, born and raised."

"Was?" he prodded, his voice low, but insistent.

Mary turned to stare at the curtained window. "She died fourteen years ago in a car wreck." Her death had been the reason Mary had stayed in North Pole as long as she had. Her father had loved his first wife completely. Olivia Claus had been a shining beacon, a consistently happy woman, content in her life in Alaska, thrilled to be a part of Christmas Towne and in love with her husband. And Santa had loved her more than life itself.

When Olivia Claus had died, Santa had needed Mary more than ever.

For the next fourteen years, she'd concentrated on making her father happy. She'd graduated with honors from high school, gone to college in Fairbanks and put off her dreams of moving to the lower forty-eight, indefinitely. Then she'd met Bradley and thought she was in love. When he'd turned out to be a cheat, her dreams of raising her children near her father fell through. That's when her father arranged for her move to Seattle, to get away from bad memories.

She shook herself out of her morose musings. "How old was the man in Brooklyn?"

"Early sixties, maybe. We're still looking into his background. I don't know much about him yet, other than he was a retired Army sergeant."

"You think he might have known my dad before he moved to Alaska? Back when he'd been in the military?" When had her father moved to North Pole? Perhaps she could ask Christmas Towne's janitor, Mr. Feegan. He'd known her dad about as long as anyone, she guessed. A glance at the clock confirmed it was too late to call now. At nearly midnight, she wouldn't get a coherent response if she got him to answer the phone at all.

And Nick still hadn't answered all her questions. "You still haven't said who you work for."

"Let's just say, I used to work for the country and in a way I still do. You better get some rest. We want to start fresh and early looking for your father."

"I don't like it."

"Like what?"

"That I still don't know what you are."

"I'm just a man here to help Santa."

"Like some kind of saint from heaven?" Mary snorted. "North Pole's very own Saint Nick?"

"I'm no saint." All humor disappeared from his face, leaving his eyes dark and fathomless.

She glanced at the gun in his hand. "How do I know you're not here to kill my father? How do I know you didn't kill Frank Richards?"

"You don't." He set the gun inside a dresser drawer and scooped her elbow with his palm. "Now, are you going to your room, or would you rather sleep here?"

Mary's heart flip-flopped in her chest at the thought of staying in the same room with this man who was sexy enough to be a model and with just enough mystery to be dangerous. A deadly combination for her under exercised libido. If she didn't leave now, it might be fatal to more than her tenuous hold on self-preservation. Who was to say he wouldn't kill her? Her skin chilled. "I'm going."

She couldn't hustle across the hallway and into her room fast enough. When she turned to close the door, she noticed Nick leaning in his doorframe. Having shed his jacket and with his black hair falling over his forehead, he could crank up any female's blood pressure and she was no different.

Damn.

Mary glared at him. "I intend to learn more about you and what's happened to my father tomorrow. So, don't go anywhere."

His lips twisted. "Don't worry. I'm not. I'm just as interested in finding your father as you are."

After closing the door with a sharp click, Mary leaned against it and wondered if Nick's reasons were much darker than hers. She tested the lock on her window and shoved her dresser in front of the door. When she fell into bed, she lay with her eyes half-open, jumping every time the heater kicked on or the walls settled. Questions raced through her mind, keeping her awake into the wee hours.

Who had bumped into her in the hallway? Was he after her father? Why hadn't her father tried harder to contact her once she was in North Pole? And what did the sexy mystery man across the hall have to do with her father's disappearance? Most of all, what did her father's clue mean?

CHAPTER 5

The incessant theme from *Mission Impossible* jarred Nick from the light doze he'd fallen into after lying awake all night listening for any sound from the room across the hall.

Mary might have been certain about the intruder in her room being her father, but it didn't account for the man who'd plowed into her in the hallway. Probably the same man who'd chased her father away on a snowmobile. Since her father had left a clue, what would keep the other man from coming back to claim it?

Nick grabbed for the cell phone on the nightstand. The display screen indicated a private number. "Yeah."

"Patch did a name search into Alaska state records." A pause lengthened as if an acknowledgment was required.

Patch was their techno-guru back at the SOS office in Texas. Royce Fontaine didn't waste words on simple pleasantries. It took two full seconds for his boss's voice to register.

"You awake?" Royce asked.

Nick scrubbed his hand down his face and glanced at the clock. The bright green digits indicated five-thirty, Alaskan time. "What did you find?"

"Not what, but who. Charles Mercer."

Nick shook his sleep-clouded head. "And Charles Mercer should ring a bell?"

"Frank Richards had contracted with a New York publishing house to sell his military memoirs. Patch hasn't been able to tap into Richards' computer. The motherboard looked pretty much like Swiss cheese. We also learned that Frank Richards had recently been diagnosed with terminal lung cancer. His doctor gave him three months to live, four months ago."

"Could his memoirs be some kind of confession?"

"If so, it wasn't just his actions he's confessing. He's got someone else scared."

"What do Richards' memoirs have to do with Santa?"

"Patch checked his phone records. He'd made two calls to North Pole, Alaska, in the past two weeks. The phone number he called belonged to our Santa Claus, aka Charles Mercer. Mr. Mercer had a legal name change twenty-eight years ago upon his arrival in Fairbanks. Your Santa's fingerprints also match the military records of Mercer."

"Branch?"

"Army. Special Forces."

Nick frowned. "Why change his name?"

"That's what we have to figure out," Royce said. "Do you need help on this one?"

"No. It's still early in the investigation."

"Yeah, but we have one man dead and another missing. I already have Tazer running a scan through military records to see if we find a connection between Mercer and Richards. I lay you odds they served together. I'll alert Kat Sikes from the Anchorage office to head your way."

"How is Kat?" Nick asked. He'd worked with Kat on a mission involving a terrorist element in Florida. The woman was a top agent until her first husband was killed in an embassy bombing in Africa a couple of years ago.

"She and Sam should be back tomorrow from their delayed honeymoon in Nome." Kat had helped keep Sam alive when an SOS agent-gone-bad had tried to end Sam's life during the previous year's Iditarod dogsled race.

Nick rolled to the side of the bed and sat up. "Nome, Alaska, in the winter? Whatever happened to honeymooning in Hawaii?"

"They never made it to Nome when they were competing in the Iditarod. Sam wanted to go, Kat went along with him." Royce laughed. "Me? I would have gone for a tropical beach, not a frozen coastline. I've got another assignment for Sam, but I can send Kat when they get back. Can you hold out for a day or two?"

"Sure. I'm working an inside connection."

"You are?"

"Yeah." Nick stood and walked across the room. "Santa's daughter."

"Santa's daughter, huh? Want Tazer to run a check on her? What's her name?"

"No. I think she's genuine. Her name's Mary...Mary Christmas." Nick grinned, imagining Royce's expression.

"I'm sorry, there must have been some static in the line. Did you say Mary Christmas?"

"That's right. These people really get into the whole Christmas theme up here." Something completely foreign to Nick.

"I knew that, but...Mary Christmas?" Royce paused. "Is she normal?"

Normal? Mary Christmas? Nick envisioned the long silky blond hair and even longer, silkier smooth legs he'd glimpsed peeking out of her robe last night. His groin tightened. "Yeah, she's normal."

"Well, keep an eye on her. If Richards thought Santa was in danger, Santa's daughter might be a target as well. Keep me informed. Kat will be there in the next day or so." Royce ended the call.

Nick slid the cell phone into his pocket. He'd already considered Mary as a target for whoever was after Santa. Thus, the restless night, listening for sounds.

The best way he could protect her and learn more about the town was to get close. A pinch of irritation gnawed at his gut. He liked working alone. Liked keeping a distance from the subjects of his mission. It spared messy goodbyes. And face it, he would be saying goodbye once he'd located Santa and neutralized the threat to the bearded elf and his family. Nick St. Claire didn't stay long in any one place.

Get in, solve the problem and leave.

Passed from foster home to foster home as a child growing up in Texas, he'd learned emotional ties only weighed you down.

Another glance at the clock. He'd promised to meet Mary at eight. In two and a half hours. Going back to sleep wasn't an option. Going for a run was.

He slipped into socks, tennis shoes and several layers of clothing before stepping out into the darkness of an early winter morning. With the cold wind biting at all exposed flesh, Nick reevaluated his decision to jog. After ducking back inside and donning his snow boots and a solid white snowsuit, goggles and hood, he left his room, feeling a bit more prepared for a brisk walk and a chance to learn the layout of the town.

* * *

Mary must have fallen asleep sometime after three because she didn't wake until thirty-five minutes after five, when she looked at her clock again. Nightmares had plagued her. All involving her father and some dark menace lurking in the shadows of the town, of her home and the bed-and-breakfast where she and Nick St. Claire were staying.

Had she scared herself awake or had something disturbed her sleep? Maybe a noise? She sat up and held her breath, straining to hear it again.

A door opened and closed in the hallway, and from the sound of it, right across from hers. She flung the covers back and ran barefoot across the carpeted floor. She took a moment to shove the dresser aside before she could yank open the door.

A man in a white snowsuit stood in the hallway, bundled up from head to toe.

Mary opened her mouth to scream, but before she could utter so much as a squeak, the man reached out, grabbed her arm and spun her around, clamping a hand over her mouth.

Her heart pounded in her chest so hard, she thought maybe she'd pass out, but she couldn't. This could be the man who was after her father. Barely able to breathe, she fought with all her might against the arm crushing her breasts beneath the thin flannel of her pajamas. No matter how much she wiggled and kicked, his hold didn't loosen.

Over the sound of her own muffled grunts, a deep baritone penetrated her frightened mind. "Be still. I'm not going to hurt you."

Too late, her foot had been in mid-swing, and she couldn't stop her heel from gouging the man's shin hard enough to make her heal radiate with the pain.

The man grunted. "It's me, Nick." He let go of her so suddenly, she almost collapsed on the cool tile of the hallway floor. She spun and faced him, ready to kick again, her breath coming in ragged pants, anger replacing fear. "Why the heck did you grab me?"

"Did you have to go and kick me so hard?" He bent, rubbing his shin, pushing his goggles up onto his forehead, exposing those brown-black eyes that sparkled like a moonlit oil-spill.

"What did you expect, after what's happened? My room's broken into—"

"—by your father, so you said—" Nick straightened, a frown denting his forehead with fine lines.

"—my father's missing, and last night a man almost ran me over in the hallway—"

The corners of Nick's lips twitched, "—who could have forgotten to turn off the stove in his house—" And the jerk had the audacity to grin.

"—and you aren't wearing your cowboy hat—" She knew she was floundering, but the man had her tied in freakin' knots!

"—which I couldn't fit under my parka hood—" His grin widened.

Mary glared at Nick, unable to stop now, "—and you expect me to welcome you with a kiss?" She jerked her bare foot back and kicked him again, hopefully in the same spot as the first time.

He yelped. "Hey, what was that for?"

"For laughing at me when, for all I know, you could be the man my father's having to hide from." She flattened both her palms on his chest and pushed. "You could have been feeding me lies all along and be the root of my problems. Give me one good reason why I should trust you." She pushed him again until his back hit the wall behind him. "Just one good reason."

His eyes darkened and his hand grasped her flannel-covered shoulders, jerking her forward.

She gasped, drawing in a deep breath to scream, only for the sound to be muffled by the force of his lips crushing hers in a lip-lock that defied breaking. Even if she'd wanted to push away from him, she couldn't. Her knees buckled and she fell against him, her breasts pressed against the cushiony thickness of his insulated jacket.

At first hard, his mouth softened, his tongue darting out to trace the line of her lips until she opened them on a sigh. He plunged in, past her teeth to her tongue. The gloves he'd had in his hands hit the floor as his fingers rose to thread through her hair, gripping the length. With a gentle tug, he tipped her head backward, exposing the long line of her throat.

Just when she thought she might never breathe again, his lips slid off the end of hers and traced a path along her jaw and downward to the pulse shooting blood up in her ears. Her fingers moved between their bodies, and she slid them inside his jacket, letting his skin warm hers. When his hands rubbed down her sides and slid beneath the hem of her flannel shirt, his warm fingers against her naked skin, Mary's body flared with red-hot desire and she moaned.

Just as quickly as he'd drawn her to him, he set her away, a smile curling his lips as his hands dropped to his sides.

Mary pressed the back of her fingers to her ravaged lips and stared up at him, too shaken to move away. "That wasn't a reason," she said, her voice a husky remnant of her prekissed tone. When she realized how weak she sounded, she forced her shoulders back. "Don't ever do that again. Just because you're stronger doesn't mean you can force unwanted advances on me."

His gaze shifted from her eyes downward to the flare of her nightshirt where the turgid tips of her nipples pressed against soft flannel. "Unwanted?" Dark eyebrows angled upward.

Mary crossed her arms over her chest, heat rising

in her neck to fill her cheeks. Best to defend with a good offense, her daddy always said. "Where were you going anyway?"

"For a walk." He stepped forward.

Mary stepped back. "At this hour?"

"Yeah."

"Honey, this ain't Virginia, or wherever you're from," Mary said. "It's probably minus twenty outside. Are you nuts?"

"I need air."

She purposely stood in his way. "If you're going out to snoop around, I'm going with you."

"I work alone."

"Not as long as I'm around." She narrowed her eyes and pointed a finger at his chest. "Stay. I'll be back in two minutes." She ducked into her room, slamming the door behind her. She dressed, shoved her hair into a ponytail and covered her body from head to toe in cold-weather gear. All the time she dressed, she prayed Nick hadn't left the building. With the snow still falling, his tracks would disappear within minutes.

Grabbing her gloves, Mary flung open her door and raced out, running face-first into Nick's chest. "Oh, well...so you stayed."

"Not that I follow your orders. I was just curious."

Mary straightened. "What do you mean, curious?"

"Whether or not any woman alive could get ready

in just two minutes." He turned and walked toward the exit door. "By the way, it was three."

As she jerked her gloves onto her hands, Mary felt the flash of irritation fade into a chuckle. The man had a sense of humor, warped as it might be.

For the next twenty minutes, they crunched through icy layers of snow along the partially cleared sidewalks lining St. Nicholas Drive, headed northwest past Christmas Towne and the twenty-foot-tall Santa Claus statue. Mary peered into every shadow, wondering where her father was or if there was someone out there watching her and Nick. Surely, even the bad guys didn't get up and out this early on a frigid morning.

They turned left onto Santa Claus Lane and took another left onto Mission Road, passing Snowman Lane and crossing Highway 2.

Mary hadn't realized it, but she'd ended up leading him past all the most famous of street names like Blitzen, Donner and Kris Kringle. The cheerful memories of her childhood lightened her footsteps and chased away the demons in the darkness.

They completed the entire walk in silence, much to Mary's relief. She still didn't have a response to Nick's kiss, and the longer she went without one, the happier she was. What could she add without sounding like a prude?

The freezing temperature served the purpose of cooling her burning cheeks, her hooded jacket hiding her expression from the man. She tucked her gloved hands beneath her armpits to keep frostbite from setting in, her breath creating frost and ice on the woolen scarf pulled up over her mouth and nose.

When she couldn't stand another step without turning into an icicle, she steered Nick back toward St. Nicolas Drive and the Christmas Towne Diner. Lights shone through the frosted windows, spreading a warm yellow glow across the fresh layer of gleaming white snow.

By six-thirty, the diner was half-full of morning customers grabbing a cup of coffee and breakfast before work.

Mary sat across from Nick in a red, vinyl-covered seat next to the frosted windows and inhaled the scents of coffee, pancakes and bacon. She'd come to the conclusion that avoidance of the kiss was the best course of action. Stick to the facts of her father's dilemma and stay clear of entanglements.

In her limited experience, short-term relationships with men she didn't really know wouldn't work. Mary wrapped her hands around the ceramic coffee mug and let the steam rise to thaw her cheeks. "Ahhh. Being warm never felt so good."

"You didn't have to walk with me."

"What, and let you get lost in this thriving metropolis?" Mary huffed softly. "Besides, I couldn't sleep. Not with all that's happened."

Nick stared out at the street and the twenty-foot Santa in all his red and white glory welcoming tourists and customers to Christmas Towne. "What's with the year-round Christmas theme?"

"With a name like North Pole, what did you expect?" She tipped her head to the side and studied the man in front of her.

Black hair, neatly trimmed on the sides, fell down over his forehead, giving him that intriguing mixture of dangerous-spy and little-boy-lost. Add fathomless brown-black eyes and impossibly broad shoulders and you had Nick St. Clair, a killer combination to any woman's self-control, including hers.

Another reason she'd been up all night. How could she even be attracted to a stranger when her father was missing, possibly on the run from a killer?

She dragged her eyes away from Nick and stared around at the groggy customers filling their bellies with warm coffee to chase off the chill. The men exchanged weather reports and news. Some chatted with the waitresses or Lenn, the short-order cook, who ran between the kitchen and the counter with plates of steaming eggs and pancakes.

One man, sitting three booths over, caught her attention, not because he had a remarkable face or anything, more because she didn't recognize him. He stared at her for a long time, his dark eyes narrowing just slightly. Eventually, he lifted his coffee mug, breaking off eye contact. He was probably in a sleep-deprived, morning coma, like half the customers pouring caffeine down their throats. A chill slithered down Mary's spine. She frowned and turned her attention back to Nick.

Nick set his mug on the table and leaned back, crossing his arms over his chest. "I just don't get it. Why make it year-round Christmas in a town so small and out of the way as North Pole?"

"It may surprise you to know that throughout the year, people come from all over the world to visit North Pole. Each year, the post office gets tons of mail addressed to Santa. And each letter is answered with another letter postmarked North Pole." She smiled, thinking of the children who opened their letters, their eyes wide with wonder and excitement.

"Isn't it carrying the commercialism of Christmas a bit far?" Nick asked, his tone crisp and biting like the wind outside the diner's door.

Mary's gaze shot up to his at the hard sound of his voice. "Don't you believe in the spirit of Christmas?"

He stared through the frost-covered window into the near-dawn of the Alaskan winter. "No."

Interesting. Mary leaned closer. "Let me guess, you've never believed in Santa Claus, have you?"

He shot her a hard look. "No."

Her heart tugged in her chest as she imagined a miniature version of Nick turning his back on the joy of Santa and Christmas. "How sad. Didn't your parents even put up a Christmas tree?"

"I didn't have parents." His tone didn't invite further questioning on the subject.

"Oh." What did she say to that?

His eyes narrowed, as if daring her to throw so much as a scrap of pity his way. Nick St. Claire wouldn't tolerate pity. Pity was for weak men, and Nick was anything but weak. The man looked as though he could chew nails with his teeth.

Anything she might have said died on her lips. Mary sat in silence. The semi truce between them shattered by her unwitting questions. Okay, so she'd hit on a sore subject. Growing up without family had to have been difficult and lonely.

If not for the well-rounded childhood she'd had with the most popular parents in the country, Mary might have been more cynical. Her own cynicism hadn't set in until her mother died when she was twelve, and she'd entered her terrible teen years. What had been every child's wish to have Santa as their dad became her constant nightmare.

Growing up as Santa and Mrs. Claus's only daughter, Mary had been teased by her peers relentlessly. Any boy who dared to date her received the same teasing. Her love life suffered and she'd resigned herself to being Santa's helper for the rest of her life.

Until Bradley Kane waltzed into her life. For a short time, she'd entertained visions of weddings and a name change. How many times had she practiced writing Mary Kane and chuckled over naming their firstborn daughter Candy.

Then she'd received the e-mail that had shattered her dreams.

Mary stuffed her hand into her pocket and felt the key she'd found beneath her pillow last night. "I don't know about you, but I need to get into my father's house and find what this key belongs to."

"You think you'll have a problem getting in?"

Mary frowned. Jasmine hadn't been ugly to her, but she'd made it more than clear that Mary was a third wheel on a cart built for two. "I don't know."

Nick pinned her with those soulful black eyes. "What's your relationship with your stepmother?"

Mary's gaze shifted to the frosty window. Blurry figures moved past on the street outside. "We don't have one."

"That bothers you?"

Mary shrugged. How could she tell him she didn't trust her father's wife without sounding like a spoiled child or jealous daughter? She glanced at her watch. "The store should be opening soon. I want to get over to the house before Jasmine leaves it for work." She pulled a bill from her purse, tossed it on the table and stood, holding up the key her father had left beneath the pillow. "Are you ready to see where this clue leads?"

"After you." He too dropped a bill on the table to cover his portion of breakfast.

When they exited the diner, one of the North Pole police cars whipped by, lights flashing, headed toward Christmas Towne and Mary's family home.

"What the hell?" Her heart choking her throat, Mary broke into a jog, careful to watch for icy patches on the sidewalk.

Snow crunched behind her, the sound of Nick following her strangely comforting with all the frightening circumstances surrounding her father's disappearance. Could it be they'd found him? Could he be hurt...maybe dead?

Mary ran faster, her lungs stinging, laboring to breathe the icy air over the two blocks she ran. *Oh, please, let him be all right.*

The store was still closed. The police SUV stood in front of Mary's childhood home. Without thinking, Mary raced through the front door. "What's happened? Where's my father?"

Jasmine, dressed in a deep red sweater pantsuit, stepped away from Officer Baskin. "Mary, I'd hoped you wouldn't have to see this, but the house was broken into last night while I was asleep."

"Who? How?" Mary asked. Nick stepped through the door behind her and slipped a hand around her waist. She leaned into him, thankfully.

Jasmine glanced from Mary to Nick, her eyebrows rising briefly. Then her attention shifted to Trey Baskin. "I don't know who, but it appears as though he crawled in through a window in the laundry room. I had a fan circulating the air in my bedroom and didn't hear a thing until almost too late. Thank goodness I keep a gun in the drawer beside my bed."

The woman's fingers twisted a tissue in her hand, her face paler than normal. A single tear slid down her cheek. "It was very distressing to know someone was in the house, what with your father missing and me all alone. There's just no telling what could have happened."

Mary forced herself not to snort. For a newlywed, Jasmine didn't seem nearly as upset by her husband's disappearance as she was about her own safety. If Mary had been the newlywed, she'd have been frantic. Unbidden, her glance strayed to Nick. As quickly as it had gone there, she pulled her attention back to Jasmine. Not that Nick would ever be her husband or anything, but if he were, she'd be worried about him to the point she wouldn't sleep at night until she knew he was okay.

"Did you notice anything missing?" Trey asked.

"No, not yet." She waved at the mess in the living area behind her. Furniture laid overturned, cushions slashed, papers scattered from what Mary could see. "I can't imagine what someone would want from our house. Everything valuable is in the store safe."

"Mind if I have a look?" Mary hated being a stranger in the house. Asking permission to enter the only place she'd ever known as home didn't seem right.

"I think we should wait until Santa returns, don't you? He'll know if anything's missing." Jasmine laid her manicured fingers on Trey's arm. "Have you heard anything?"

Officer Baskin patted her hand and stepped out of reach. "If we hear anything about Santa, you'll be the first to know."

Her teeth grinding together, Mary bit hard on her tongue to keep from saying that if anyone had a right to be the first notified, it was Santa's daughter. She shouldn't care if she was first, just as long as she heard.

The hand around her waist tightened and Nick moved closer, bending to whisper in her ear. "The key." The warmth of his breath stirred the loose tendrils of her hair across her neck, heating her blood and sending unnerving sensations throughout her body.

Mary sucked in a breath to clear her mind, then pulled off her glove and stuck her hand in her pocket. With the tips of her fingers, she turned the key over, the cool metal reminding her that she needed to focus on her goal and get into the house, most likely the basement where she and her father had always stored their memorabilia. She stepped toward her stepmother and away from Nick. "Jasmine, this might not be a good time, but I had some things in the basement I need to collect. Would it be too much of a bother?"

Jasmine shredded the tissue between her red-tipped nails. "I don't think now is a good time. Officer Baskin will want to look around, won't you?" She sent Officer Baskin a wide-eyed, questioning look, inviting him to agree. "I haven't had time to glance over everything to make sure nothing's missing. Maybe another day?" She hooked her hand through Trey's arm. "Come, Officer, let me show you the window he came through." She glanced over her shoulder. "Do you mind showing yourself out, Mary?"

Steam rose under Mary's turtleneck collar. She waited until her stepmother disappeared into the laundry room before turning to Nick. "Want to make a run for it?" She eyed the hallway, her brows dipping low.

"No. We'll come back when there isn't a police officer around. I wonder what she's hiding that she won't let you in?"

"I don't know, but I'd bet my last dollar she has something to do with my father's disappearance." Mary shoved her hands into her gloves. "And if she's hurt him in any way..."

"You'll let the law handle it." Nick grabbed Mary's arm and led her toward the door. "Who are your father's closest friends? Maybe they know of his whereabouts."

Her feet dragging, Mary stepped out of the house, the arctic air cooling her fevered cheeks. "Friends. My father has lots of friends. He knows everyone in town."

"Who is he closest to? Who would he confide in?" Nick tucked her gloved hand in his and strode toward the B and B.

Mary liked to think her father would confide in her. And he'd tried. "His poker buddies, Reuben Tyler, Bob Feegan and Jimmy Janovich. He's known them since forever."

"Good. We'll start with Reuben."

"Don't you think the police would have started there?" Mary asked.

"Yeah, but if your father's in trouble, they might not be as willing to share his location with the authorities as with his daughter." He lengthened his stride, practically dragging her along behind him.

Mary dug her boots in the snow. "And you think they'll talk to me with you along? Maybe I should go by myself?"

"I'm not letting you out of my sight. Someone might be after you if they can't get to your father. Now, where does this Reuben guy live?" He stopped next to the rental car that had brought them to North Pole from the airport.

"Four blocks over." Mary pointed east, looking out over the rooftops.

"Hop in. We'll drive—"

A thundering boom blasted the morning air. The earth rocked beneath Mary's feet, throwing her against Nick.

CHAPTER 6

"Get down!" Nick shoved Mary to the ground, throwing his body over hers. Explosions and the rapid report of firefighting in Iraq surfaced in his memories. When silence settled over the town again, he dared to look up.

"What was that? What's happening?" Mary's muffled voice rose from the snow.

"Stay down." Nick pressed a hand to Mary's back to keep her from popping up as he rose to his haunches and scanned the street.

"Oh God." She tried to move beneath his hand. "Let me up, the snow's cold."

"Cold is better than dead." Then he spotted a plume of smoke rising from the direction Mary had pointed moments before. A heavy weight settled in his gut. "Where did you say Reuben lives?" He released the pressure on Mary's back and climbed to his feet, extending a hand to pull her to hers.

"Over there—" Mary's gaze panned the rooftops and her face paled. "You don't think..."

Sirens wailed and a fire truck appeared from around a corner, lights blazing.

Mary jerked open the car door. "Come on!"

Nick rounded the vehicle and slid into the driver's seat.

"This can't be happening." Mary shook her head. "Reuben Tyler is one of the nicest men I know. Why would anyone want to hurt him? Could you hurry?" She rocked in the seat beside him, a single tear rolling from her eye and making a long track down her cheek. "If they would hurt Reuben, what will they do to my father?" She stared across at Nick, her blue eyes swimming in still more tears. "We have to make this stop before anyone else is hurt."

A wave of protectiveness washed over him and made him want to wrap this woman, this stranger, in his arms and shield her from the ugliness of what was happening. A mental image of Frank Richards appeared in Nick's memory. Instead of reaching out to take Mary in his arms, he shoved the car in reverse and backed out of the parking space, slammed the shift into drive and shot out onto the icy street.

Focus, St. Claire.

Focus, or Mary might end up like Richards.

He could have run the four blocks, as much

adrenaline as he had racing through his veins, as much from the explosion as from surfacing battle memories and frustration. Damn! Why did she have to cry? Had she ranted and raved, he could have handled it. "We'll find your father," he said through gritted teeth.

"Alive?"

He didn't answer—couldn't. How could he make a promise he had no idea whether or not he could keep? Until they located Santa Claus, all bets were off. For all he knew, the killer could have gotten to him already.

Rescue personnel jumped from the fire truck as Nick pulled onto the street. He slowed, but before he could shift into park, Mary flung her door open and leaped out of the car.

"Damn!" Nick parked and jumped out, racing to catch up. "Mary." He grabbed her arm, pulling her to a halt. "What if whoever did this is still hanging around? You could be his next target."

"I don't care. Reuben's family." She jerked her arm free and continued toward the blasted shell of what used to be a house.

Emergency medical technicians wheeled a stretcher across the ground with a man draped in thick blankets.

"Reuben!" Mary caught up with them when they stopped at the rear of the ambulance.

"Ma'am." A young technician blocked her from

coming closer. "You'll have to stay back. He's pretty badly burned."

A soot-covered hand rose from the blankets, reaching out for her.

Mary pushed past the technician and grasped the hand, staring down into the man's battered face.

Nick stepped up beside her and circled her waist with one arm.

"What happened, Reuben?" Mary asked. "Who did this?"

The injured man shook his head, his lips remaining closed.

"Does this have anything to do with my father?" she implored.

He nodded.

"Oh, Reuben. I know you can't talk." She lifted his bunched fist to her cheek. "But do you know where he is? Do you know where my father is?"

The man never uttered a word, his glassy gaze fixed on Mary, his mouth pressed into a thin, pain-filled line.

"We need to get him to the hospital." The EMT at the end of the stretcher moved it closer to the ambulance. "I'm sorry, but he needs immediate attention for the burns and other injuries."

When Mary stepped away, the old man on the stretcher pressed his hand into hers, then let it fall, his eyes closing.

Mary gasped, her eyes widening. "Is he—"

SAINT NICK

The other EMT touched a stethoscope to Reuben's chest. "He passed out. Let's load him up. Fairbanks has been alerted and they're waiting."

The fire chief stopped to speak with the ambulance driver. "Looks like a busted gas line. Is Reuben gonna be okay?"

The driver shrugged. "We'll keep ya posted." Then he climbed into the front seat and closed the door.

A busted gas line. Nick wanted to know if someone had busted it or if it had been an accident. He was about to ask when Mary backed into his arms. He couldn't move with her tucked against him, watching the doors close behind Reuben and the technicians. Then she buried her face in Nick's winter jacket, silent sobs shaking her body.

Nick stood transfixed for several long moments. Every cell in his body warred between SOS training and his own body's reaction to Mary leaning against him. Finally, his physical instincts won out, and he pulled her to him, cradling her head against his chest. The urge to carry her away from this town and all its madness almost overwhelmed him. As he touched his lips to the top of her head, he realized he was getting in too deep.

While the firemen worked to extinguish the blaze, the ambulance pulled away, the siren blaring to life, filling the quiet street with its urgent wail.

After a moment, Mary's sobs subsided and she grew still. "I'm sorry." She looked up into his eyes, her own red rimmed, her skin blotchy, but no less beautiful. "You don't even know me and here I am..."

His arms tightened around her. "It's okay," he told her, though he was feeling anything but okay. Holding her in his arms had only stirred the feelings he'd had earlier when he'd kissed her to make her shut up. He wanted to keep on holding her and kissing her until the world stopped spinning.

That wasn't the way an SOS agent worked. Ever since Elaina, he'd sworn off getting involved with anyone on a case. He'd learned his lesson. You love. You lose.

Deep down, he knew Mary wasn't like her. Elaina had been trained to deceive. Mary was innocent, naïve to the tricks people played on each other. Still, Nick knew better than to get involved while working a case. Involvement made you lose focus.

Snow drifted from the sky in heavy, fat flakes as Nick set Mary away from him. "We should check in with your father's other friends."

Mary's face blanched, her hand rising to her mouth, her fingers curled into a bulky fist. "Do you think..."

"We should check," he repeated. Nick turned toward the rental car, but when he looked back over his shoulder, Mary hadn't moved. He grabbed her hand and tugged her behind him, but her fingers wouldn't unbend. "What have you got?"

She stared down at her hand, her fingers opening

to display a soot-covered figure of a moose. "Reuben must have given this to me. I was so upset, I didn't even realize." A sad smile played around her lips. "He's our master toy maker at the store. He makes the most amazing toys and carves animals out of wood."

"Why would he give it to you?"

Mary stared at the moose, her brow furrowing. "Reuben can't talk, hasn't ever since I've known him." She spoke slowly as if piecing together the significance of the moose a word at a time. "He doesn't tell me things..." she looked up at Nick, a smile breaking through the frown. "He shows me. This moose must mean something." Then her frown returned. "But what?"

Nick glanced at the gawkers gathering around the smoldering house. "Let's get in the car."

Mary clutched the moose to her chest and climbed into the vehicle. Once in the passenger seat, she clipped on her seat belt, then opened her fist.

Nick settled in the seat beside her. "What were you asking him when he gave you that?"

"I was asking him if the explosion had anything to do with my father." Her forehead crinkled. "He nodded in answer to that question."

Nick reached across and grabbed Mary's arms. "What else did you ask?"

"If he knew where my father was. This moose has something to do with where my father is." She squeezed her eyes shut. "Where would my father be that has anything to do with a moose? Where?" Then her eyes opened. "Moose Lodge!"

"Moose Lodge?" Nick let go of Mary's arms. "Where is it?" He shifted into gear and pulled out on the street.

She laid a hand on his arm. "Nick, you can't get there in this car. But I know how we can. Go two blocks and turn right on Dennis Road, then take another right on Aztec. I have a friend I think can help." Mary's tears had dried and her jaw set in a firm line.

Nick's attention shifted from the road to this more determined Mary, admiration swelling in his chest. Most women would fall apart at this point. Not Mary. A few tears and she was back on top of it.

"Here! Stop here." Mary was out of the car before Nick came to a complete stop.

"Gotta talk to her about basic driving safety," he muttered beneath his breath.

A man met Mary outside a weather-weary garage where snowmobiles of all shapes and sizes lined the parking spaces in various stages of repair. Some had For Sale signs tied to them.

Mary stood slightly behind the man, but facing Nick. "Ed, this is Nick, my...boyfriend." She gave Nick a pointed stare. When Ed shot a narrow-eyed glance down at her, she smiled up at him. "Ed and I dated back in high school, didn't we Ed? But that was ages ago." Mary sidled up to Nick and tucked her arm in his. "You aren't going to get jealous, are you?" She batted her eyes at Nick and squeezed his arm hard.

His body hardened in response to Mary pressing against him. "Maybe." Nick studied Ed. The man looked none too pleased to meet him and Nick felt likewise, a sensation he wasn't familiar with on a first meeting with a complete stranger.

"Chris said you were back in town." Ed's gaze moved from Mary to run the length of Nick. "But I thought you were alone."

"Nope. I brought Nick." She smiled at Ed. "I promised Nick I'd take him on a snowmobile ride around the area. I don't suppose you have a couple we could rent, do you?"

Ed wiped his hands on a greasy rag. "I don't rent snowmobiles. I fix them."

"Then do you have a couple we could borrow?" Mary looked up at Ed. "Please?"

Nick could have laughed at Ed the way Mary's blue-eyed gaze melted his anger so easily. Then again, Nick was ready to give her just about anything if she'd look at him with that much pleading in her eyes. Damned female.

Ed looked from Mary to Nick and back to Mary before answering, "Oh, all right. You can take mine. It's a two-seater that I've refurbished. It'll do." Ed led the way into the shop. "Did you hear the explosion a while ago? I heard from Millie at the convenience store that Reuben Tyler's place blew."

Mary ducked her head. "Yeah. He's on his way to the hospital in Fairbanks."

"Probably a busted gas line." Ed collected a set of keys from a hook on the wall in the office inside. Piles of paper littered the desk, and dark handprints coated the walls and doorframes. "Been thinking about converting to electric heat, myself. What with the price of propane and all. Might be worth checkin' into. Gas can be dangerous." Ed walked through the shop to the back door.

"When do you need it back?" Mary asked.

"No hurry. I ain't goin' for no joyride in this weather." He motioned toward the thick clouds dumping snowflakes like so much confetti at a Thanksgiving Day parade in the city. He slogged through the dirty snow in back of the shop and brushed the loose white powder from a vinyl snowmobile seat. "You know how to run one of these?" Ed pushed the key in the ignition, his gaze raking Nick as if questioning his manhood.

"Yeah." To prove it, Nick climbed on the seat, flicked the key and pressed the start switch. The engine chugged and died. On his second attempt, the engine roared to life.

"Hmph. Just don't stop in a snowdrift." Ed turned his attention to Mary and spoke in a lower tone. "What say you ditch this guy and go out with me, Mary? We can pick up where we left off in high school."

Nick caught the gist of what Ed was saying, and despite himself he strained to hear Mary's answer.

"Ed, I appreciate the loan of the snowmobile, but I can't go out with you. I'm with Nick now."

Nick caught Mary's smile and returned it as if he couldn't hear a word they were saying.

Ed glared at Nick. "That could change."

Mary touched the other man's arm and smiled gently. "I like you, Ed, but I'm not interested in dating you."

Nick grinned and waved. "Thanks, Ed. The engine sounds good. Mary and I will have it back to you before dark." He raised his brows. "You ready, darlin'?" he said in his best southern drawl.

Her cheeks bloomed with color. "Yes, I am." She climbed on the back of the machine and wrapped her arms around his waist. "See you later, Ed."

When Nick took off, the surge of the machine forced Mary to squeeze her arms tighter around his waist. A gloved hand covered hers for a brief, reassuring moment.

Mary directed him west, heading out of town toward the Tanana River, parts of which were frozen over by a month of freezing temperatures. The machine raced down streets until the roads turned to paths through the trees. How long had it been since Mary had been out to Moose Lodge? Would she be able to get them there safely?

. . .

As the trails wound through valleys and over hills, across frozen creeks and farther out into the wilds, Mary wondered if she was headed in the right direction. Her most recent memory of Moose Lodge was from a fishing trip with her father during the summer seven years ago.

Snow blurred the terrain, limiting visibility to less than ten feet in front of them. Nick slowed the machine to keep from ramming into a tree or boulder submerged beneath the fluffy white blanket.

Perched on the back, her arms clutched around a stranger, Mary questioned her sanity. What was she thinking heading out into the wilderness at the mercy of a man she'd known less than twenty-four hours? Was she so concerned about her father she'd failed to consider her own safety? Her arms tightened and Nick's hand covered hers as if reassuring her that he wouldn't let anything happen to her.

That little bit of reassurance went a long way. If Nick was going to hurt her, he'd had plenty of opportunities before now to do so. Deep down, Mary believed that he was there to help. Which left her on the backseat of a snowmobile, her legs wrapped around a man she'd seen nearly naked only last night. The image of him in nothing but a towel surfaced and the juncture of her thighs ached, rubbing against his backside.

Though her hands and feet were freezing, a fire deep inside warmed her body. *Just what I need. To fall for another transient. A man who has no intention of sticking around, another man I know nothing about.*

Mary shook her head. No way. Hadn't she had her heart broken already? Wasn't once enough?

Still the solid feel of Nick in front of her, the breadth of his shoulders shielding her from the worst of the snow pelting her face and eyes, was downright sexy. Her cheeks flushed with heat about the time Nick slowed at a fork in the road.

"What do you want to do?" he yelled.

Wrong question. She wanted to take him to bed and explore what she hadn't seen beneath the towel the night before. "Wh-what?"

"Which way?"

"Oh." Her face burned hotter.

Nick swiveled in the seat to stare at her. "Are you all right?"

No. She wasn't all right, she was falling in lust with him and she couldn't stop herself, like being swept over the edge of a cliff. Damn, she was going to crash and burn all over again. "Yes, yes, of course." She nodded to the left. "Take the left fork." *And please quit staring at me with those brown-black eyes that could melt my resolve to stay clear of men like you.*

After what felt like an eternity, probably only a second or two, Nick returned his attention to the trail and sped forward along the route she'd indicated.

Mary lifted her face to the wind, the icy air

chilling the fire in her cheeks. Did the man have this effect on all women? Or just this one? Mary wasn't sure what answer she preferred.

Nick hit the brakes and the snowmobile skidded sideways on the crusty snow beneath the fresh layer, before coming to a halt. If she hadn't been holding on so tightly, she'd have ended up flying into a tree. With a quick flick of his wrist, Nick turned the key, cutting the engine.

"What the heck?" Mary swiveled around to stare at the trail ahead. Barely masked under the thin layer of new-fallen snow were tracks left by another snowmobile.

"Shh!" Nick leaped from the machine, grabbed Mary's arm and yanked her off. He tugged her through three feet of snow and shoved her into a drift behind a large spruce tree. She fell face-first into the snow. The more she struggled, the deeper she went. After several clumsy seconds, Mary struggled her way out of the drift and brushed off the snow clinging to her eyelashes. She fought her first inclination to shove Nick for slinging her around like a rag doll.

Nick crouched beside the tree, his hands holding a pistol, aimed at the trail in front of him.

Forget shoving him. Mary's heart slammed against her rib cage. The man had brought his gun. Why hadn't she noticed it? Wouldn't she have felt it beneath his jacket? Was he going to shoot her father?

She took a steadying breath and asked in what she hoped was a calm voice, "What's wrong?"

"Fresh tracks beneath the new snow." He nodded toward the trail. The tracks appeared to lead in from another direction, converging several yards ahead of them. "How much farther to the lodge?"

Mary studied the trail, the creek running alongside and through the trees. "Should be just around that hill ahead." Despite her best effort, her voice shook. "You aren't going to hurt my father, are you? Tell me again you're not one of the bad guys." Her words faded away when Nick turned toward her, a frown making him look even fiercer, more deadly with the gun in his hand.

"Now wouldn't be the time to ask."

Mary inhaled sharply, all the blood rushing from her head.

Nick shook his head. "Calm down. I told you, I'm here to help your father. Now, will you shut up and let me do my job?"

She let go of the breath she held and sagged with relief. "Why didn't you tell me you brought your gun?"

"It didn't come up." His attention focused on the woods around and ahead of them. After a long moment, he stood. "Stay here."

Hugging the side of the hill and staying in the dark shadows of the trees, Nick moved forward like a thief on the prowl, his footsteps muffled by thick snow.

Mary huddled next to the spruce for all of a minute before concern for Nick and her father drove her out of hiding to follow in Nick's footprints. Only for her it was more wading through the heavy snow than stepping.

What if something had happened to her father? What if whoever had set off the explosion at Reuben's had a similar fate awaiting Nick or her father at the lodge?

Nick rounded the edge of the hill and disappeared, leaving Mary alone in the near dark, the cold seeping through her jacket like the hand of death. She shivered and stumbled, breaking her fall by grabbing a low-hanging tree branch. Snow shook off and plopped onto her head. She brushed it from her face and stared ahead.

Losing sight of Nick made the wilderness seem even more vast, unyielding and treacherous. Every snap of a twig, every rustle of dried leaves made her jump until she found herself running, slogging through the snow to catch up with the man and his gun.

Nestled in a stand of trees, a faint trickle of smoke rising from the stone chimney, stood a ramshackle one-room shack her father had affectionately named Moose Lodge.

Could her father be there? Where had Nick gone?

Mary ran forward, desperate to find her father and stop the craziness. Abandoning the side of the hill for the path, she ran toward the cabin.

Before she had gone ten feet, something hit her from the side, then picked her up and tossed her into another huge snowbank. She fell on her back, the wind knocked from her, opening her eyes just as a large object landed on top of her.

CHAPTER 7

"I THOUGHT I told you to stay put." Nick's heart thundered inside his chest. He'd been studying the shack, searching for signs of habitation, when he'd heard someone running up behind him.

His first instinct was to shoot first and ask questions later. When he'd turned his weapon on his pursuer, he recognized the powder-blue jacket and snowpants.

As quickly as he recognized her, he realized she was running right for a cabin that could be occupied by a killer, waiting for just this kind of opportunity. He'd done the only thing he could think to do. He'd knocked her off the trail and behind a tree, out of sight and hopefully out of target range.

"Get. Off. Me," she forced out between wheezing breaths.

Nick rolled to the side and up onto his haunches,

alert for any movement from the shack and nearby. "How am I supposed to protect you if you don't do as I tell you?" he hissed.

"My father could be in there." She lay on her back for another moment, sucking in a deep breath before sitting up.

"I take it this is Moose Lodge?" He leaned out from the trunk of the tree, his pistol in the lead. "Not much of a lodge."

"Yeah. My dad and his buddies spend their weekends fishing from here in the summer."

Nick sat back on his heels behind the tree. "If I go check things out, can I count on you to stay still?" He focused the full intensity of his gaze on her.

A glazed look formed over Mary's eyes, and she nodded.

As if he'd believe she'd stay put. She'd chased after him on the trail. "I won't leave if I think you'll run out like an idiot again."

Her back stiffened. "I'm not an idiot."

"Then don't put yourself in harm's way." He couldn't help himself. The hurt doe-eyed look she gave him, followed by the stubborn set of her jaw made him want to kiss her.

Despite his best judgment, he leaned forward and pressed his lips to hers. Before he could deepen the contact and forget his mission, he jumped to his feet and ran toward the house.

His soldier training kicking in, he hugged the

trees surrounding the clearing and zigzagged to limit the targeting experience of a would-be assassin.

The clearing remained silent, snow falling in thick waves, the wind lifting and swirling the white flakes to slap against his face. His passage didn't stir human, bird or animal. He was alone. Or was he?

When he reached the door, he studied the shadows in the woods to the left and right of the structure. His hand closed on the latch holding the door shut, and he eased up on it, careful not to make a sound. Nick sucked in a deep breath and slammed his heel against the wooden planks. The door flung open, crashing against the wall with the force of his kick.

Nick held back a second and then, crouching low, ducked inside, his eyes adjusting to the gloom within. The room was warm as though someone had been there recently. The glowing coals of a dying fire smoldered in the roughed-in fireplace.

"He's not here, is he?"

Nick swung around, his weapon pointed at Mary's chest, her powder-blue jacket covered in a light dusting of white.

Her hands whipped up in a defensive position, her eyes wide, her pretty mouth formed in the shape of a startled O.

"Do you have a death wish, woman?" He yanked her out of the doorframe into the room and shut the door behind her.

"No, but I want to know what happened to my father." Her voice shook as she stared at the gun. "You would have shot me, wouldn't you?"

"Maybe I should have." He shook his head. "You seem hell-bent on getting yourself killed today." His gaze shifted from her back to the room.

"I'm just concerned about my father." Her unspoken message told him more than her words.

"You don't trust me, do you?" His head tipped to the side.

"Would you trust you if you were me?"

Nick chuckled, the absurdity of her words lightening his anger.

"You don't have to laugh at me. You're the one carrying a gun. What am I supposed to do, let you shoot my father?"

Lowering his gun, Nick walked over to her and grabbed her shoulders. "I'm not here to kill your father. The sooner you believe me, the sooner we can get on with finding him." He shouldn't have moved that close. It only made him want to get closer and he still hadn't ascertained the safety of their current position. Nick sighed and let go of her.

"I'm trying hard to believe you, but I don't have much to go on. You haven't shown me any credentials."

"We don't carry them. I work for a secret organization. Emphasis on *secret*."

"And that's supposed to set my mind at ease?" She

snorted, rubbing her gloved hands over her arms as if chasing away a chill. "People who live with secrets are only covering nasty truths."

"Or protecting others." Nick lifted a book from a makeshift kitchen table. He opened it, fanning through the pages. Dust wafted through the room. "It's as much as you'll get. You'll just have to go on blind faith."

"That's a tough sell." She circled the tiny room in four steps, lifting a sleeping bag from a cot in the corner. "He was here. This is his.

"Are you sure it wasn't left here and someone else used it?"

Mary lifted the bag and sniffed. "No, that's Dad's cologne. I'd know it anywhere." She hugged the sleeping bag to her chest and stared across the floor at him. "What's happening, Nick? Who would want to hurt my father?"

"I don't know any more than I know who killed Frank Richards, but we need to get out of here. If I'm not mistaken, there was more than one set of snowmobile tracks in the snow outside."

Mary tossed the bag on the cot, and something fell to the floor between the cot and the wall. She reached for it and straightened, a newspaper clutched in her hand. "This is odd."

"What is?" Nick crossed to stand beside her, staring down at a copy of the *Fairbanks Daily News Miner*, dated the day before.

"Dad's on the run and he takes the time to read the newspaper?" A shiver shook her body, and she tucked the paper inside her jacket. "We'd better get back before this snowstorm gets any worse. The temperature is falling fast."

Nick shook his head. And he thought it couldn't get any colder. He'd been on missions in frigid climates, but he was fast learning a new meaning for the word cold. "Let me." He pushed her to the side of the door and opened it, standing away from the entrance. Nothing moved but the continuous downpour of heavy snowflakes.

He glanced at her. "Do I have to tie you up to make you wait for my signal?"

Mary sighed. "No. I'll wait."

He didn't have any rope, but if he did, he'd sure as hell tie her up. Twice now she'd jumped the gun before he'd secured the perimeter. All he could go on was her word, which hadn't been very reliable thus far. Nick slipped through the door and made a complete circle around the cabin, looking for footprints or any other sign of someone lurking, waiting to pounce.

When he reached the front of the cabin he paused and listened.

"Whoever was here is gone. Aren't you giving it a little overkill?" Mary asked from deep in the shadows of the cabin.

A surge of anger came and went. She was probably right. If her father had been there, he'd definitely left.

Unbidden, an image of Frank Richards' blood-soaked body rose in his mind. Nick's chest tightened as he imagined Mary dead because he didn't take precautions. No, his actions weren't overkill.

An arctic blast reminded him they weren't in the clear yet. The best they could hope for was to get back to town before they couldn't see the trail at all. Nick studied the snow falling in the dusky shadows. Hell, they might already be too late. "Let's go."

Mary hurried out of the cabin, her blue gaze darting to the left and right.

Hiding a grin, Nick turned and slogged his way through the mounting snow to the snowmobile they'd left down the trail. Mary might make a good agent if she weren't so impetuous. She was growing on him, and he had to admit he liked it when she fit snugly against him on the back of the snowmobile.

His snowsuit tightened at the thought and tightened even more when he slid in place on the vinyl seat.

Mary hopped on behind him, slipped her arms around his waist and tucked her body against his. Okay, maybe riding double wasn't such a good idea. At this rate, he'd run into a tree if he couldn't keep his mind off the blond beauty with the bizarre name.

In his head, Nick reminded himself about rule

number one of being a special agent: never fall for the beautiful woman. They're always trouble.

Remember Elaina?

Nick turned the key and revved the engine, spinning the snowmobile around in a circle.

Mary's arms tightened around his middle.

Maybe he wasn't being fair to Mary. Elaina had been a dark-haired, sultry beauty, working as a double agent. He'd fallen for all her lies and, because of his lapse in judgment, almost got himself and fellow agent Casanova Valdez killed. Nick had deserved to die for his lapse in common sense, but his mistake shouldn't have endangered his friend. Of course, Mary wasn't Elaina.

Mary's bright blue eyes and silky blond hair gave her the appearance of an angel, innocent and gullible. But he'd seen the strength of devotion to her father. She'd be a force to reckon with if someone threatened her or her father.

Nick wondered what it felt like to love a father the way Mary loved hers. He hadn't stayed long enough in any foster home to form an attachment to a father figure. The closest he'd come was his respect for Royce Fontaine, his friend and mentor.

With the thickening snow drowning out any bit of light from the winter sun, the going was slow and took twice as long as the trip out. The wind kicked up, biting through his gloves, making his fingers numb.

Mary shivered behind him, her face buried in the back of his jacket. His hands and feet were cold, even with the miniature heaters on the hand- and footrests. Mary had to be freezing. He increased his speed, carefully negotiating the turns in the trail.

So intent on avoiding a head-on collision with a boulder or giant spruce, Nick wasn't prepared when another snowmobile erupted from a side trail, swerving within inches of their front end.

Nick jerked the handlebar too late to miss the other vehicle. The front runner of their snowmobile clipped the back of the other machine. At the edge of an embankment, the sudden movement sent them over and sliding down a twenty-foot slope toward a frozen creek.

Holding on with everything he had, Nick tried to steer the machine to a halt, but they were moving too fast toward a huge boulder.

"Jump!" he yelled, kicked against the footrest and threw himself to the side.

At the same time, Mary's arms let go of his waist.

Nick crashed into the snow, his shoulder hitting a rock before he rolled and continued his wild tumble down the hillside. Pain radiated from each point he rammed into an obstacle beneath the snowy surface. He reached out, grasping for something to slow his fall, but his gloved fingers couldn't find anything but snow and loose rocks.

More snow and debris slipped down the hillside

with him. If he continued to fall, he wouldn't stop until he crashed through the ice in the creek. And if he didn't break all his bones getting there, he'd die of hypothermia before he got back to civilization. As this thought crossed his mind, his back hit against something solid and his downward spiral ended in a bone-jarring halt. The rest of the hillside continued tumbling down on top of him, pelting him with rocks, snow and sticks. Then Mary's powder-blue-clad body slammed into him and knocked the air out of his lungs.

MARY LAY with her face smashed against the solid wall she'd crashed into, her nose smarting from hitting it. Nerves throughout her body reported in, detailing all the aches and pains collected on her death slide down the embankment. She'd lost her gloves somewhere on the hillside, knocked from her hands as she scrambled to find a handhold. Too soon, the cold seeped into her fingertips, spreading up her arms into her body, and she shivered.

The wall beneath her moved, a coat-padded arm curling around her. "You okay?" Nick's breath warmed the top of her head, her hood having fallen off in her fall.

"I just fell twenty feet down a rocky slope—you do the math." She tried to move but felt wedged against him, her chest and torso firmly smashed into his. The shock of the attack, on top of the terror of free-falling, made her movements slow and unwieldy.

An engine revved on the trail above them.

Nick seized her shoulders and shoved her away from him, then rolled behind the tree he'd been leaning against.

One minute Mary was sitting on a hillside wondering what the hell had just happened, the next, she was thrown on her back into the snow behind the tree. Nick's body slammed down on top of her, squeezing the air from her lungs.

A loud bang echoed through the treetops and a splinter of wood bit into her cheek. "Crap!" Mary yelled. "Is that what I think that is?"

"Shut up and be still." Nick covered her head with his face and arms, his body completely burying her in the snow.

Another bang split the air, the sharpness of the report sent fear searing through Mary. Someone was shooting at them. The snow beneath her didn't chill her nearly as much as knowing someone wanted to kill her or Nick, or both of them. Mary lay still, her ears straining to hear what her eyes couldn't see.

The rumbling engine revved again and roared off into the distance.

Nick lifted his head enough to peer around the edge of the tree trunk.

"I think he left," Mary whispered. The chill of a

moment ago transformed into a slow, steady boil as her body became increasingly aware of Nick's on top of hers. His chest rested against her, his hips pressing into her hips, a hard ridge evident beneath the bulky snowsuit, pressing into her lower belly.

Heaven help her. She'd just been shot at and all she could think about was the way Nick felt lying on top of her.

Nick dragged his gaze back to her. "You're right, he's gone." Still, he didn't make a move.

With Nick's lips a few short inches from hers, and adrenaline pinging through her veins like a pinball, Mary's mouth dried, her heartbeat increasing to a mad pace. She ran her tongue over her lips, searching for something to say, coming up with nada. Every ounce of her energy seemed to pour into her arms, urging her to...to...

She reached out, cupped the sides of Nick's cheeks and pulled his face down to hers.

He didn't put up a fight, didn't resist.

When their lips met, Nick took control, jerking off his gloves to tangle his fingers in her hair. His lips slanted over hers, his tongue scraping across her teeth, pushing through to toy with hers.

The ridge between them hardened and Mary squirmed to get closer, cursing the layers of clothing in the way.

Her body ached to be next to his, skin-to-skin. She wanted to touch him, feel him, run her fingers over the hard muscles of his chest and down his washboard abs to...

Nick's lips left hers and trailed a path along her chin to the sensitive area beneath her earlobe.

Without his head shielding her face, a large fat snowflake landed on her eyelid, melting against her heated skin. Another flake followed the first until the cool air and direness of the situation penetrated her lust-clouded brain.

Was she absolutely insane? What was she doing? She slid her hands between them and pushed against his chest.

When Nick's lips left the curve of her neck, Mary's entire body chilled. She wanted more but knew she'd be a fool to continue down this path.

Nick stared down at her, his eyes black and glassy. Then he was on his feet, racing up the side of the hill, his gun drawn.

Although she'd heard the snowmobile drive away, Mary couldn't stop the rush of fear washing over her. What if he hadn't gone far? What if he was gunning for Nick?

Mary scrambled to her knees and peered around the tree trunk.

Nick had reached the top of the hill, holding close to the tree trunks, barely visible through the thickening snowfall. Then he was sliding down the hill again, headed for the snowmobile that had come to a rest on its side against a large boulder.

Mary worked her way across the slope, collecting their gloves before heading for the machine. She reached it at the same time as Nick.

If not for the cushioning of the seat where it hit, the machine would probably be a complete wreck. As it was, it had sustained considerable damage to the runners and body in the tumble down the steep slope. Ed Scruggs would not be happy.

With Nick on the handlebars and Mary at the other end, they tugged and leaned hard on the machine, pushing it into the upright position. Once on its skids, the snowmobile slid downward again.

Nick and Mary braced against it until it came to rest again on the boulder that had stopped its initial fall. Nick climbed aboard and pressed the starter.

Nothing.

Mary envisioned a really long, cold walk back to North Pole. Her body, already soaked from lying in the snow, shook violently.

After fiddling with the starter and lifting the seat to wiggle the battery connection, Nick pressed the start button again and the engine sputtered to life.

Now all they had to do was get it back up the hill to the road. Mary stared up at the very steep slope and groaned.

"Can you make it to the top on your own?"

Mary stared up the hill. Her ankle throbbed but held under her weight. "Yes."

"Go."

She stared at him. "What about you?"

"I'll be right behind you."

Mary looked from him to the road high above and back. "Are you sure?"

"We don't have time to argue. Just do it."

His bark sent her scrambling up the hill. Her fingertips stung. Frostbite would set in all too soon as the temperature dropped deeper into the negatives. When the engine revved behind her, Mary forced herself to concentrate on getting herself up the hill, amazed at how worried she was about a man she barely knew and was just beginning to trust.

The roaring increased, along with the clashing sound of runners on rocks.

Almost to the top Mary couldn't stand it. She turned in time to see the snowmobile fly into the air, Nick clinging to the handlebars, his feet flying free of the footrests.

CHAPTER 8

WITH THE THROTTLE WIDE OPEN, Nick shot up the hill, bouncing over rocks and logs buried beneath two feet of snow. He couldn't avoid them without losing control of the machine, so he rode the worst of the bumps, his teeth jarring against each other, his head aching from the constant banging. As he neared the top of the hill, he held his breath. On a practically vertical slope, he knew he risked flipping the machine and tumbling back to the bottom.

Nowhere else along the side of the embankment was much better. He had to make a run for it or they'd freeze to death.

His breath held in his throat. Nick leaned all his weight as far forward as possible and gunned the throttle. The snowmobile shot straight up.

For a second, Nick was suspended in midair, his feet flying free of the footrests, all that connected him to the snowmobile were his hands on the grips. Gravity kicked in, and the machine fell forward, the skids slamming against the flat trail. Nick landed hard on the seat, his chest bouncing off the handlebars, the breath knocked from his lungs. Immediately his hands loosened on the throttle and the snowmobile slid to a stop against the opposite side of the trail, the front runner bumping softly against the base of a massive spruce tree. When he found his breath and his feet shifted back to the footrests, Nick shot a look through the blowing snow for Mary, his pulse hammering.

He found her on the side of the trail, her eyes wide, her face blanched.

"Get on." He jerked his head toward the back of the vehicle.

Mary stood transfixed for another moment, then shook her head, as if shaking off the fear of the past few minutes and hurried toward him. "I truly think you have a death wish. Promise me you won't do that while I'm on the back." She slid onto the seat and wrapped her arms around his waist, squeezing tighter than necessary to hang on.

A grin twitched the corners of Nick's mouth, a rush of relief-induced endorphins making him feel as if he could conquer the world. "I make no promises. Hold on."

Mary's hands clenched around his gut, her breasts smashing against his back.

With adrenaline pulsing through his system, a beautiful woman with her arms and legs wrapped around him and a powerful engine rumbling between his legs...life didn't get much better than this.

The rest of the trip back to town Nick kept a sharp eye out for further attacks from rogue snowmobile operators. He'd let his guard down once too often for his own good, but they'd survived and now was the time to neutralize their attacker.

When they inched into town, the snowstorm had hit full force, blinding in its intensity. Not to be deterred, Nick headed for the police department they'd passed earlier that morning walking along Snowman Lane with Mary. Hard to believe it had only been that morning when so much had happened in between.

He parked the snowmobile in the snow-covered parking lot and hurried Mary through the door, a blast of wind and snow shoving them through to the inside warmth.

Mary stood in the entry, pulling the gloves from her hands, her entire body shaking.

"Mary, what are you doing out in this storm? I thought everyone would be holing up until it passed." An older man in a police uniform hurried forward.

"Ch-Chief Landham, we j-just came in from M-Moose Lodge out on the T-Tanana River," Mary stammered through chattering teeth.

"You were where?" He grabbed her arms and ushered her to a chair beside a space heater. "You're frozen." He clasped his hands over hers and rubbed them.

"This is my...f-fiancé, Nick St. Claire." Mary nodded toward Nick, her brow dipping in warning.

The chief stood and extended a hand. "Dale Landham, nice to meet you." He turned back to Mary. "Did you go out to the lodge looking for your father?"

"Yes, but we found more than we bargained for." She explained about the cabin being used. "We were on the way back when someone on a snowmobile ran us off the trail."

"You sure it wasn't an accident? With the snow falling the way it is, it would be hard to see another rider."

Mary's lips pressed together. "Maybe so, but that doesn't account for the rider shooting at us."

"Shooting!" The chief sat back in the chair behind his desk, his brows rising into the thatch of salt-and-pepper hair hanging down over his forehead. "Good Lord, has this town gone crazy? What with your father missing, Reuben's house exploding and now this. Makes a man wish he hadn't gotten up this morning." He pulled a pad of paper across his desk and fished a pen from a drawer. "Give me the details."

"Nick was on the front of the snowmobile. He had a better look at the driver."

"What little I saw when he flashed by was a white

coat and white pants that blended in with the snow. He also wore a white helmet with a face shield."

"Would you say he was short or tall, small or big?"

"Hard to tell with him sitting on the snowmobile, bulked out in a snowsuit, and it was snowing pretty hard. Whoever it was knew his way around in the snow."

"I didn't even see him coming." Mary shook her head, staring down at her reddened fingertips.

"Did you get a look at the machine?" the chief asked.

"White," Nick said.

"I don't know of a lot of snowmobiles in North Pole that are white. Most people want to see it against the snow. We could start there."

Mary leaned forward. "Any word of my dad?"

The chief shook his head. "No. Nothing."

"You'll let me know—"

"As soon as I hear anything, you'll be the first to know." He grinned. "Even before I talk to Mrs. Claus."

"Thanks." Mary gave him a weak smile, before turning to Nick. "Ready?"

"Yeah."

The phone on the chief's desk rang as Mary headed for the door. Nick could tell by the droop of her shoulders that she was exhausted from fright and cold. "Want me to take you back to the B and B?"

"No, let's go over to the Christmas Towne Diner."

"It's pretty bad out, you think they're open?"

"Positive. Those who can't get home will wait out the storm with a cup of Lenn's coffee." She fumbled with her zipper, her fingers clumsy and stiff. She looked as though she needed a warm bath more than a cup of coffee.

The thought of a naked Mary in a warm bath, heated Nick's afterburners. He coughed, clearing the sudden lump of lust blocking his airway. "Coffee sounds good about now." Anxious to step back out into the frigid snowstorm to cool his rising desire, Nick turned Mary to face him and zipped her jacket. He took her gloves from her and helped her slide them onto her stiff fingers. Then he pulled her faux-fur-trimmed hood over her head and tightened the string. "There. Now you're ready."

She looked up at him with those pale blue eyes and gave him a lopsided smile. "Thanks."

"See? It's not so hard to trust me, is it?"

Her smile turned downward. "No. It's too easy." She pushed through the door the wind whipping it out of her hands and jerking it wide. A blast of arctic air and snow, mixed with hard pellets of sleet, slashed at Nick's face and exposed hands. He pulled on his own gloves and walked out behind Mary. The woman had him alternating between hot and cold.

. . .

MARY STOOD by the snowmobile waiting for Nick to climb on before she did. Normally a two-block walk wasn't bad, but she could barely see past a hand in front of her face. She opted for motor vehicle transportation to the diner, when she'd rather go back to her room and crawl into a hot shower.

With Nick.

Mary lifted her face to the biting wind, willing the heat in her cheeks to freeze.

Her father could be out in this miserable storm, having been chased from his hideout at Moose Lodge. And here Mary was dreaming of getting naked with a stranger.

An outsider who'd saved her life. A man she was afraid to trust, not so much with her life, but because she highly suspected he could break her heart. The chill wind did nothing to cool the heat raging inside. If she didn't need Nick's help to find her father, Mary would have ditched the secret agent—or whatever he was.

Nick St. Claire had disaster written all over him. At least for Mary. She'd made the mistake of falling for a man with a boatload of secrets once before, and Nick had secrets...lots of them. All of which he wasn't willing to share.

Bradley had seduced her into false dreams of happily ever after. They'd made love on the banks of the Tanana River that summer two years ago. Summer ended when his wife e-mailed Mary.

Bradley swore he didn't know her. By then, Mary knew he'd lied, yet again.

She'd had nightmares about Bradley, dreaming up all manner of horrible things she wanted to do to him for duping her and his wife. Although the pain had faded, she'd never gotten over the shame of being the other woman who'd broken up a marriage.

Mary refused to land in a trap that deep ever again. If she had a relationship with any man, that man would have to come clean with all his secrets.

As they arrived at the diner, Mary shot a look at Nick. She'd get a few of her questions answered here and now, or she'd take him down with his own gun.

"Miss Mary!" A little girl with dark ringlets spilling down the back of her pink flannel dress raced up to Mary as soon as she stepped through the diner door.

"Lissa!" Mary moved out of the draft and scooped up the little girl in her arms. "How's my favorite elf?"

"I'm going to be six on my next birthday." She wrapped her skinny, little arms around Mary's neck.

"Already? Hey, loosen up there. I need to breathe." Mary pulled the tiny arms from around her neck and stared into the girl's dark brown eyes.

"I'm sorry, she got away from me before I could stop her." A pretty woman with shoulder-length hair the exact shade of Lissa's hurried over. "She's just been beside herself since she heard Santa was missing."

Lissa planted her hands on Mary's cheeks and forced her to look straight at her. "Is Santa gone? Will he miss Christmas?"

"Oh, baby, yes, Santa's gone right now. But he'll be back in time for Christmas. Don't you worry. He'll be back." Mary was proud of herself. She hugged the little girl and handed her back to her mother before a single tear could slip down her cheeks. She made it all the way over to a booth on the opposite end of the diner before the first one fell.

Nick yanked a napkin from the shiny metal napkin holder and handed it to her. "Do all the kids in North Pole believe in Santa?"

She looked at him over the napkin. "Of course. All the children love my father. He's an icon for the community." She dabbed at her drying tears, then flapped the napkin. "Children from all over the world visit here and he takes time with every one of them to listen to their wishes."

"I bet it makes for great sales." Nick's flat tone said it all.

Mary's hand slammed down on the table in front of him. "It's not all about the sales." She glared across the table at Nick. "You don't get Christmas at all, do you?"

"Okay, okay, I'm coming with the coffee." Betty Reedy hurried across the floor, her plump face flushed.

"I'm sorry, Betty. I was just explaining to Mr. St.

Claire that my father being gone means more than a drop in revenue."

Betty's eyes widened at Nick. "Is that what you think?"

Nick's jaw tightened. "Isn't that what Christmas is all about? Massive amounts of sales to make up for the rest of a dismal year in the retail world?"

"My poor Mr. St. Claire, you must have had a very sad childhood if you've never believed in Santa." She set two mugs on the table, her tongue tsking the entire time. "Santa is more than just making a sale. He brings hope, love and happiness for many children and adults. I've heard that Mrs. Attebury's Sunday school class is writing prayer requests to bring him home safely. The children all over Alaska will be sorely disappointed if he doesn't get back in time to participate with the National Guard in Operation Santa."

"Operation Santa?" Nick shook his head.

"Yes, Operation Santa." Mary sat forward. "Fifty years ago, the Alaskan National Guard started a program called Operation Santa to take the joy of Christmas and Santa out to the remote villages. Many of those children would never have seen Santa or received gifts without it. And my father spends time and his own money on each of those children."

"Charity." Nick snorted. "Charity only makes the *giver* feel good about himself."

"Says who?" Mary and Betty both spoke at once.

"It's not important. Forget I said anything." He lifted the menu blocking Mary's view of his face.

Betty huffed and opened her mouth to say something more, but a customer called out her name. With a wrinkled nose and a flounce in her step, she left to help.

Mary reached out and plucked the menu from Nick's hands. "Apparently it is important if you think charity is all about the giver. You obviously haven't seen the faces of all those children when they see Santa for the first time."

The oaf sat back against the vinyl cushion, his fingers tapping on the table. "Probably scares them half to death."

"Wow, someone must have put coal in your stocking when you were a kid to make you so down on Christmas." Mary stared at Nick, realization dawning and a huge lump of remorse choking her throat like a dry sock. For a long moment, she fought off a rise of tears before she could steady her voice enough to ask, "You didn't have happy Christmases, did you?"

Nick scowled. "Look, whether or not I hate Christmas has nothing to do with your father's disappearance. Can we just stick to the case?"

"Yes, of course." Obviously, he was very touchy about his childhood and hated sympathy more than Christmas.

"Do you still have that newspaper you picked up at Moose Lodge?" Nick asked.

His words didn't sink in at first. All Mary could do was stare at Nick, seeing a sad, dark-haired little boy looking through a store window at all the Christmas decorations, knowing he wouldn't be included.

His frown deepened. "The newspaper?"

"Oh, yeah." She fumbled in her jacket for the crumpled paper and spread it out on the table between them. If she didn't get back on task, she'd find more reasons to fall for the interloper who pretended not to care.

On the front page a smiling senator waved from the door of an airplane, the caption reading California Senator Seeks Alaskan Vote.

"Gordon Thomas. He's a highly decorated war veteran. In the running for the presidential race," Nick stated.

"What could Gordon Thomas have to do with my father's disappearance?"

"All I can do is to speculate at this point. Frank Richards was a war veteran as well. But then so were a lot of men their age."

The roar of snowmobile engines outside the window made Mary and Nick look up at the same time. The frost on the outside of the windows plus the condensation on the inside blocked their view. They rose from their seats to get a better look.

Two snowmobiles raced down the street, one man wearing a navy-blue snowsuit, the other dressed all in white.

Nick reached the door before Mary. When he jerked it open, Chris Moss fell into the diner.

"Thanks, but I could have gotten it myself." He grinned at Mary and Nick.

Nick brushed past him and ran outside coatless.

Mary followed.

The two snowmobiles disappeared around a corner in a veil of heavy snow.

By the time Nick and Mary got their coats on and followed, the riders would be long gone.

Nick muttered a curse beneath his breath.

Cold sliced through the sweatshirt and turtleneck Mary wore, driving her back inside.

"For a moment I thought the diner was on fire. What gives?" Chris slipped out of his jacket and hung it on a hook by the door.

"Any idea who those two men were on the snowmobiles that just passed by?" Mary asked.

"Looked like Silas Grentch and that man he's been showing around town, Nelson Barney or Bailey or something. Not the best weather for a tour, if you ask me. But a great day to be off work."

"Did Jasmine close the store early?" Mary asked.

"Not early...all day." Chris grimaced. "I didn't need a day off. I could use the money to make my truck payment."

"All day?" Her father only closed the store on Monday and during really bad weather. But the weather hadn't been bad *all* day. "Is she ill?"

"No, she said she had business in Fairbanks, something about hiring a private investigator because the police couldn't find snow in a snowdrift. She didn't want to be bothered opening. I told her I'd be happy to hold down the fort, but she didn't take me up on it." Chris shrugged.

Mary stared out at the raging blizzard. "She'll be stuck in Fairbanks until this storm passes and the roads are clear."

Chris bit down on his lip. "Think I should open on my own tomorrow? Your dad would have let me."

"You better let Jasmine call the shots. It's her store in Dad's absence. She's the wife, I'm just the daughter." Jasmine had made that pretty clear from the time her father brought her home after their surprise elopement.

Chris nodded. "Yeah."

"Where are you headed now?" Mary asked.

"I needed to talk to Miss Betty." He looked away. Too quickly.

Chris's parents had ditched him, headed for the lower forty-eight, leaving him without food or money in the trailer they'd rented. He'd taken to stealing from the local grocery store to survive until Santa had caught him in the act of stuffing a package of hot dogs in his jacket.

Mary could tell when Chris was hiding something. Normally when she asked him questions, he looked at her with an open, curious expression. Now he dodged her gaze and ducked around her and Nick. "Gotta go. See ya later."

Mary moved to follow him, but a hand on her arm held her back.

Nick leaned close, the scent of his aftershave filling Mary's senses. "If Jasmine's stuck in Fairbanks for the night, it's our chance to try that key."

A thrill of excitement flashed through her, heating her skin. "I know where my father kept a spare key to get in."

"I have a few things I want to check on back in my room. Then we can head over to Christmas Towne. You still have the key your father left under your pillow, don't you?"

Fear lodged in her throat. They'd been through hell in the tumble down the hillside. Mary shoved her hand in her pocket. When her fingers scraped against contoured edges of metal, she breathed a sigh. "Yeah. I also want to call Ed about the snowmobile and let him know we want to keep it a little longer."

"Are you going to tell him it's been wrecked?" The edges of Nick's lips twitched, his eyes shining.

The look had her face flushing with heat. "No, no. I think I can wait that bit of news." Darn, she was letting his deep brown eyes and wicked grin get to her. She walked back to the table, gathered her winter coat and gloves and handed Nick's to him. "Let's go." The sooner they were in their own rooms, the better off she would be. By herself, back in control.

She almost volunteered to walk back to the B and B rather than tempt herself all over by sliding her legs around Nick on the snowmobile. Granted there were several layers of clothes between them but having him that close only made her weak in the knees and lose track of her main goals: to find her father and never fall for a guy with more secrets than she could shake a stick at.

Nick St. Claire wasn't just any guy passing through. Every inch of him was lean, defined muscles down to the ripples across his abdomen. What girl wouldn't be attracted?

The man was good eye candy. She found movie stars attractive and she didn't get all jelly-legged over them. What was it about Nick?

Maybe it was his innate toughness, his ability to take charge of a situation. Or the way he protected her from harm. No, she was avoiding the real reason. The kiss. She'd never before been kissed the way Nick had kissed her today. He had tapped into every one of her female fantasies and erogenous zones in the two long, sexy slides of his lips against hers.

Nick made short work of slipping into his coat and gloves. "Ready?"

Boy was she.

Mary jerked out of her lust-induced stupor and slung her jacket over her shoulders, shoving her hands into the sleeves while ducking to hide her burning face. "Yeah." No, she wasn't ready for another dose of the super sexy secret agent, but what choice did she have?

Outside the full force of the icy wind stung Mary's cheeks, chilling them in a second. Good. Cool was good. Maybe she could make it back to the B and B without succumbing to Nick's killer magnetism.

The two blocks passed in a flash, but her hands were already freezing by the time she climbed off the snowmobile. A hot shower would help to thaw her.

Nick entered the B and B first to check for any bad guys lurking in the corners. At her room, he took her key from her and unlocked the door, checking the room before she entered. "Knock when you're ready to go to Christmas Towne. Dress warm. We'll be walking." Then he shut the door in her face.

Mary stood staring at the wood paneling long after the door closed. He'd been in a hurry to get rid of her. A flush of anger warmed her insides. Granted, she'd wanted to leave his company as soon as possible, but she had a good excuse—she was committing the ultimate folly and falling for the guy.

Still, he'd ditched her like last year's old tennis shoes. That stung. Apparently, the kiss hadn't meant as much to him as it had to her.

Hmmph!

Mary turned and faced the empty room, dragging her jacket from her shoulders and her sweatshirt over her head. The shower wasn't calling to her as loudly as it had a moment before. All she wanted was to see Nick again and give him a piece of her mind. But she couldn't. What would she say? "Hey, Nick, that kiss didn't mean anything to me either!" And by so saying, she'd be admitting that she'd been thinking about it and that it had meant more to her than she wanted him to know.

With each passing second, the urgency to march across the hall and say something to the man built inside her like a surging volcano, but she had nothing to say. Knock on his door when she was ready. She was ready now. But not for another walk in the snow. More likely, a romp in the sheets.

Knock on the door? When? What time? Mary spun and raced through her door, her body primed for another close encounter of the Nick kind, the kisses of earlier that day fresh on her mind.

She knocked and waited. The sound of someone shuffling about inside made her heartbeat quicken. Maybe she'd catch him half undressed. Fire burned in her belly and spread lower.

Finally, the door opened.

A beautiful dark-haired female smiled at her. "Can I help you?"

Nick lay on the bed behind her, his chest bare, his

jeans unbuttoned, a frown marring his handsome, two-timing face.

CHAPTER 9

Nick swung his legs over the side of the bed and flipped the laptop closed. "Mary, I thought you were going for a shower."

Mary stood framed in the doorway. Minus the bulk of her winter jacket and sweatshirt, her pale blue turtleneck sweater hugged her body, accentuating the curve of her waist and the swell of her breasts. Light blond hair swung down around her shoulders in straight, silky strands despite their earlier tumble in the snow.

Nick's pulse leaped and his jeans tightened. He hadn't realized how much he liked having her around.

But her ready smile was absent, in its place her lush lips firmed into a thin line and her usually sky-blue eyes darkened into the color of a winter gray storm cloud. "You didn't give me a time." She shot a glance at the other woman in the room. "You're busy. I can make it over to my father's house on my own."

She backed into the hallway. "In fact, it would probably be better if I did this alone. I have more right to be there than you. If I'm caught, I don't think the police would do anything to me. So, I'll just go." She turned and made a run for her door.

Nick snagged her arm before she could twist the doorknob. "I want to go with you. A fresh pair of eyes might see something different than someone familiar with Santa's belongings. Come back across the hall, I want you to meet Kat."

Mary resisted the pressure he exerted on her arm, refusing to make eye contact with him. "No, I don't want to interrupt anything between the two of you." Her gaze connected with his bare chest and bounced to the woman standing in the doorway.

Kat had the insensitivity to grin. "Nick, I think you're shocking her with your nakedness." She grabbed his shirt from the bed and tossed it at him. "Put this on."

Nick kept his hold on Mary's arm, catching the shirt with his other hand. "I was just about to hit the shower but had to answer a call. Please, come back over, I've got some news."

Mary hesitated, her gaze narrowing at the woman he'd called Kat and then him. What was wrong with her? She'd been much more willing to work with him a few minutes ago. What had changed? She was acting strange. Then again, he'd only seen her with people she knew.

Mary glanced at Kat, standing just inside his room.

Was Kat making her nervous? Although she was an SOS agent, she didn't *look* threatening.

Kat nodded toward the shirt in Nick's hand. "Ahem. The shirt?" When he just stood and stared at her, she rolled her eyes. "Even my husband might take offense at seeing me with you half-dressed." She motioned toward Mary, who was staring down the hallway now, her face flushed pink.

A dim lightbulb clicked in Nick's head. "Did you think that Kat and I were..."

The pink in Mary's face deepened. "What you do is your own business." She pried at Nick's hand holding her arm. "Let go."

Was Mary jealous of Kat? Nick laughed out loud. "Mary, Kat is a co-worker, not my lover."

"Heaven forbid." Kat grinned and stuck out her hand, drawing Mary through the door and shutting it behind her. "I'm Kat Si—er, Russell. Just got married. I'm not used to the new last name."

"I'm surprised you didn't keep your own," Nick said. "What with women's rights and all."

"Sam wanted me to, but I kinda like the guy." Kat's face faded to a rosy shade of pink and she smiled at Mary. "I just got back from my honeymoon when our boss assigned me to help with this case."

She waved toward the laptop on the desk. "The manager of the B and B is getting a room ready for me. In the meantime, I'm using Nick's room and WIFI."

Mary's stiff shoulders sagged. "You work with Nick?"

"That's right. Although it's been a while since we've been on assignment together."

Mary crossed her arms over her chest. "And just what do you do?"

Kat laughed. "Nick's given you the spiel I take it? Can't tell you, secret organization, kinda like the CIA and FBI, but not?" She frowned. Although, we're no longer a part of the US government. We've struck out on our own."

Mary nodded. "Yeah. I take it you're not going to tell me any more than that, are you?

The short, dark-haired woman shrugged. "Can't. If I told you—"

"You'd have to kill me." Mary shivered.

Nick wanted to wrap her in his arms and warm her up. Instead, he slipped the shirt over his head and pulled it down, covering his naked chest. "Maybe not kill you, but it might put us and others in our organization in danger."

Mary's glance traveled from Nick to Kat and back. "Okay, keep your secrets, but don't expect me to trust you overly much. Like I've told Nick, you could be the bad guys for all I know." She squared her shoulders. "Which makes me all the more determined to go to the house by myself tonight."

Nick's chest tightened at her words. "Somebody shot at us today. I don't know if they were shooting at you or me or both of us because we're looking for your father. Either way, you're in danger."

"Right." Kat stepped forward. "You might consider sending me and Nick in rather than going yourself. At least we're trained in this kind of operation."

Even before Kat finished her sentence, Mary's head shook. "It's my father who's missing. He left me the clue in this key. I know the house. I know my father. The key goes with me."

Kat nodded. "Fair enough. At least let Nick go with you to provide protection."

Nick lifted Mary's empty hand. "Look, if you're hurt trying to help your father, he'll have no one he can trust to figure this out for him. Let me help. I swear on the twenty-foot Santa standing out in the snow that I'm one of the good guys." He squeezed her hand gently. "What do you say?"

Pearly white teeth gnawed on her lower lip as she stared up into his eyes, her own blue ones gray and troubled. She tugged her hand free. "Okay. But I'll take care of the key. You have to promise to keep me informed with as much as you know about what's going on. Promise?"

Nick held his hand up like a Boy Scout. "I swear."

Kat snorted. "Like you were ever a Boy Scout.

Give me a break." Kat ushered Mary over to the computer. "As soon as I got here, I went to work on a background check on some of the people of interest Nick mentioned."

Mary shot a look at Nick as Kat spun the laptop around so that they all could see the screen. On it was a picture of the man who'd accused Santa of being a criminal the night Nick and Mary arrived in North Pole. "What do you know about this man?" Kat asked.

"Silas Grentch is a businessman and real estate salesman, and whatever else he can find to do in town that makes money. He sold this land and building to Dad thirty years ago and has regretted it since. My dad made it a success. Silas has been trying to get Dad to sell it back to him for as long as I can remember."

Kat leaned back in the desk chair, crossing her arms over her chest. "I did a credit check on our man Silas. He's in debt up to his eyeballs from gambling in Vegas."

Mary's eyes widened and then narrowed. "I wouldn't put it past the man. He likes to spend too freely. Always the most expensive car, the fanciest house, the latest gadgets."

Tapping a finger to her chin, Kat nodded. "That doesn't mean he's our man, but he bears watching."

"It also doesn't explain the connection between my father and the man who died in New York City."

Nick smiled. Mary's reasoning skills impressed him. "Right. Grentch also served in the military. I have our people searching through military records to see if he served at the same time as your father and Frank Richards."

Kat displayed another face on the screen. "Know this man?"

"Ed Scruggs." Mary shot a look at Nick. "But you know that. We borrowed a snowmobile from him earlier today."

Nick ignored her direct look and stared at the photo. "Your old boyfriend was arrested for the murder of a buddy of his on a hunting trip."

"I remember. He shot Lance Rankin," Mary said. "The jury ruled it an accident."

Nick's fist tightened. In his opinion, they couldn't discount Ed just because a jury ruled his friend's death an accident. According to the write up, Ed Scruggs had been hunting every year since he was four years old. He'd won several shooting competitions in his teens and early twenties. A man that experienced with a gun didn't have hunting accidents. He'd rather have known about the "accident" before he'd allowed Mary to be in the same town as Scruggs, much less on the same street. "Scruggs knew we were going out on the snowmobile and could just as easily have followed us out to the cabin."

"Why would he do that?" Mary asked. "Besides, Ed likes me. He always has."

Nick's brows rose. "Why would someone follow us just to take potshots at us?"

Mary's mouth opened and closed without uttering a word.

"Both men are familiar with snowmobiles, guns and the lay of the land. Both have questionable circumstances. Therefore, both need to be watched." Kat tapped the mouse and Ed Scruggs's face disappeared.

"I think you're wrong about Ed." Mary's forehead furrowed. "He's not a murderer."

Nick's gut clenched. Mary had been involved with the man when she was younger. When he was working a case with someone else, prior relationships didn't normally bother him. It did with Mary. And it gnawed at his belly even more that she'd stick up for the guy.

"And I really don't think Silas has it in him to kill. And it all comes back to what do they have to do with Frank Richards?"

"Your father's disappearance may have nothing to do with Frank Richards. It could all be one big coincidence." Kat turned the laptop around and closed the lid.

Nick growled. "There's no such thing as coincidence," he muttered beneath his breath.

"What did you say?" Mary's blue gaze held his.

"We need to run a check on the man riding snowmobiles with Silas today."

Mary's eyes narrowed, but she didn't press for the truth. "Fine. Want to meet at midnight to go to my father's house?"

"Midnight it is." Nick opened the door and waved her toward it. He'd had enough temptation in the room for now. "If you plan to shower, I suggest you do it. I'm next."

"Ah, here's my room key." Kat stepped out in the hallway to greet Nancy Petri, the owner, operator and number one housecleaner of the B and B.

Mary ducked back into her room and closed the door, mulling over what Kat and Nick had said about Ed and Silas. If these were the only two suspects they could come up with, they were in trouble. Mary just couldn't see either one as threatening to her father. Santa had dealt firmly and fairly with everyone in this town for years.

Mary wasn't familiar with the strong-arm tactics of Las Vegas bookmakers. Had Silas gotten himself into a pinch over his gambling? Everyone knew he made frequent trips south. Mary hadn't known where, until today. Was a gambling debt enough to drive a man over the edge? Would her father have run from Silas, a man he'd known for years?

Mary grabbed a towel, her shampoo and clean underwear and dashed down the hall for her shower, determined not to run into Nick until the appointed hour of midnight.

She stood under the hot spray, letting the water

jet over her skin, beating away the stress of the day. The heat and steam eased the bruising from the tumble down the hillside and drained away the tension and what was left of her energy, leaving her tired and sleepy. She wondered how she'd ever wake up enough to perform the next mission.

All her sleepiness disappeared the moment she stepped out of the bathroom.

Nick leaned against the hallway wall in only his jeans, having tossed his shirt again. A towel draped over his shoulder and a small smile tugged at his lips. "Did you leave me any hot water?"

It wasn't so much the words as the way they rolled off Nick's lips so effortlessly and with such a deep, resonant tone that made Mary's bones turn to soup. "Uh, yeah." She stood transfixed and tongue-tied, unable to drag her gaze from the mat of hair sprinkled across his chest. What would it feel like to run her fingers through the springy curls?

Mary licked her bottom lip which had gone suddenly dry.

Nick's eyebrows rose into the dark hair drooping over his forehead. "Mary?"

"What?" She shifted her gaze from his chest back up to his face and fell into twinkling dark eyes.

The smile at the corners of his lips spread across his face. He nodded to the door behind her. "The shower?"

Her face flamed and she scooted out of the bathroom door, hurrying down the hallway as fast as she could go without running.

A low chuckle followed her, echoing off the walls.

Mary slammed her door behind her. "Jerk." She pressed a hand to her heated cheeks, ignoring the way her breasts felt ultrasensitive against the abrasion of the soft terry cloth. She yanked the bathrobe off and strode across the room in her panties, searching for dark, concealing clothes, her heart hammering in her chest and not from sprinting down the hall.

The man infuriated her.

She paused with her hand on a black turtleneck sweater.

"Why?" she wondered aloud. Why did he infuriate her? All he'd done was stand in front of her without a shirt.

It was the smile. That freakin' sexy smile of his had completely thrown her for a loop.

Mary smacked her hand against her forehead. "Get over it. The man isn't going to be around once we find Dad." Even if he was, he'd never tell her what she wanted to know about him. She couldn't trust Nick any more than she could trust her ex-boyfriend, Bradley.

She tugged the sweater over her head and slipped into a pair of black, lined leggings and thick socks. Completely covered, her body still tingled with awareness for Nick.

Damn. Why did she do this to herself? Why did she let her emotions get the better of her when she knew nothing would come of it? Was that it? Was she always going after the unavailable men to save her from ever committing to one?

She lifted the photo frame on her nightstand. It was the one picture she'd carried with her everywhere. The last family photo of her mother, father and herself together.

Mary had inherited her blond hair from her mother and her blue eyes from her father. They stood in the snow outside the Christmas Towne store, her father in his full Santa outfit, his long white beard the real deal. Her mother wore a full-length dress trimmed around the collar and hems in faux fur, her long blond hair pinned on the top of her head in a neat bun. Mary wore a miniature version of her mother's dress. They were all smiling.

Had that been the last time she and her father had been happy? Olivia Claus's death had been a blow to everyone in North Pole. She'd been the driving force behind Christmas Towne's involvement in Operation Santa. If someone had a need, her gentle smile and humble presence brought peace and blessings to all.

Tears welled in Mary's eyes. She missed having a mother. Missed her at her senior prom and high school graduation. Missed being tucked in at night. Mary's father did the best he could to make her teen years tolerable, loving her and providing the support she needed.

Now he was gone.

A knock startled her out of her memories. The clock on the nightstand glared a bright green 12:00.

She shot from morose depression to jagged nerves in two seconds flat. Tucking her blond hair into a black knit hat, she shrugged into her powder-blue jacket and snowpants, cursing its brightness when she needed a dark coat to move through the night unseen. With the temperature outside somewhere in the negative digits, she couldn't just walk two blocks without one.

Another knock sounded.

Her hand on the doorknob, Mary inhaled and let it out slowly. She could handle this. Nick was just a man. They were going to her home, the place she'd grown up. Jasmine wasn't there. No big deal.

With a calm she didn't feel, she opened the door.

"Ready?" His shoulders, clad in a black leather jacket, filled the doorway, sending a shiver across Mary's senses. He hadn't bothered to shave, a shadow of beard making him look like a real badass instead of the good guys he alleged to be.

Black gloves, black pants and a black hat enhanced his black eyes. The man oozed danger from every pore.

As she stepped through the door, a thrill of excitement filled her. "I'm ready."

CHAPTER 10

Nick grabbed Mary's gloved hand. "Let's go out the back way."

"You're the expert, lead the way." Her cheeks were flushed a rosy pink, her eyes sparkling in the dimly lit hallway. Nick could think of a lot better things to do with her than tromp through the snow in subzero temperatures. Not that she'd go for any of them. He had a little more work to do to gain her full trust. Keeping secrets didn't help.

That was the nature of the SOS operative. Always a life undercover. Never free to share your work, talk about people you've met, interesting places you've been. Never committing to lasting relationships outside of the people he worked with. Up until now, he'd been okay with the rules.

With this diminutive blonde poking a hole

through his shell, he found himself questioning his lonely life. Not a good thing in his profession.

Mary had almost everything he'd never had. A father who loved her, a town full of people who looked out for her. A home she'd grown up in. She'd had everything until her stepmother moved in, and her father disappeared.

As a child, Nick would have given anything to have half of what Mary had. Without his help, she stood a chance of losing it all. Nick couldn't let that happen. Finding Santa had become more than his job —more of an obsession.

He moved quickly in the darkness with wind blowing through the only dark jacket he owned, the cold seeping through as though he wore nothing at all. They kept to well-trodden paths to avoid leaving new footprints, which meant walking down the edge of the road. Snowdrifts crept up the buildings, some more than three feet tall. Thick snow swirled, dimming the efforts of the few candy cane streetlights. A twin set of headlight beams speared the darkness from the south on Highway 2, headed their direction.

Nick jerked Mary between buildings and ducked behind a snow-laden bush.

The beams grew brighter until they could make out the body of a police vehicle, creeping along the road on a routine drive-by.

Nick kept Mary crouched behind the bush until

the SUV turned left onto Santa Claus Lane and disappeared.

Nick straightened. "Come on."

Only one light shone in front of Christmas Towne. Mary tugged Nick's hand and led him around to the back entrance where delivery trucks unloaded during the day onto the dock. "Dad kept a spare key back here under a statue of an elf." She pulled a penlight from her pocket and shone it toward the ground by the back door. A four-foot drift blocked it. Mary sighed. "So much for getting in without leaving a trace."

"What do you mean?"

"The elf is under that snowbank."

"Then we'll just have to make it look like someone from the shop shoveled it out before they left for the day. Besides, it's still snowing, our tracks will be covered by morning." Nick dug into the snow with his gloved hands, burrowing down until he revealed a two-foot-tall concrete elf, painted in bright green and red.

"The key is tucked into the bottom of the statue." Mary brushed more snow away from the back door with her foot until she'd cleared the entrance.

"I thought you wanted to get into the house. Why are we breaking into the shop?"

"We *are* going to the house. First, we have to get into the shop."

"You're the expert on Christmas Towne, lead the way." He handed her the key.

When they were inside, a beeping sound alerted Nick to trouble. An alarm.

"Don't worry. It's the security system. Let's just hope they haven't changed the code." On a wall next to the door was a plastic box with a numerical keypad. She punched in numbers, then stood back, biting her lip. The machine immediately stopped beeping and Mary sighed. "Whew."

Low lights illuminated the interior with a soft glow, allowing them to move through the shadowy aisles in the back storage area. Mary came to a halt in front of another door. "I used to play hide-and-seek down here." She opened the door and descended wooden steps into the basement.

It was as large as the building above. Wooden and metal shelves lined the walls and formed more aisles, stacked with everything from boxing materials for shipping products to additional inventory.

Mary hurried through the shelves and aisles until she came to what looked like a closet door on the south side of the building. When she opened it, a water heater and furnace filled the small space with little room to spare for the mop bucket and mop leaning to the side of the water heater.

Nick checked his watch. It was already twelve-thirty. "We need to hurry."

Mary smiled back at him, her teeth shining in the

glow of her penlight. "Don't worry, we're almost there. I told you. I used to play down here when I was a little girl. It was my secret place."

Nick's brows rose. "A secret?"

Mary frowned. "A secret that didn't hurt anyone."

"Still, it's a secret."

"A different kind of secret." She grabbed the mop handle and rolled the mop bucket out, setting it against the opposite wall. Then she removed her bulky jacket, hung it on a nail on the inside wall of the tiny room. Turning sideways, she scooted past the water heater and disappeared.

Nick's heart dropped into his gut like a lead rock. "Mary?"

"It's okay. I think you can fit. My father could."

A hinge creaked and a waft of cooler air caressed Nick's cheeks.

"Your turn, come on," Mary said, her words a fading echo as if she was moving away.

Nick removed his jacket and, mimicking Mary's movements, flattened his back against the wall next to the water heater. The space was tight, but Nick made it around the metal tank and found an open wooden door behind it. He pulled a small flashlight from his pocket and pointed it in the direction Mary had gone. The passageway was a narrow burrow through the earth lined with river stone and sturdy timbers. A light blinked on at the end of the tunnel and Mary appeared as a dark silhouette framed in the tunnel.

"This way."

Nick emerged into a room the size of a large walk-in closet, lit by a single exposed bulb hanging from a socket in the ceiling. Old trunks and cardboard boxes full of discarded toys lay in disarray. In the corner sat a child-size vanity mirror with a matching seat covered in faded roses.

"This was my secret cubby." Mary sat on the floor in the middle of the cubby, her gaze panning the room, a shining glaze making her blue eyes glisten in the dim lighting. "I remember the last time I came down here. It was after my mother died. I was only twelve." She squatted next to the vanity and ran her finger over the wood, tracing a path through the dust. "She would spend hours playing dress-up with me."

"You look like her," Nick said without thinking. Based on the photo in her room, she was the spitting image of Olivia Claus.

"I know." Mary glanced in the mirror, a sad smile curving her lips. "But I have my father's eyes."

Nick's chest tightened. He'd never known his own mother or father, having been left with social services at the age of three. Witnessing Mary's sorrow over the loss of the mother she'd known all her young life, Nick thought perhaps he'd been more fortunate to never have known his parents, than to have loved and lost them.

Mary turned away from the mirror and lifted a stuffed teddy bear. "I remember the year I got this bear. I'd been with my mother and father delivering toys to the remote villages. One of the little boys received a bear just like this one." She laughed, but it sounded more like a choked sob. "I wanted one so badly, I cried until I fell asleep on the plane." Tears slipped down her cheeks. She crushed the bear to her face. "I woke up on Christmas morning a month later and found this bear under the tree. My parents had remembered." Tears fell in earnest, dampening her cheeks and the teddy bear.

Nick stood in silence, his professional rules and work ethic battling with the uncontrollable urge to sweep Mary into his arms and hug away all the sorrow. The uncontrollable urge won out. Nick sat on the dusty floor and pulled Mary into his arms. "We'll find your father," he promised. And if it was the last thing he did, he'd keep that promise.

Mary turned her face from the bear into his chest, her shoulders shaking with silent sobs, her fingers clutching his thick sweater.

Nick pushed the black hat from her head and ran his hand across hair as fine as silk. With each stroke, he felt himself falling deeper into trouble than he'd ever been before, and it scared him more than having an AK-47 pointed at his head. No matter how scared, he couldn't stop himself.

Mary needed him to hold her and tell her that everything would be all right. She needed to know that someone was in this battle with her and would see her through. She needed him and that need humbled him.

When her sobs subsided, he tilted her head back and stared down into watery blue eyes. "It's going to be okay." He kissed the tip of her damp nose.

Mary stared up at him, her lush lips parting on a sigh.

Rational thought escaped him as his mouth covered hers, the taste of salty tears fueling the fire in him. He crushed her to his chest, his fingers sliding over her arms to circle behind her back, drawing her closer. The kiss deepened, their tongues entwined, tasting and thrusting in a primal rhythm.

Mary's fingers combed through Nick's hair, holding him close. Her body fit snugly against his, heat building with each passing moment.

When the kiss ended, they both sat back, breathing hard.

What was he thinking? Nick's brain reengaged as cool air came between them. "I shouldn't have—"

A slim, pale finger touched his lips. "Don't."

She had enough to deal with at the moment, without hearing Nick express regret for a beautiful kiss.

SAINT NICK

Mary climbed to her feet and fished in her pocket for the key her father had left beneath her pillow. "Just help me find my dad, will you?"

She left the tiny room by ducking through a door too short for an adult, but just right for a child. A chuckle bubbled up in her chest when Nick practically duck-walked out of her secret room.

They entered another basement, closing the cubby door behind them. The door was cleverly hidden by a large, framed picture of George Washington. Unless someone knew the door was there, he'd never think to look behind old George. That had been her father's idea.

Smaller than the first one, this basement lay beneath the house she'd grown up in and was as familiar to her as her old room upstairs. With snow covering the ground sometimes six months out of the year, Alaskans made full use of all inside space. Especially curious kids with active imaginations. The house and the store had been Mary's castle, complete with hidden passages and secret rooms with its trove of fabulous treasures hidden beneath the earth.

Swallowing a lump of nostalgia, Mary worked her way through the room, stopping at old trunks and boxes with locks on them. One by one she fitted the key into locks only to be disappointed when the locks didn't open.

When she came upon a pale lilac trunk she paused. It didn't have a lock, but she couldn't resist opening it anyway. "This trunk belonged to my mother." She lifted the lid, a wave of longing washing over her as she stared down at the things her mother had cherished. Things neither she nor her father could part with.

Mary lifted the bottle of perfume her father had bought for her mother's last birthday. Knowing she was a fool for doing it, she sprayed some on her wrist, the scent surrounding her, reminding her of happier times. Pain squeezed hard in her chest, making it hard for her to breathe.

"She must have been a remarkable woman," Nick said.

"I miss her so much." Mary set the bottle back in the trunk and closed the lid. "But we're here to help Dad." She wove her way through boxes and discarded furniture, old tools and car parts until she came to a row of shelves. A wooden footlocker, painted Army green, perched on the top shelf. A footlocker with a shiny new lock securing the latch on the front. A knot of excitement filled her belly, and she rose up on her tiptoes to reach for it.

"Let me."

Mary stood back while Nick, standing flat-footed, hefted the box from the shelf and softly laid it on the floor.

Without a doubt, she was certain she had the right trunk. A new silver padlock secured the rusty latch. When Mary inserted the key, it turned effortlessly, popping the hasp free. Within seconds the lid was opened and they both stared down into the footlocker.

Mary lifted an old Army dress uniform draped in an envelope of sheer dry-cleaning plastic. She laid it on the open lid of the footlocker and placed her penlight on top of it, shining down into the interior space. Inside was a collection of medals, hats, and various souvenirs from foreign countries. In the right corner was a stack of documents with Charles Mercer's name written on each. An Army Commendation Medal, a Meritorious Service Medal, a Bronze Star for bravery in battle and a Purple Heart for an injury in Bosnia.

Intermixed among the documents were a stack of old letters and photographs of a man in his late teens wearing a crisp new uniform, probably fresh out of Basic Combat Training. Another picture was of the same youth with more lines on his face than a man in his early twenties should have. He wore the full combat gear of a soldier serving in war torn country, right down to the leaves and branches tucked into the strap of his helmet—camouflaged to protect him from enemy view. He held a rifle and hand grenades were strapped to his web belt—a young soldier prepared to die for his country; in a war no one believed in back home.

"These are my dad," Mary said, her voice catching. She leaned closer, studying the print on his name tag.

"Charles Mercer. He never told me his real name. I wonder why?" She flipped through the photographs, one at a time. There was a shot of her father in a jeep, a shot of him standing in front of a large Army tent and one of him with the men of his platoon. They all looked brave, young and happy, despite the deplorable conditions of their camp. Their uniforms consisted of dirty uniforms, helmets, rifles and a webbed harnesses with grenades and ammo pouches stuck through loops.

Mary could make out bits of the camp in the background and a Bosnian woman standing behind the men, her face barely visible to the camera.

"Let me see that one." Nick took the group shot from her hands. "If I'm not mistaken, that's Frank Richards." He pointed at a man in the second row. "I have a copy of an old photo on my computer of Frank Richards in his uniform during the Bosnia peacekeeping mission with NATO. Let's take this back to the room. Do you mind if I have a look through this stuff?"

"No, go ahead." Mary moved back, clutching the other photographs.

Nick picked through the contents of the trunk, setting things to the side on the lid until the trunk was empty. Then he felt along the base of the trunk.

"What are you doing?"

"Seeing if there are any hidden compartments." He shook his head. "None here that I can tell." He placed all the war memorabilia back in the trunk and ran his fingers over the lid. "No. Nothing." He pulled a large plastic bag from his back pocket and slid the documents and the group photo inside. "Want me to carry those as well?"

Mary stared down at the photos, taking one more look before handing them over. "Thanks."

Somewhere above them, a door closed.

Mary jumped. "Someone's upstairs. Do you think Jasmine made it home in this weather?"

Nick handed her the bag while he closed the lid to the trunk. "Want me to check it out?"

Mary shook her head. The lighter sound of a woman's heels clicked toward the door to the kitchen. The door that led to the basement. "No, we need to hide. She's headed this way."

Nick bent to lift the trunk.

Mary's hand on his arm stopped him. "No time. We have to hurry."

Nick shoved the trunk against the shelf and used a discarded rag to brush at the dust on the trunk and floor in a weak attempt to hide their hand- and footprints.

Mary grabbed his hand. "No time, come on."

"Where to?"

"Back to my cubby." With nothing but Nick's flashlight beam to guide her, Mary raced across the basement, trying not to make too much noise. She leaped over tools and dodged boxes making it to her cubby just as the kitchen door opened, lighting the dark stairs.

Nick bumped into her and flicked his flashlight off.

Mary fumbled in her pocket for her own penlight, but it wasn't there. Then she remembered she'd left it on the lid of the trunk. It must have fallen in when they closed it in a hurry. She hadn't turned it off.

Before the footsteps finished descending the steps, Mary pulled on the corner of the framed George Washington and ducked back inside the cubby, dragging Nick with her.

As soon as Nick made it through, she closed the door, hoping they hadn't been seen or heard.

Mary reached over her head and pulled the string next to the lightbulb, plunging them into darkness. Scooting around Nick's hulking frame, she pressed her ear to the door. "I can't hear anything," she whispered.

"Good. Maybe she didn't see us."

"We need to get out of here, just in case she goes over to the shop and sees that the security alarm has been disabled." Mary left the tiny door and felt her way in the dark back toward the tunnel entrance. "Two break-ins in as many days will freak her out and have the police crawling all over the place." Thank goodness they'd been wearing gloves. No fingerprints to trace back to them.

"Hold on just a minute." Nick captured Mary's

hand. "I want to know what she's looking for in the basement."

"You want what?" Mary bit into her lower lip, her heart racing beneath her ribs. "We need to leave now."

Nick gently squeezed her hand. "What reason could she have to come down to the basement right after getting back from Fairbanks? And in the dead of the night?"

"How do I know? I never have understood my stepmother." Nor had she really tried. She hadn't wanted to acknowledge that her father could love someone other than her mother. Selfish, she knew, but she couldn't change the way she felt. "The only thing I know for certain is that she never wanted me in the house from the get-go."

Nick dropped her hand and squatted onto his haunches. Pushing against the spring-loaded cubby door, he poked his head out.

Mary leaned over his shoulder and looked out as well.

Jasmine Claus had reached the bottom of the stairs, her hand holding a cell phone to her ear as she spoke in another language.

"Sounds Slavic," Nick said.

"You speak Slavic?" Mary stared at the man inches from her. She knew nothing about him.

"A little Croatian. Not enough to converse."

Jasmine ended the call, reached out and tripped

the light switch, illuminating the interior of the basement.

Mary automatically backed into the cubby, the fear of discovery tingling down her spine. Though why she should be afraid of Jasmine, she didn't know. She knew, deep down, she didn't want to like the woman, mostly because she'd come between Mary and her father.

Jasmine, wearing heeled boots and a long red sweater dress, picked her way through the boxes and storage tubs just as Mary and Nick had a few minutes before.

Mary held her breath, hoping the woman didn't see any footprints or traces of their earlier foray through the basement. And she hoped she wouldn't find the—

Her stepmother must have read Mary's mind because she zeroed in on the footlocker as if that was exactly what she'd been searching for.

"Uh, Nick," Mary whispered, tapping lightly on his shoulder.

"What?" he answered without pulling his gaze off Jasmine.

"Did you put the lock back on the footlocker?"

"Yes."

"Do you have the key?"

"In my pocket."

Mary let out a sigh.

"Why?"

"I think my penlight is in that footlocker and still shining."

Nick looked up at her in the shadows. "Let's hope she's not smart enough to figure out how to get into that lock."

"Yeah."

Jasmine squatted next to the footlocker and tugged at the lock. When it didn't open, she straightened and looked around the basement. As if spotting what she was looking for, she moved across to the workbench Mary's father kept his tools on and lifted a large tool off a nail on the wall.

"It's time to leave," Nick said.

"Why?"

"She's got a pair of bolt cutters. When she finds that light on in there, she's bound to call the police."

CHAPTER 11

Nick let the picture frame door close, plunging the cubby into complete darkness.

"How are we supposed to see without turning on the light?" Mary's whisper was like a disembodied voice.

"Hang on." Nick switched the flashlight to the red setting, giving them enough light to navigate, but not enough to give away their location. "Let's get out of here."

"It's handy having an agent around with nifty gadgets." Mary picked her way across the cubby and into the tunnel. Free to move without knocking into anything, she sprinted to the end.

Nick followed, impressed by her light-footedness and ability to recognize when not to argue.

When they came to the closet at the other end,

Mary waited for Nick. "You go first. I'll shut the door."

Nick edged around her, his body bumping against hers in more places than one, reminding him of the kiss in the cubby. How had this woman gotten beneath his skin in so short a time? He sucked in a breath, the scent of her hair making him hot in the cool tunnel.

Not good. Not good at all.

He was transient, a secret agent destined to leave when he found her father. He had nothing to offer the beauty from North Pole, Alaska. A woman who still believed in Santa and happy families. Mary deserved a husband like her father, full of goodness and optimism. Not someone like Nick who'd seen the worst in people, poisoned by life in the foster care system. If he ever had kids, he'd want them to be happy, with a mother like Mary and a grandfather like—

"Are you going through or what?" Mary's voice shook him out of his daydream. He'd stopped halfway through the narrow space, blocking her way out. With a mental shake, he slipped through and shone the red light for her to see by.

Mary hurried through the tight space, her breasts skimming the water tank.

Next thing Nick knew, he'd find himself jealous of a stupid hot water heater.

While Mary grabbed for her coat, Nick shrugged into his jacket and stood outside the closet, shining his light in until she was jacketed and ready. "We might only have a few minutes to get out of here and back to the B and B before she sounds the alarm—assuming she sounds the alarm." Nick closed the closet door.

"Right. Let's go." Mary led the way through the aisles to the back of the building. "You go on out. I'll set the alarm."

Nick stepped outside, the bitter wind an immediate reminder of his lack of appropriate clothing for a midnight stroll in subzero temps.

Mary closed the door between them so that she could reset the motion sensors and enter the code to activate the alarm.

With Mary out of his sights, tension peaked and Nick looked around for something with which to cover their tracks. A young spruce tree stood at the edge of the paved area, its branches laden with snow. Nick broke off a limb, shook the snow free and returned to the back door.

What was taking Mary so long?

Holding his breath, Nick leaned close to the door, trying to hear anything over the wail of the wind. Nothing. Had she been waylaid? Had she forgotten the code? What if someone hadn't changed the off code but had changed the alarm reset code?

Certainly, lights and sirens would have gone off by now and the police would be notified. But would the door lock automatically, trapping Mary inside?

Nick had seen security systems like that. But who would need one so robust in this forgotten corner of the world? Still, he reached for the doorknob, intent on pulling Mary out prior to the door locking.

Before he wrapped his gloved hand around the handle, the door opened and Mary hurried through.

Branch in hand, he stared at her, the desire to hug her foremost in his mind.

Her brow furrowed and she pointed at the branch in his hand. "What's that for?"

Her question pulled him back to the task at hand. "To cover our tracks. You go first. I'll follow." Nick gestured with his free hand for her to lead the way.

Mary skipped down the steps and around the side of the building where someone had cleared the drive earlier. Unfortunately, snow lay another two inches deep since that time and every step she took left a glaring footprint.

Nick followed behind her, sweeping the snow gently with the spruce branch, effectively obliterating their trail.

All the way back to the B and B, Nick dragged the branch behind him. With the continuous snowfall, their path would be completely covered in the next ten minutes.

When they reached the B and B, Mary was first through the back door.

Nick tossed the branch behind nearby bushes and entered behind her.

Mary pulled the package of papers and photographs from her jacket. "My place or yours," she whispered.

With thoughts of activities other than looking at faded pictures of GIs springing into his head, Nick brushed past her, fishing for the key in his pocket. "Mine. I want to compare that picture with the one I have of a younger Frank Richards."

Once inside, Nick shed his jacket, pulled out his cell phone and called Kat.

"Back already?" Kat answered on the first ring. "What did you find?"

"Some photos and documents from the Bosnia NATO peacekeeping operation."

"Anything interesting?"

"Maybe. We'll know more after I scan and send them to the office."

"Good. Need me for anything?"

He glanced across to Mary. who watched him closely. Oh yeah, he needed Kat to run interference between him and his crazy desire for Santa's daughter. "Not yet. Get some rest. We have a lot of ground to cover in the morning."

"If you're sure." Kat yawned in Nick's ear. "I haven't caught up on sleep since my honeymoon."

"See ya in the morning." Nick hung up, opened his laptop with one hand and held out the other toward Mary. "Let me have the group photo first. I want to scan it and send it to headquarters."

Mary unzipped the plastic bag and laid all the papers across the bed. When she located the group photo, she handed it over, pointing to the man on the left side. "That's my dad."

"At least we know one of the guys in the picture."

She returned to the bed, her fingers skimming across the documents and the individual photos of her father. "Do you think that's what my father wanted us to find?"

"I don't know," he murmured, "but it's a good start."

"Why would he want us to look at stuff that happened thirty years ago? Surely all this is old news. Who would be a threat to him after so long?"

"That's what we have to find out." Nick clicked the mouse and brought up the picture of Frank Richards in his uniform as a young man. "That's Richards." He pointed to the group photo and the man standing in the back row behind Charles Mercer.

Nick peered closely at the name tags on the other uniforms. Yellowed and fading, the letters were blurred. Reaching into a computer accessories bag, he extracted a magnifying glass and held it over the photograph.

Without turning, he sensed Mary's presence behind him. She'd shed her heavy winter coat and stood in the formfitting black turtleneck sweater, the scent of her shampoo completely wrecking Nick's concentration.

When she leaned over him, her breast touched his shoulder.

Nick caught himself before he groaned.

"You come prepared, don't you?" she said, her breath warming his neck and the back of his ear.

An image of a foil packet tucked in his nightstand jumped into his mind until he realized, with a bit of disappointment, she'd been talking about the magnifying glass. "Part of the job description." He held the glass out to her. "Can you make out any of the names?"

As soon as she took the glass, Nick swiveled and stood, inserting distance between him and Mary.

Who'd have thought a woman with a name like Mary Christmas could turn him on so utterly?

He touched the document scanner icon on his cell phone, ready to start the scanning process. Keeping his hands busy excluded him from touching anything else. Namely one curvy little blonde.

"Let me scan the photo." Nick held out his hand. "My people can run a check on your father's military records and see if they can find the names of the men in his unit."

When she handed him the picture, their hands touched.

Something like an electric shock, more intense than the static electricity normal to the dry winter Alaskan climates shot through his arm and into his chest, making his entire body tense.

She looked up, her eyes wide. Had she felt it too? "Nick?"

Her blue eyes mesmerized him, making him forget what he was supposed to do. When her tongue darted out to moisten her bottom lip, he almost came unglued.

Before he lost his mind and perspective, he snatched the photo and laid it on the dark surface of the dresser. "I can take care of this if you want to go back to your room and get some sleep."

"I'm not really sleepy. I'd rather look at the picture and see if I can read some of the names. I think there were two or three of the name tags I could make out. Give me a few more minutes with the magnifying glass." As if to belie her words, she yawned, slapping a hand over her mouth.

"Yeah, you're not sleepy and it's not two in the morning." He strode to the door. "Go on, hit the sack. I might need you coherent in the morning."

"I can go without a little sleep. It won't kill me."

"Maybe so, but I can't. And if you stay in my room, I know I won't get any sleep." He gave her a heated look, his gaze panning her body from her blue eyes to the flare of her hips.

"Oh." She stared at him, wide-eyed. "Okay." Her feet dragged toward the door, her hand reaching slowly for the knob.

Nick almost felt home free. If she'd just leave, his unreasonable attraction would subside.

Instead of opening the door, she turned back toward him, her face rosy. "If you find out anything...anything at all..., will you wake me?"

"You bet," he lied.

Not on your life.

An image of Mary coming to her door in her flannel pajamas stirred more desire than a silky, sheer negligee, sabotaging his attempt to stay neutral. "Now, go to bed." He hadn't meant his tone to sound so mean, but it had the desired effect.

Mary scampered through the door and closed it behind her.

After one split second, Nick realized he hadn't cleared her room. His heart leaped into his throat. He grabbed his gun from the desktop, and he sprung across the room, flinging open his door.

Mary spun, her hand frozen with the key poised to go in the lock, her gaze going to the gun in his hand. "What? I'm going to bed. You don't have to threaten me."

Nick's face heated. "Sorry, didn't mean to scare

you. I just haven't cleared your room," he said quiet enough so as not to disturb the other guests.

He removed the key from her hand and inserted it in the lock, careful not to make a sound. "Stand to the side."

Mary moved down the hallway and waited.

Crouched low, he unlocked the door and swung it open. Nothing moved inside, but he didn't trust the silence. He reached up and flipped the light switch, ducking back out of range. Again, nothing moved, no shots were fired. All good signs but not enough to bet your life on. With a deep breath, he somersaulted into the room and rolled to his feet, his SIG Sauer preceding him.

"No one's here," Mary said from the doorway.

"Jeez, woman." Nick jumped in front of her. His gun still pointed toward the interior of the room. "Do you just *want* to get yourself killed?" he hissed over his shoulder. A quick glance proved her right. No one lurked in the shadows, or under the bed.

"There's no one in here, but someone was." Mary crossed the room and lifted something from the pillow.

"What is it?"

"Another clue." Mary handed him a photocopy of an old newspaper article dating back to 1995.

Charges of treason in enemy arms sales case dropped for lack of evidence. The article listed Taylor Rayburn as the soldier in question.

"Taylor Rayburn?" Mary's brows rose. "That might have been one of the names in the picture."

She raced into Nick's room.

Nick followed.

Mary grabbed the photograph and the magnifying glass from the desk. "There!" She pointed to the man standing in the back, the one with the civilian woman hovering behind him. "Do you see it?"

Nick took the glass from her and held it over the faded photograph. "Could be. I'll have my guys run a check on that name and see what they come up with."

Mary took the picture from him and sat in one of the lounge chairs next to the bed. "I swear Taylor Rayburn looks like someone I should know." She tipped her head, squinting. "If it is, he'd be thirty years older. But I swear I've seen a picture of this man before. Let me have the magnifying glass." She held out her hand.

"Mary, we have a computer guru who specializes in this kind of thing. Let him do the hard stuff."

"What about these documents, the letter?" Mary grabbed the stack of letters and rifled through them.

"You're stalling."

"No, I'm trying to figure this out." Her hands stilled and her face blanched. "Oh my God."

Nick dropped down on the bed beside her and took the letter she held open in her hand. "What?"

"These are love letters to my father." Mary's eyes filled and she stared up at Nick. "From Jasmine."

Nick read through several. "There's nothing worth killing a man over in these." When he finally glanced across at Mary, he noted her pallor.

"She wasn't lying. She really did know my father before he met my mother."

"He was barely out of his teens when he went to Bosnia. All young men think they're in love when they're that young."

"I didn't want to believe her." Mary shook her head, a tear slipping from the corner of her eyes. "I guess I always thought my mother was his first and only love."

Nick's chest tightened and he tossed the letters onto the bed. "It was a long time ago."

"He never forgot her." Another tear followed the first and Mary swiped at the offensive drop. "He never told me."

The second tear made Nick's chest squeeze even more, until he could barely breathe. If Mary didn't leave soon, he'd be holding her in his arms telling her everything was all right. And he didn't want to go there. "Go to bed, Mary. You'll feel better about it in the morning."

"But—"

"Go to bed." He took the last letter from her and, grasping her hand, pulled her to her feet.

And right into his arms. That was his first mistake. His second was when he didn't back up immediately. The heat of her body pressed to his ignited a flame so hot he couldn't escape being burned through his clothing.

Her hands fluttered to his chest, her sky-blue eyes smoldering to gray. "I should go now." But she didn't make a move toward the door.

Nick didn't bother to release her, his errant arms locking around her waist. Anger mixed with overpowering desire. "Damn it, Mary. You're a complication."

Her pretty brow furrowed. "No, I'm a woman."

Her breathy response and the way she pressed against him only fueled the fire. "Which automatically makes you a complication." He tipped her chin with his thumb, his gaze focusing on the plump swell of her lips. "I can't get involved with subjects in my work."

Her gaze left his and moved downward to his lips. "Who's asking you to get involved?" Her fingers climbed up his chest to slip around his neck and feather into his hair. "I just want my dad back. I'm not promising you anything and I'm not asking for any other guarantees." Pressure on the back of his neck drew him inexorably closer to her.

Damn the rules.

They were just guidelines anyway. He had to taste her, had to feel her lips on his just once more. "Good, because I don't have any guarantees to give." His mouth crushed hers, slanting across her lips, his tongue darting out to slide between her teeth and duel with hers. Anger, lust, passion and something more pushed him further.

His hands skimmed downward, cupping her buttocks, pressing her against the pulsing evidence of his quickly loosening grip on control. The solid ridge beneath his fly strained for release from the confines of his jeans.

How could he let her go now? How could he send her back across the hall to the safety of her room? She couldn't be safe with him when he had only one thing on his mind, and it wasn't tucking her in bed with a good night kiss.

He turned her, backing her against the mattress on his bed, until the backs of her legs hit and buckled. She sprawled across the bed, dragging him down with her.

Nick rolled to her side to keep from crushing her beneath his weight, and she rolled with him, their lips locked in a kiss that lasted until he remembered to come up for air.

When he did, his breath came in ragged gulps, his pulse leaping beneath his skin. "I've never wanted someone as much as I want you now."

NICK'S WORDS made Mary's insides burn like a red-hot inferno, consuming her thoughts and destroying all common sense. When she should be pushing him away, she pulled him closer. Her mind had given up on its pathetic attempts to show her reason. Nick had secrets he'd never tell, and he was only passing through. He'd leave. She'd be heartbroken. The end.

But it wasn't the end yet, and her body didn't give a damn. It wanted satisfaction only Nick could give her. How long had it been since she'd made love with a man? Two years? She'd waited. hoping for someone who'd love her and whom she could love back. Someone who could be honest, no secrets, no lies to stand between them. Why had she fallen for someone who couldn't tell the truth, couldn't love her forever? Wouldn't be around for tomorrow?

Why didn't these thoughts stop her?

His hand cupped her chin and slid down her throat, pushing aside the collar of her sweater. His lips followed the path of his fingers.

Suddenly, Mary felt suffocated by the heavy turtleneck sweater she'd worn for their clandestine mission to her dad's basement. She reached for the hem, dragging it up over her belly.

A large hand stopped hers. "Are you sure? Don't start something you can't finish."

"I'm sure." From stark uncertainty to positive confirmation, she made up her mind. If this was a one-night stand, so be it. A woman had to grab for happiness when it came. Damn the consequences. Her hand paused beneath her breasts. "Before we do, tell me two things."

His lips twitched. "If I can."

Her eyes narrowed. "You better."

He nodded.

"You don't have a wife hiding somewhere in the lower forty-eight states, do you?"

"What?" His eyes widened, his surprise evident. "No. I don't."

"Promise?" she asked.

"Scout's honor."

She stared long and hard into his eyes.

He smiled and kissed the tip of her nose. "That one was easy."

"I still have a second question."

"Shoot."

"Don't tempt me."

Nick captured her lips in a long, heated kiss. "Your question?" he murmured against her lips.

Her heart fluttered and she found this question both harder than the first, and even more urgent with the rise of longing claiming her body. "Do you have protection?"

Nick reached into the nightstand and lifted out a foil package.

A smile spread across Mary's face and an exquisite ache built between her legs. She jerked the sweater up and over her head, dropping it to the side of the bed.

Leaning over her, Nick kissed the swell of her left breast peeking out of her black lace bra. His fingers slid around her back to unclasp the hooks. With deliberately slow movements, he eased the straps from her shoulders, tugging them down her arms until her breasts sprang free.

Mary shivered, her nipples puckering at Nick's heated gaze. She wanted to see him naked, to feel his skin against hers. She pushed his shirt up his chest, eager to touch bare skin, feel his strength and warmth beneath her fingertips.

Nick sat up and removed his shirt, tossing it to the floor. Then he was on his feet beside the bed, loosening the button at her waistband and easing the zipper downward. He kissed her belly, his fingers sliding beneath the elastic of her black bikini panties with slow, sensual care. Mary almost screamed with frustration. She wanted him inside her. Now. Hard and fast.

At last, he tugged her pants and panties down her legs. Completely exposed to his view, Mary had never felt more desirable.

Then Nick removed his own clothing, his gaze locked with hers, as each item dropped to the floor until he stood in all his naked glory.

Mary's mouth watered as though anticipating a tasty dessert.

Nick St. Claire was a perfect specimen of all that was incredibly male and sexy. From his smoldering eyes, broad shoulders, ripped muscles and well-defined abs to that part of him standing at bold and beautiful attention. "Are you sure?" he asked.

"Never more certain in my life." A thrill of power surged through Mary. She'd made him that hard. He wanted her. She scrambled to her knees and reached out for him, dragging him back to the bed, where he lay down beside her.

Nick held out his hand, the foil packet between his thumb and forefinger.

Mary grabbed it and ripped it open with her teeth.

A smile spread across Nick's lips. "Anxious?"

"Shut up." Back on her knees beside him, she ran her hands over his chest, down his rock-hard abdomen and lower, until she clasped that needy part of him in her hands. She loved the velvety smooth hardness between her fingers. She stroked him, marveling at how big and straight he was.

Nick's hands caressed the insides of her thighs, his index finger delving between her folds, stroking her until an electric jolt of energy speared through her loins.

She couldn't take much more before she shot over the edge and came undone. Mary slipped the condom over him and straddled his waist, poised over him. "Nick." Her legs spread wider, lowering her down until he entered her.

"Yes?" He grabbed her hips and stared up into her eyes, his own deep pools of ink. He pushed upward, entering her slowly.

Mary gasped. "This doesn't change anything with us, does it?"

Still partially embedded, he paused, his eyes widening, then narrowing. Then he flipped her over onto her back.

The movement was so sudden, Mary squealed.

"My sweet Mary." He smoothed the hair from her face and touched his lips to hers. Then he settled between her legs, pressing deep, filling her to full. "This changes everything."

CHAPTER 12

NICK WOKE before Mary the next morning and stared down at her in the light shining across her face from the edge of the curtain covering the window. His mind raged that he'd broken the cardinal rule he'd imposed on himself when he'd become an SOS agent, *never get involved*. At the same time, he couldn't ignore the feel of her soft curves spooned against the harder planes of his body.

After seeing her in her father's basement, surrounded by traces of her happy past, he'd have a hard time walking away at the end of this case. Her love for her family shone through, the memories invested in each object evident in the way she caressed them.

A gnaw of envy ate at his gut. He found himself wishing she would caress him as lovingly and remember him the way she did her family. His desire stirred, an ache growing low in his belly. If he didn't get up soon, he'd throw the case to the winds and make love to her all over again.

He couldn't, not when he would leave soon. How could a woman who still believed in Santa Claus understand why a man would leave her after making love to her as he had? No matter that he'd told her he couldn't commit. If she was fool enough to fall for him, he'd surely hurt her. Knowing that he might be the cause of putting tears in Mary's eyes wrenched at his gut, quenching his rising excitement. He'd done wrong by taking her to bed.

Mary slept peacefully unaware of Nick's churning thoughts. Her straight blond hair splayed across the white pillowcase like a halo of spun gold, her lips parted as if on a sigh. She looked thoroughly kissed, her mouth slightly swollen from their long night of lovemaking.

Nick slipped from the sheets, drawing them up over Mary's naked breasts, reasoning that it was best to hide temptation. The sooner he found Santa, the sooner he'd leave. Before Mary got hurt.

Before he fell for her so hard he couldn't leave.

Moving around in the dark, he located the jeans he'd worn the night before and slid the cold denim over his legs. Once he had a sweater on, he padded barefoot across the room to the laptop and booted it to life.

The first message in his in-box was one from

Royce. Patch, their techno-geek, had enhanced the photograph to the point he could make out a majority of the name tags on the uniforms. Using the names from the tags, they'd performed a cross-check against information from the military database. He'd listed the names of soldiers based on their position in the photograph.

Nick compared the names to the faces. As he suspected the man he'd pegged as Frank Richards was the one he'd identified from the picture he had stored online. Mary had been right about the one she'd identified as her father, Charles Mercer. But there was another that nagged at him. Gordon Thomas, the senator campaigning for President of the United States.

If he'd learned one thing in his life as an agent for both the FBI and the SOS, never assume something is a coincidence. Charles Mercer had been studying that article about the senator before he'd fled the cabin. Why? If Frank Richards' death had anything to do with this squad, it made sense that the others might be in danger. Since Gordon Thomas was campaigning in Alaska, he might also be in danger. Royce needed to send a warning to the presidential candidate.

Footsteps rang out in the hallway, and someone pounded on a door across the hall from Nick's room. That person was pounding on Mary's door.

"Mary! Wake up, Mary!" a woman called out.

Mary sat up straight, blinking the sleep from her eyes. "What? What's that noise?" The cool air must have made her aware of her nakedness and she pulled the sheet up over her breasts, her face flushing a sexy pink. "What's going on?"

"Mary!" the voice carried through the wood paneling of the door.

Nick peeked through the peephole. "Looks like your friend Betty from the diner."

"Something must have happened." Mary jumped from the bed dragging the sheet with her as she snatched her clothes from the floor.

"Let me handle it." Nick waited, his hand on the doorknob, until Mary had ducked into the bathroom. Then he opened the door. "Ms. Reedy, what's the trouble?"

"I need to find Mary. Someone tried to kill Reuben last night at the hospital!" Betty wrung her hands. Her eyes glazed with tears. "I'm so scared I just don't know what to do." She threw herself at Nick and, clutching his sweater, burst into tears.

Nick froze for a second, then did the only thing he could think to do. He wrapped the woman in his arms and patted her back until the tears subsided enough, that he could be heard. "How is Mr. Tyler now?"

"He's alive. But barely. They have police protection on him now." Betty looked up into Nick's face. "Who would do such a thing to Reuben? He's never been anything but kind." The woman buried her face in Nick's shirt again, her tears soaking through to his skin. "He couldn't even shout for help."

Mary stepped out of Nick's room and swung around behind Betty Reedy. She laid a hand on the older woman's shoulder. "Ms. Betty, Reuben's a trouper, he'll pull through."

"Oh, Mary!" She turned and threw herself at Mary.

Mary held her until the next round of tears faded. "What happened? How did they try to kill him?"

"Someone tried to smother him, but he was able to press his call button for help. Whoever it was got away."

"Poor Reuben." Mary's troubled gaze met Nick's.

"That isn't the worst part." Betty sniffed and rubbed her eyes on her sleeve. "The scare was too much for Reuben and he went into cardiac arrest. They moved him into the cardiac care unit at Fairbanks Memorial."

Ms. Reedy pulled away and gave a shaky laugh. "Look at me. I never fall apart." She pulled a clean tissue from her coat pocket and blew her nose. "Your father wanted you to know about Reuben." The woman's eyes widened. "I mean with your father, being out of pocket and all, I didn't know who to turn to. I just knew he'd want you to know."

Nick schooled his face to keep from showing any reaction to her stumble and cover-up. What did Betty know about Charles Mercer's disappearance? Could she know where he hid?

Mary wrapped an arm around the woman and hugged her to her side. "I'm glad you came to tell me."

"I'd better get on over to Fairbanks. Lenn is filling in for me at the diner." She dried her eyes on yet another tissue. "Be careful, will you, Mary? We'd hate anything to happen to anyone else in town." She gave a mirthless laugh. "And this used to be such a nice place to live."

"And still is." Mary patted the woman's arm. "I'll drop by the hospital later."

Before Betty had taken two steps toward the exit, Nick laid a hand on her shoulder. "Ms. Reedy, if you need someone to talk to or you need assistance, you can count on us. We're here to help Santa. If he's in any kind of trouble, we want to get to the bottom of it."

Betty's gaze narrowed and she opened her mouth, but nothing came out. She snapped her lips shut and shook her head. "I sure wish I knew where he was. He's got us all worried half to death."

Nick nodded. "I'd hate for what happened to Reuben to happen to Santa. Just remember, we're here."

Betty nodded, a flush rising in her cheeks. "Well, uh, thanks. I suppose I'd better get going. I want to make sure they're treating Reuben right at that hospital." She walked away still muttering to herself. "Hard to believe a killer could just walk right in..."

After Betty left, Mary planted a hand on Nick's chest and guided him back into the room. "What was that all about?"

Nick captured her hand and, before he could think, turned it palm upward, pressing a kiss to the smooth, warm skin. "I think Betty knows more about your father's disappearance than she's letting on."

"Just because she made that comment about my father wanting me to know?" Mary stared at the closed door leading to the hallway. "Do you really think she does?" She turned as if to follow the older woman.

Nick stopped her by tugging on the hand he still held. "Don't push her. I'll have Kat keep an eye on her. If Ms. Reedy knows anything, Kat will find out. In the meantime..." He strode across the room and touched the trackpad on the laptop. He brought up the e-mail Royce had sent.

"In the meantime what?" Mary moved up behind him, her body warm, the scent of her hair and skin sending miniature shock waves through him, reminding him how good it had been between them the night before. He turned, not realizing just how close she stood, and found himself bumping into her, body to body. He reached out to steady her, his fingers gripping her shoulders. The urge to pull her into his arms was so strong, he ached with the need.

A soft knock sounded on his door, followed by Kat's voice. "Nick?"

"We need to talk." Nick stared down into Mary's smoky blue eyes. "Just not now." He dropped his hold.

Mary stepped back, wrapping her arms around her middle. "You better get the door." Her gaze didn't meet his, instead she stared at the door. She'd already backed away physically and now mentally.

Good. At least one of them had sense enough to know a relationship between them was destined to fail. Nick yanked the door open.

Kat stood on the other side balancing a cardboard tray containing three foam cups and a newspaper. Her glance skimmed past Nick to Mary. "Oh, good, I hoped you'd be here, seeing as the folks at the diner gave me three coffees instead of two."

Mary's face flushed. "Good morning, Kat."

Nick took the tray and pulled her through the door.

Kat's brow furrowed. "What's going on?"

"Someone tried to kill Reuben Tyler at the Fairbanks hospital, and I have info from headquarters." He set the coffee on the table next to the laptop.

"Is Taylor going to make it?" Kat asked.

"Tyler," Mary corrected. "And yes, so far. They've got him in the cardiac unit with a police guard." Mary's eyes widened. "Taylor. Oh my God."

Kat gave Mary a half smile. "I meant Tyler."

"Reuben Tyler." Mary's head lifted and she stared up at Nick. "Taylor Rayburn. That's why I know him. They're the same. Reuben Tyler is Taylor Rayburn."

"Did I miss something?" Kat glanced from Nick to Mary and back to Nick.

"Are you sure?" Nick's gaze never left Mary's face.

"Positive. Sometimes I'd go with Dad on poker night at Rueben's house. Mr. Tyler had a photograph on his mantel of himself as a young soldier." She lifted the photograph and pointed at the man in the picture identified as Taylor Rayburn. Her eyes narrowed. "But that doesn't make sense."

"What doesn't make sense?"

"The article we found in the trunk. The one about illegal arms sales involving Taylor Rayburn."

"Why?"

"The man I know as Reuben Tyler would never do anything wrong, never commit treason."

"War makes a man different, Mary."

Mary glared at Kat. "Not that different. Reuben Tyler may not talk, but he would never hurt his own people or country. Ever."

Kat raised her hands in surrender. "Okay, okay. I'll take your word for it. And from what the article said, he wasn't convicted."

Mary's glare receded only slightly. Her back stiffened and her hands clenched into fists. Her pale blue eyes fired up when she was mad. He'd be honored if

Mary showed that much loyalty to him. Anyone would.

Nick fought a smile. "If Reuben was one of the men in Santa's, aka Charles Mercer, unit back in Bosnia, then his house exploding wasn't an accident." Nick forced himself to look at Kat. "And Royce confirmed our stiff in Brooklyn, Frank Richards, was a member of the same unit."

"Okay then, we have something to go on." Kat reached across the table and snagged a cup from the holder. She pulled the top off and a cloud of steam rose, the air filling with the rich aroma of fresh coffee.

Nick turned to Mary. "Which makes it even more imperative that we find your father before whoever has it in for the unit does. We haven't checked out your father's other poker players, Bob Feegan and James Janovich. Do you think they might be harboring him?"

Mary's face paled. "Do you think they might be in danger because of Dad? If he's hiding out with them, they well could be." She pulled her cell phone from her pocket and selected a number. She waited, her gaze connecting with Nick's. After a long minute, she shook her head and ended the attempted call. "No answer at Mr. Feegan's."

"Try Janovich." Kat nodded toward the phone resting in Mary's hand.

Mary dialed and waited. After a while, she shook

her head. "Sill no answer. Same as yesterday." She slipped the phone in her pocket and rubbed her hands over her arms a worried frown pushing her brows together. "I have to go."

Nick grabbed her before she made it outside. "You're not going anywhere without me."

"Mr. Feegan lives in a cabin north of town. Chris Moss lives with him. Mr. Janovich lives in a house east of here on Highway 2. What if my dad is staying with them? A killer could find them by asking around. They could be hurt or..."

"Or nothing. Don't borrow trouble, Mary." Nick smoothed a hand down her arm.

Mary's blue eyes glazed with tears. "If you're right, and Ms. Betty knows anything about where my father is, she'll be in trouble too." She pried at Nick's hand. "Let me go. I have to go check on them. They're as much a part of my family as my father."

"We will," Nick said. "Ms. Betty is on her way to Fairbanks. Does she have a cell phone?"

Her brow furrowing, Mary answered, "Yes."

Nick handed her a pen and paper. "Give me the number. I'll call her and let her know to be careful. We'll also need addresses for Janovich and Feegan."

Mary scribbled down the number and addresses.

Kat set her coffee on the table. "I'll take Janovich."

"And we'll drop in on Feegan." Nick gathered his jacket and gloves from the bed. "After you've checked on Janovich, catch up with Betty Reedy in Fairbanks and tail her. She might know something about Santa's whereabouts."

"Roger." Kat's hand dove under her jacket and she pulled out her nine-millimeter SIG Sauer. She released the clip, tapped it once in her palm, shoved it into the handle and stuck the weapon back in the holster in under three seconds. "I'm ready."

Mary's eyes rounded, her face paled.

Nick hid a smile.

Kat must have realized Mary was staring at her. "What? Haven't you ever fired a pistol?"

"No, I mean yes. My father taught me when I was a teen." Mary laughed, the sound shaky at best. "I just didn't expect everyone around me to be carrying one." Her gaze shot to Nick's pistol lying on the dresser where he'd left it last night. A shiver shook her body.

Everything that was happening was a lot for Mary to handle. If he could have, Nick would have left her in town, but he didn't trust her not to do something stupid like try to find her father on her own. "Come on."

Mary grabbed her coat, gloves and hat from her bedroom and slipped into her snowpants and boots.

"You doing her?" Kat tipped her head toward Mary's door.

"For a married woman, you're very crude," he replied without taking his gaze off Mary's door.

"It's a tough life being an SOS agent, whether as

part of the government or not. It's hard to manage a relationship even when you're both on the inside."

"Who said we're in a relationship?"

Kat rolled her eyes and slipped into her jacket. "Whatever, St. Claire. I'm beginning to think you don't know what the hell you're getting into." She left the room and jogged down the hallway to the exit.

Nick clenched his fists, his gut knotting as tightly as his fingers. "I'm beginning to think that myself."

THE WINTER STORM had let up from the day before, but the clouds hovered, blocking out the few short hours of dusky daylight, making the sky a thick smoky gray. At least the wind was still for the moment. Mary could deal with the cold a lot better when the wind wasn't blowing through her clothes like an air pressure hose.

The snowplows had been hard at work early that morning clearing the main streets and highways. Taking Highway 2 out of town would have been easy in a car. But they weren't taking the more traveled route. Mary passed the rental car and headed for the snowmobile.

Nick zipped his jacket and pulled gloves onto his hands before he climbed aboard the vehicle. "I don't suppose our man Feegan lives out on a river somewhere, does he?"

"No. Normally, you can get to his place by car or a

four-wheel-drive vehicle, but with the recent snow, we can't count on the plows having made it out that far yet. They get the main roads between Fairbanks and North Pole cleared out first."

"Fair enough." He turned the key and hit the start switch.

Mary's body tingled at the thought of getting close to Nick again. Why she should be shy after what they'd done last night, she didn't know, but damn it, she was. Or was it the memories of their lovemaking that made sliding on the back of a snowmobile with Nick more intense?

Nick's lips twitched as if he could read her thoughts. "Are you coming?"

Her cheeks burning, Mary clambered on and wrapped her arms around Nick. There. That wasn't so bad. In fact, it felt pretty darned good. Too good.

Mary slid her goggles in place, blaming the negative temperatures for the stinging in her eyes. What did she care if Nick St. Claire left? Hell, he'd only been here a couple of days. She couldn't have fallen for the guy so soon. It was just sex. A one-night stand. No emotional attachments, right? She wasn't that stupid.

As they sped out of town, Mary leaned into Nick's strong back, letting him block the cold wind stirred by the snowmobile, moving forty-five miles an hour over the snow.

Right or wrong, being with Nick gave her a

certain sense of security and reassurance. She didn't know what she would have done if she'd had to look for her father on her own. That bleak thought gave her a chill that shook her from head to toe.

Nick slowed. "Doing okay back there?"

"Yeah, no problem. Just hurry."

Nick still hadn't told her who he worked for and likely never would. Mary had no reason to trust him. But she did. He'd saved her life on the trail yesterday. Of course he was saving his own life at the same time.

He'd made passionate love to her through the night.

A sinking feeling settled in her gut. Mary supposed sexy special agents always slept with the girl. That's how it worked in all the James Bond movies. Granted, Nick was no James Bond. He was much more appealing in a rugged, tough-guy way. She much preferred Nick's hardness. He banked around a corner in the road, and she squeezed tighter around his middle.

Even through the thick layers of the snowsuit he wore, the solid core of muscles couldn't be missed. She'd run her hands across them in the privacy of his bedroom last night. Not an ounce of fat on that man's body.

Her blood warmed beneath her clothes, and she almost missed the turn to Bob Feegan's place. "Here! Turn left here!"

Nick whipped the machine to the left.

If Mary hadn't been holding on tightly, she'd have been flung off.

The snow hadn't been cleared off this road yet, but someone had been out this way since the snowstorm ended. A clear set of skid marks and tracks indicated a snowmobile had passed through not long ago.

Nick gunned the accelerator and sped along the road. Mary was used to being in the driver's seat on a snowmobile. The lack of control made her hold on for dear life.

As they approached the last bend in the road before the cabin, Mary squeezed tighter. "Slow down!"

Letting off on the accelerator, Nick slowed immediately and brought the vehicle to a halt on the edge of a clearing where a log cabin stood. He killed the engine.

Without the sound of the motor, the silence in the picture-postcard setting was eerie. No smoke poured from the chimney, nothing moved, no signs of life.

Mary shivered, a cold lump of dread settling in her belly.

Nick pulled her off the snowmobile and behind a tree.

"What's wrong?" she whispered, scrambling to get her feet under her in the snow.

"See that window on the right?" He pointed to a window on the front of the house.

Mary squinted in the near dark, trying to see what Nick saw. Then she did. A perfectly round hole, the size a bullet would make, in the glass, six inches from the left side.

"Mr. Feegan. Chris!" Mary lunged toward the house.

A hand grabbed the back of her jacket and yanked her back so hard, she stumbled against Nick's chest.

Nick's lips moved against Mary's ear. "Whoever put that hole there might still be around."

Her gaze darted around the shadowed clearing. Nothing moved.

"Look." Nick pointed to the ground around the house. Footprints marred the freshly fallen snow. Footprints that led around to the back but not out into the trees. Whoever made them had come from either inside or the rear of the house. "If he's still here, he knows we are."

Mary hunkered lower to the ground. "What if Mr. Feegan or Chris is inside and hurt? We need to get in there."

"Not yet." Nick moved her closer to the tree. "Stay here. And I mean stay." He gave her a stern look. His lips pressed into a straight line. Then his long body bent low as he scanned the shadows beneath the trees.

Fear jolted through Mary. "You can't go out

there." She grabbed his sleeve and held on. Images of Nick being gunned down tightened her grip.

Nick faced her, laying his hand over hers on his arm. "Gonna miss me?"

"No—yes—oh, hell." She let go. "You could get hurt..."

"I'm trained in this kind of thing. I'm just going to have a look around. I'll be back in five minutes." He leaned forward and kissed her. "Promise me you'll stay?"

With the warm promise of his kiss still on her lips, Mary stood back behind the tree and trained her eyes on Nick as he moved through the trees on the edge of the clearing. He had the grace of a cat, slipping from shadow to shadow, zigzagging from one large tree trunk to another, his white coat blending into the snow.

When Nick had gone halfway around the clearing, Mary lost him. The darkness of the Alaskan winter wrapped her in a frigid shroud. She shivered, counting the seconds until the five minutes were up. She couldn't wait any longer. He should be behind the house by now.

A loud crack killed the silence, echoing off the tree trunks.

A shout bounced off the treetops. "Get back!" It sounded like Nick.

Mary leaned around the trunk. Dusk was

claiming the minimal daylight, and she couldn't see a damned thing in the tree line.

Another crack pierced the air. A man cried out, his voice cut off in a gurgling sort of grunt. Was it Nick? Had he been hit?

Mary staggered away from the safety of the tree and ran toward the house.

An engine revved on the other side of it.

More guns popped off, one after the other until the engine noise faded away.

By now Mary had reached the back corner of the house. A figure lay crumpled on the ground in front of a shed out behind the house. A river of blood stained the virgin white snow.

A moaning wail rose from her throat and Mary threw herself toward the inert form. "Nick!"

CHAPTER 13

NICK LAY at the edge of the woods in the snow, his back to the clearing where the house stood, his weapon trained on the disappearing blur of snowmobile. Damn it! He'd missed, and the son of a bitch had gotten away.

"Nick!"

Mary's voice jerked his concentration back to the area behind him. He sprang to his feet and scanned the area for more potential threats. Deep down, he knew the lone rider of the speeding snowmobile had been the only bad guy here.

Mary ran across the open space toward the downed man. Apparently, she hadn't seen Nick in the shadows. When she reached the figure, she dropped to her knees.

The man's hat lay in the snow beside him,

exposing a shock of gray-white hair Nick could see from where he stood.

"Mr. Feegan?" Mary's voice cracked. She rolled the man to his back, shucked her gloves and felt for a pulse in his neck.

Nick strode across the snow, angry he hadn't been able to help Feegan, angry at the man who'd gotten away, angry at himself and angry at Mary. "I thought I told you to stay put."

"It's Mr. Feegan," she said in a choked whisper. "I...I think he's dead." She looked up into Nick's face as if begging him to prove her wrong. Her blue eyes swam in tears, one fat drop trickling down her cheek.

Nick dropped to his haunches beside her and pushed her hand away. He pulled his gloves off with his teeth and pressed two fingers to the man's neck.

Already the man's body temperature was falling, the cold air leaching the warmth right out of him. The gunshot had hit him square in the chest. He never had a chance. Still, Nick prayed for the soft thud of a pulse pumping against his fingers.

After several long seconds, he shook his head. "He should have stayed put in the shed. I warned him, but he was standing between me and the shooter. I couldn't get a clean shot." He didn't know why he was explaining, but the sadness in Mary's eyes made him do things totally out of the tough-guy character for him.

Tears spilled over and tumbled down Mary's

cheeks, the moisture chilling as they touched the icy air, making crystallized trails on her skin. "He was one of my father's closest friends. I've known him all my life. He was an uncle to me."

Never having known an uncle, Nick could only guess at the depth of her loss. He supposed if Royce died, he'd miss the man. He'd been a mentor to Nick, bringing him back from the self-destructive bent he'd been on before joining SOS. Whatever Mary felt was hurting her and the more Nick knew Mary, the more her pain manifested itself in him.

Nick pulled her into his arms. "I'm sorry, Mary."

Mary leaned her forehead into his chest, the tears falling faster. "Is this what's going to happen to my father?"

"Not if I can help it." Nick smoothed his hand down her back and tugged her closer. He wanted to hold her there until all the bad guys were dead and gone.

Mary gripped the front of Nick's jacket and stared up at him, her teeth clenched. "Who the hell wants him dead? And why? Tell me," she begged, her words choked.

Nick shook his head, his mouth twisted. "I don't know. But let's make sure Chris isn't here."

Mary's eyes rounded. "Oh my God." She jumped to her feet. "You don't think...oh God. And what about Uncle Jimmy?"

"Kat's got him covered. Let's check inside for

Chris." Nick motioned toward the back door. "The shooter came out of the house."

Mary lifted Mr. Feegan's hat from the ground and covered his face with it. "We have to notify the police." Her attention shifted to the house, her breath ragged and shaky.

"Does Feegan have a phone line?"

"Yes."

"Maybe you should wait outside."

"No way."

Nick knocked the snow off his boots before stepping up on the back porch. The door stood open.

Tapping her boots on the corner rail, Mary knocked the loose snow from the treads.

Nick entered first and did a quick once-over. "Chris isn't here."

Mary inhaled and let the air out slowly. "Thank God."

"Try not to touch anything. The police will want to collect evidence."

"Why would that man be after my father and his friends?"

"Maybe your father was hiding out here."

Mary blinked back tears. Anger flared in her pale blue eyes. She turned into Nick's chest, pounding a fist against him. "But why would they want to kill my father?"

He grabbed her wrist and held her. "Easy there."

"I'm sorry." She stared at where his hand held her wrist. "I just don't understand."

"I think it has to do with his time in Bosnia." Nick held her at arm's length. "He never talked to you about it?"

"No, never." Mary brushed tears from her eyes. "Until yesterday, I didn't even know his other name. How stupid is that?"

Nick sighed. "We all have secrets. I'm sure your father had a good reason for keeping them."

"But why now? It's been over thirty years. Why are the secrets surfacing?"

Nick stepped inside the small cabin with the hardwood floors hewn of split logs. The furniture was handmade of smoothed cedar with leather cushions. A stuffed moose head hung over the smooth river stone fireplace. Blankets draped the back of the sofa. In the corner, a tall safe like the ones men used to store guns in stood open, the lock having been blown off. All the contents spilled out on the floor, including several shotguns, rifles and documents. The documents had been scattered across the room. Throughout the two-room cabin, cabinets and dresser drawers hung open, the contents shoved out on the floor.

"He was looking for something." Mary spoke Nick's thoughts aloud.

"Yeah, but what?"

"I don't know. Obviously, he thought it was worth killing for."

Nick lifted a telephone receiver off the kitchen counter and listened for a dial tone.

Nothing.

"Line's dead." He dropped the receiver in the cradle. "Come on, let's get back to North Pole. I want to check in with Kat." Nick grabbed Mary's hand and pulled her out the back door.

"What about Mr. Feegan?"

"We'll send the police out to take care of him." Nick wanted to talk to Royce. He pulled his cell phone out of his pocket. No reception. A satellite phone would come in real handy about now. He should have known his cell phone wouldn't work this far out of town. Maybe Royce would have more information for him. They couldn't keep losing people to this hit man.

Mary trotted to keep up with Nick. "I don't feel right leaving him here."

The sorrow in Mary's voice tugged at Nick's heart, but he pushed aside the unwanted feelings. He had a job to do. Find Santa and keep Mary from being killed. "It can't be helped."

Mary's feet slowed. "Maybe I should stay with him."

Fear tightened Nick's chest. Not for himself, but at the thought of Mary alone in the wilderness with a dead man, exposed to the machinations of a killer. "No."

"But—"

"Not an option." He climbed on board the snowmobile and pushed the start button. The sooner he got her back to town, the better. If he could lock her in a room for the duration of the case, he would. "Get on."

Mary frowned but did as directed. Her gaze strayed to the house, behind which Robert Feegan's body lay. Tears swam over blue eyes.

Nick's grip on the handlebars loosened and he grabbed one of her hands and squeezed. "The sooner we get to the police station, the sooner he'll be taken care of."

Mary sighed. "I know, but it still doesn't feel right. As far as I know, Mr. Feegan didn't have family. Dad and the other poker players were all he had. I hadn't realized how much I'd missed them all until I moved to Seattle." She settled on the back of the machine, wrapped her arms around his waist and laid her cheek against his back.

Bob Feegan had lived a lonely life with no family, yet he had friends who were like family.

Nick found himself envying Feegan's connections. In his line of work, Nick was destined to live an even lonelier life, never forming lasting relationships, never having a family or a little blond-haired girl bouncing on his lap, calling him Daddy. When had the action and stimulation of life as an SOS agent lost its glamour and become less fulfilling?

When he'd come to North Pole and met a woman who loved her father enough to risk her own life to save him.

Nick ground his teeth together. Something about this place and this woman was getting under his skin. Still, he refused to acknowledge Mary's hold on him. To acknowledge was to admit he cared. In Nick's books, caring got you in trouble. Caring made you vulnerable to the enemy.

Unwilling to switch the headlamps on and create a more visible target, Nick left them off and hugged the edge of the roads on the way back to town. The clouds had cleared sufficiently to allow light from the stars to guide them.

When they pulled up in front of the bed-and-breakfast, Kat ran out. "I talked to Janovich."

Mary's face brightened. "Is he all right?"

"Alive and kickin'." Kat's mouth twisted into a crooked smile. "I had to convince him I wasn't a threat. He had a gun big enough to shoot an elephant pointed at me the entire time."

Mary laughed. "Sounds like Uncle Jimmy. He and Dad used to hunt bear together."

"I'd be scared if I were a bear." Kat grinned. "I was just about to scout out Ms. Reedy."

"Let's move this discussion inside."

When Kat opened the glass door to the bed-and-breakfast, it shattered into a million shards.

Nick dove for Mary, but she jerked and he clipped her side, taking her down into a snowbank beside the building.

"I didn't hear anything, did you?" Kat asked.

"No. He must be using a silencer." Nick rolled off Mary, placing his body between her and the shooter. "Mary, are you all right?"

She gave him a half smile. Her brows creased in a strained frown. "I'll live." He didn't like the way her voice shook, but she didn't appear injured.

"Kat, cover me. I'm going after him." Nick leaped to his feet, crouching low in the shadows. "As soon as I draw his attention, get Mary inside."

"Roger." Kat lay prone in the snow, her nine-millimeter SIG Sauer drawn and aimed into the dark shadows between the buildings across the road.

Headlights appeared around a corner. Nick waited until the car passed. He kept one eye closed to the lights to maintain his night vision. With the car out of the way, he hunched low and raced across the street, heading for the darkest shadows between the buildings. If a shooter was out there, that's where he'd be hiding.

Once he'd crossed the street, he pressed his back to the wood siding of a storefront, making his silhouette as small as possible. He risked a glance back in

Mary's and Kat's direction. They still lay low in the snow, waiting for the best moment to duck inside.

Nick moved out of the shadows and across the sidewalk, hugging the storefront. The next space between buildings yielded fresh footprints. The snow was packed down at the corner. Prints led toward the rear of the building. The shooter had probably fled.

If Nick didn't hurry, the bastard would get away again. He threw caution to the winds and jogged along the tracks, alert for attack.

When he emerged behind the buildings, a dark shape, hunkering low, ran around a corner.

Nick picked up speed, sprinting full out. When he reached the same corner, he paused only long enough to catch sight of the assailant thirty yards away. The man ran across an open field dropping down into a ditch and then back up again, five more yards and he'd be hidden in the trees.

"Stop!" Nick shouted.

The shooter dropped, rolled and came to his feet, facing Nick.

Nick dove behind a tree. Bark splintered from the trunk next to where his head had been.

Staying well within the shadows, Nick leaned out, checked for movement downrange of his target, then squeezed the trigger.

At the last moment, the shooter spun and darted to the left. Instead of hitting him in the chest, the bullet hit him in the side.

The force of the impact jerked the shooter around. But it didn't slow him down. Clutching his midsection, the killer loped for the tree line.

Nick knew if the man made it, he'd lose him. He fired again, the distance and the darkness limiting his accuracy. The bullet spat up snow at the man's heels, spurring him to run even faster.

Nick sprinted after him, the freezing air biting his lungs. By the time he reached the ditch, the other man had disappeared into the forest. Without hesitation, Nick dropped down into the ditch climbing the other side in two giant steps.

Once he reached the trees, he ground to a halt, allowing his night vision to adjust to even darker shadows. The man's footprints led deeper still.

His vision adjusted, Nick picked up the pace. After several minutes, Nick emerged onto another road that had been freshly plowed. He lost him there.

Nick loped along the street, his gun drawn, peering between buildings, searching for footprints or any sign of movement. After five minutes, he knew he'd been bested.

And the longer he stayed away from Mary, the more anxious he was to get back and make sure she'd made it safely indoors.

Nick followed the street to where it intersected with Highway 2 and headed back to the bed and breakfast, his feet numb from exposure. A burning sensation, like that of sharp, poker-hot needles, jabbed into his toes. If he didn't get inside soon, frostbite would follow.

He headed straight for his room, hoping Kat and Mary would be waiting there for him. He slid his key in the lock and flung the door open. The dark room stood empty.

"You didn't get him, did you?" Kat leaned against a doorjamb down the hall Her arms crossed over her chest.

Nick resisted the urge to look around her for Mary. "I hit him, but it wasn't enough to take him down. Where's Mary?"

Kat jerked her head toward Mary's room across the hall.

"I need to talk to her." He didn't really need to talk to her, but something close to an anxiety attack threatened to overwhelm his senses where Mary was concerned.

Nick crossed to Mary's door.

"She said something about getting a shower."

Nick pressed an ear to the door and didn't hear anything. He knocked.

Kat stood by, her brows rising. "I contacted the police about Feegan."

Nick didn't respond. He'd give Mary ten seconds more before he broke down the door. Ten...nine...eight...

"The chief said he'd be by after they collected the body and dusted for fingerprints."

Seven...six...five... His heartbeat ratcheted up another notch. What was keeping her?

"Oh, and Royce called. He wants a status report."

Four...three... Nick backed up a step, bending at the knee, breathing in, then out. Two...One...

Before he had a chance to cock his leg and slam it into the door, it opened.

Mary stood in the door wrapped in her fluffy pink robe, her face pale, a scrap of paper clutched in one hand, the other arm clamped around her side. "It's another note from my father."

Nick wrapped an arm around Mary's shoulder and led her into the room. Kat followed, closing the door behind her.

"I was about to—to take a shower." She glanced away. "When I reached into my toiletries kit, I found this."

Her robe parted at the knee and Nick noted she still wore her snowpants. "You were about to shower?"

"Yes." She stepped away from him, her gaze darting around the room.

"Without undressing first?" Nick stalked toward her. What wasn't she telling him?

Mary's eyes widened and she held the note out in front of her like a shield. "Aren't you interested in what the note says?"

Kat snatched it. "I am."

Nick held Mary's gaze another second, and then

he looked down at where her arm clenched around her middle. "What's wrong with your arm?"

"Nothing." Mary stepped backward, her back hitting the wall behind her, jolting her elbow. She winced.

"Nothing, huh?" Nick peeled her arm away from her side. Red stained the fluffy pink terrycloth robe.

Kat gasped. "Girl, you're bleeding."

Mary gave a very shaky laugh. "It's just a flesh wound. I'm fine."

Nick's lips thinned. The bastard who'd hurt Mary had to die. But first, the wound needed tending. He let go of her arm his fingers going to the opening of her robe. "I'll bet it hurt to get that shirt off, didn't it?" He glanced into Mary's eyes.

Pain made her pupils black pools in the center of sky-blue irises. "You don't know the half of it."

"Want me to do that?" Kat asked.

"No," Nick shot back, his voice gruffer than he'd intended. With the utmost care, he eased the robe open, peeling the terry cloth out of the sticky red blood.

"See? Just a flesh wound. I'll be just fine."

"Jeez, Mary. Even if it's just a flesh wound, bullets aren't necessarily sterile." Kat hurried into the bathroom and ran a clean washrag under the tap.

Nick slid the robe off Mary's shoulders and down her arms. She'd managed to get her shirt off, leaving her standing in blue snowpants and a lacy black bra.

"I can handle this, Kat." Nick took the cloth from Kat, his gaze fully connecting with Mary's.

"Are you sure, Mary?" Kat's brows angled to a V on her forehead. "I can call an ambulance if you want."

"No. It's really nothing." Mary winced when the cloth touched the gash in her side. "It's just more blood than anything."

"At least let me get my first aid kit. I'll be right back." Kat ran for the door and paused to throw Nick a stern look. "Don't do anything I wouldn't do, Nick. The girl's injured."

"Go."

Kat loped down the hallway.

Nick dabbed at the wound until he'd cleaned all the blood away. The bullet had only nicked her side, leaving a two-inch slash across her pale skin.

"I told you it wasn't much."

Nick's hand shook as he pressed the cloth to the wound, applying enough pressure to stop the bleeding. Then he pushed his other hand through her hair, his palm cupping the back of her head. "Promise me you won't ever hide something like this again." His mouth hovered over hers, his lips a breath away. "Promise."

She stared up at him, her gaze dropping to his lips, her hands inching up his chest clenching his jacket. "I promise."

Then a dam burst inside Nick. He had to possess

her, hold her, claim her as his own and leave his mark on her. He crushed her lips beneath his, slanting across their fullness. She tasted of peppermint, her mouth wet and hot. Nick dove in, plundering, ravaging, and taking no prisoners.

Mary's hand circled the back of his neck, pulling him closer until he could feel the lace of her bra pressing through his shirt.

A cough at the door broke through Nick's madness.

CHAPTER 14

"Here's the antibiotic ointment and bandages I had in my kit. I notified the police about the attack. They'll have someone here within the next fifteen minutes. Someone has to come in from out at Feegan's." Kat shoved the first-aid items into Nick's hands and pulled the note from her pocket. "Maybe you can tell me what whoever left this note meant."

Scratched in her father's crisp print were the words *Shop Around the Corner* and a group of numbers.

Kat turned the paper over. It was blank on the back. "Is this some kind of shopping list?"

"No, *The Shop Around the Corner* was a 1940s movie my mother and I used to watch when I was little." Mary shook her head. "When I was growing up, my father and I used to play games with each other using clues based on lines from the classics or old movies. Then we'd have to figure it out. Usually there was prize at the end. I just have to figure out what the movie stands for, then how the numbers relate."

"Could the numbers be a date?"

"Maybe. But I don't think so. There aren't enough numbers."

Nick's cell phone played the tune from *Mission: Impossible*.

Mary smiled. Nick always seemed so intense. To poke fun at spy movies made him seem more human.

Kat rolled her eyes. "You really need to get a new ring tone."

Nick slid his phone open. "Yeah."

Mary grabbed for the ointment in his hands, but he held it out of reach. Instead of handing it to her, he propped the cell phone between his ear and shoulder and unscrewed the cap on the ointment.

The whole time he talked on the phone, he tended her wound, gently applying the clear gel to her cut. When she winced, his hand jerked back, a frown deepening between his brows.

Mary found it all too personal and tried again to grab the tube from his hands. She felt exposed to him and shy of Kat watching her standing there in her bra.

Nick tipped her chin with a clean finger and shook his head. He pressed another glob of ointment to the wound, his concentration shifting for a moment to the caller. "Interesting."

Mary backed out of his reach and collected a package of gauze from the kit. She peeled back the paper and laid the pad over her cut. The gentle contact hurt. Mary bit down on her lip to keep from crying out. She could be just as tough as the agents, when she had to.

"Even more interesting." Nick fished out a roll of adhesive tape and tore off a piece. "A Purple Heart and a Silver Star? Pretty impressive."

Mary wanted to throw the first aid kit at Nick. She wished he'd hurry and end the conversation and fill in her and Kat. She fumbled one-handed with the adhesive tape, while holding the gauze to her wound, she only managed to get it tangled.

"I'll have Kat run over to Fairbanks and alert his people. No, we won't clue them in on who's involved over here. Roger."

Kat pulled her keys from her pocket. "I take it I'm on the road to warn Gordon Thomas about Frank Richards' death?"

"You got it."

The small, dark-haired woman slipped her arms into her jacket. "I'll drop by the hospital afterward and see if I can catch Ms. Reedy."

"We'll check for her on this end too, in case she's already back." Nick snagged the role of adhesive, tore off a length of tape and applied it to the gauze Mary held in place.

Kat's gaze centered on the work Nick was doing on Mary's side, her lips twisting into a wry smile. "In the event I don't make it back tonight, are you two going to be all right on your own?"

"We'll be fine," Nick replied.

Mary glanced up at Nick. When had she gone from mistrust to full confidence in the man? Was it when he'd saved her from the kamikaze snowmobile rider or when he'd thrown himself on top of her to save her from sniper fire? Whenever it happened didn't matter. What did matter was that she trusted him with her life. Not something she normally did with a stranger.

And she'd done even more extraordinary things with this stranger than she cared to enumerate. Her face flushed with heat. She dragged her gaze away from Nick. "We'll be all right."

"Good. There's supposed to be another storm headed this way later this evening. I should just make it to Fairbanks before it hits." She gave Nick a stern look. "Don't do anything stupid."

A smile quirked the edges of his lips. "Do I look like I'd do something stupid?"

"Love has a way of making a person stupid." Kat's look switched from Nick to Mary, her brows winging upward. "Just keep your eyes open and your shirts on."

Mary's face burned hotter. As if Nick was falling in love with her. *Ha!* Not when he could have any girl he wanted in the lower forty-eight states just by crooking his finger. No. Nick wouldn't fall in love with a girl from the backwoods of Alaska. He was married to the job. A woman didn't fit into his lifestyle on a permanent basis.

No matter how much she told herself that Nick wouldn't fall in love with a bumpkin like her, she couldn't stop the hope flowing up into her chest.

Great. Mary Christmas had committed the ultimate folly. She'd fallen for a guy she'd known only a few days. And here she was dreaming about happily ever after with a man who would soon be gone.

Yeah, Kat had it right. Love had a way of making you stupid. Mary caught herself before she smacked her palm to her forehead. She. Was. Not. In. Love. With. Nick. No one fell in love that fast. Mary squared her shoulders. "While Kat's on her way to Fairbanks, let's go see if Ms. Betty is back from visiting Reuben in the hospital. I'm worried about her."

"After we talk to this police officer." An SUV with police markings had just pulled into the parking lot.

After she'd given her statement, Kat left for Fairbanks in her black four-wheel-drive SUV.

Mary walked beside Nick to the diner, intent on finding Betty and getting a few answers. The smells of coffee, bread and chili filled the air, reminding

Mary she hadn't had lunch and all she'd had for breakfast was the coffee Kat brought early that morning.

Once inside, Nick ordered two sandwiches to go from the bar.

Mary looked around. No sign of Betty. When Lenn brought out their sandwiches, she asked, "Has Betty made it back from Fairbanks yet?"

"Yeah, she got in about an hour ago, grabbed a bag of burgers and left. Said she had some errands to run, but that she'd be back in time for the dinner crowd." Lenn wiped a meaty arm across his forehead. "Sure hope she does. Lunch was a bear. You want me to give her a message when I see her?"

"No, thanks." As soon as Nick paid, Mary hooked his arm and steered him toward the door. "Did you hear that? A bag of burgers."

Nick handed her a sandwich and slipped his gloves on while juggling his own. "Must have been hungry."

"Or she was getting extras for a guest."

"Let's find out. Where does she live?"

"In a little house on Flight Street."

"Do we have to take a snowmobile?"

Mary smiled. "A car will make it."

They hiked back to the rental car at the B and B and made the short drive to Flight Street in complete silence, each munching on their sandwiches.

When they pulled up the snowy drive, Betty

Reedy flung open the door and ran out to greet them. She wore her house slippers but no coat, her forehead creased in a deep frown. "Mary, I'm so glad you're here. I don't know what to do. I can't find Chris. He's missing. And your father hasn't checked in like he said he would."

"What? Wait a minute." Mary held the woman at arm's length. "Did you say my father hasn't checked in?"

Betty's hand clapped over her mouth, her eyes widening. The older woman dropped her hand and sighed. "Oh, shoot-fire. What does it matter anyway? You might as well know it all." She shot a narrow-eyed glare at Nick and then turned her gaze to Mary. "Can he be trusted?"

Mary stared up at Nick. The silence lengthened.

His brows rose. "Do you trust me, Mary?"

Her gaze collided with his and she nodded. "With my life." As she spoke the words, she knew beyond a doubt the truth of them. But she didn't trust him or any man with her heart. Oh, she wanted to, but the nature of the situation excluded him from the happily-ever-after scenarios.

Frigid wind blasted through the trees. A violent shiver shook Betty's frame. "What am I thinking? Come inside, come inside before we all catch our deaths." She shot a glance in a three-hundred-sixty-degree circle before hustling them through the front door, closing it firmly behind them. She didn't stop herding them until they were standing in the living room.

Mary brushed off Betty's attempt to take her coat. "What's going on, Ms. Betty?"

Betty Reedy crossed the floor to the couch where what looked like a thirty-pound yellow tabby lay sprawled across the seat cushion. She lifted the cat in her arms and ran her hand across the animal's fur. "Cookie, oh, Cookie, what else can we do?"

When she finally turned to Mary, she hugged the cat to her face and sighed. "Your father's been in hiding since he was reported missing the other day. He'd been holing up in my house and amongst other friends for the past few days. He was here earlier today. I guess until he heard about Bob Feegan." Betty's eyes filled. "I just wonder if Ch-Santa was out there when the gunman shot Bob?"

Nick shook his head. "We didn't see Santa and we were there. Too late to help Mr. Feegan, though."

"Oh, dear Lord." Betty set the cat on the floor and grasped Mary's hands. "Tell me you didn't put yourself in danger. Your father never would have had you come home if he'd known you'd be in danger. He's beside himself with worry for everyone in North Pole."

Mary held tight to Betty's hands. "I couldn't be anywhere else, you know that. If my father is in trouble, I have to do everything I can to help. That's what family does." Her gaze shifted from Betty to Nick.

His dark-eyed stare gave nothing away. For a long moment, his gaze held hers. Then he nodded. "We have to find Mr. Claus."

"He's not the only person I'm anxious to find." A tear slipped down Ms. Betty's cheek. "Chris is missing now."

"Chris?" The cold seemed to infiltrate Mary's body, filling her belly with dread. Her father was a grown man with a military background, capable of defending himself to some extent. Chris was a teen, friendly to everyone. "What do you mean Chris is missing?"

"He went to the post office in Fairbanks. I haven't seen him since."

Santa in hiding, Chris missing, mysterious visits to post offices in other towns...all the conspiracies jumbled in Mary's mind until she couldn't make heads or tails of any of it. "Why was Chris in Fairbanks?"

"I dropped Chris off before I went in to see Reuben. The boy was supposed to check for a package your father expected and meet me at the hospital. I waited for four hours and he never showed. I drove by the post office and didn't see him. That's when I came back here."

"Why wouldn't my father have his package delivered to the North Pole post office?"

"He didn't want anyone to intercept it. He said it was very important."

Important enough to kill for. Mary squeezed Betty's fingers, warming them with her own, trying to reassure the older woman, when she felt no certainty of her own. "What time of day did you drop Chris off in Fairbanks?"

"An hour after we talked this morning. He should have been back by now." Betty dropped Mary's hands, crossed to the windows and peered around the curtains. "I'm so afraid for him."

A thought sprang to the forefront of her mind and Mary glanced at Nick. "We'll see what we can find out. If you hear from Chris, will you call us as soon as possible?"

Nick scribbled his cell number on a piece of paper and handed it to Betty. "Lock your doors and windows. If anyone tries to get in, call 9-1-1 immediately."

"Am I in danger?"

As if sensing her owner's distress, the yellow tabby wound herself around Ms. Betty's legs, mewling softly.

"Until we catch Mr. Feegan's killer, assume the worst." Nick strode for the door.

Mary shrugged and zipped her coat halfway up. "If someone saw fit to kill Mr. Feegan for harboring my father, who knows what else he might be willing to do? Stay safe. We'll find Chris." She hugged her close.

"Would you? I'm so afraid for the boy. He's never

out of pocket without telling someone where he's going."

Once outside, with the door firmly closed between them and Ms. Betty, Mary marched for the car. "My bet is that the package contains Frank Richards' memoirs."

Nick nodded. "Agreed. And whatever is in them must be controversial enough to kill for."

"Someone has incentive to stop that manuscript from being seen, but who?"

Nick's cell phone played the *Mission: Impossible* theme. He unlocked the car and seated Mary before he answered the call. "Yeah."

"Got the ballistics on the bullet that killed Frank Richards. It's a match with a murder in Dallas two months ago. The man killed was one of the men in the photograph.

"Have you located the others?"

"Two of the men died of heart attacks within the past ten years and another died in a car wreck shortly after he returned from his tour in Bosnia. That leaves just three."

Nick's fingers tightened on the cell phone as he rounded the back of the car. "Charles Mercer, Taylor Rayburn and Gordon Thomas."

"That's right. And Nick." Royce paused. "Both Richards and the Dallas murders were precision exterminations. We've seen five others like it. Using the same weapon and M.O."

"Are the other victims linked to our men from Charles Mercer's unit?" Nick reached for the car door handle.

"No. One of them was the wife of a foreign diplomat. The diplomat eventually confessed to hiring a hit man to eliminate her. He said he'd hired a man going by the name Cobra."

Nick's hand froze, anger and fear welling up in his chest.

Mary rubbed her hands up and down her arms to keep warm.

A chill settled over Nick, colder than any arctic blast.

"Nick? Did you copy?"

"Copy."

"Clue Kat in. I'm pulling Sam off his current assignment in Portland. He should be there by tomorrow morning. I'm hopping a plane as we speak. I should be there early tomorrow as well. Don't be a hero, wait for backup."

"Roger." Like hell. If Cobra was anywhere around, every man, woman and child in a one-hundred-mile radius could be in danger. Collateral damage was part of the fun to the psycho hit man.

A wave of anger and nausea rolled over him. Nick's former FBI partner had gotten in the way of Cobra's paycheck when he'd took a security detail for a federal witness in a Bethesda, Maryland. The witness, her child and Nick's partner didn't live to tell what exactly happened, but the compromised safehouse was a bloodbath on all fronts. An FBI insider had leaked the location but was never identified. He'd arrived at the end of the shooting. Too late to save anyone. Too late to catch Cobra. Devastated and suffering severe survivor's guilt, Nick lost his stomach for the FBI. He'd turned in his service weapon and credentials and walked away.

Royce had found him working a bodyguard-for-hire assignment in D.C. and offered him a job he couldn't refuse. Nick never looked back. He didn't have to look back, images of what Cobra had done to his partner, the woman and the child would live on forever in his memories. And to think, the maniac was here.

Nick jerked open the car door and climbed in. His heart raced, pounding blood against his eardrums.

Mary leaned across the console and laid a hand on his arm.

He inhaled slowly and released the air.

"Who was that on the phone?" Mary's fingers gripped Nick's arm.

"That was my boss. The man after your father is a monster and he won't stop until he eliminates his target."

Mary's face blanched, her hand sliding off Nick's arm into her lap. "Eliminates? Like Bob Feegan?"

"And Frank Richards."

Her head shook back and forth as if in slow

motion. "I knew he was in trouble, especially after what happened to Reuben and Mr. Feegan, but you're really scaring me now." Her eyes remained dry, but the color didn't return to her face.

"I'm taking you to the chief's office and you're going to stay there until Kat and I find the man behind all this." He shifted into drive.

Before he could pull out into the street, Mary grabbed his arm. "We have to bring Ms. Betty. She's not any safer than me or the others."

Nick nodded. "I'll be right back." He opened his door but didn't get out. "Maybe you should come with me."

"You're only going to be a moment. I'll be fine. I'll duck low in the seat, so no one sees me." She leaned toward the console. "See? No problem. Just hurry, it's cold out here."

Nick stared at the house and back at Mary.

She smiled and waved at him. "Go on."

He climbed out of the car and half ran, half slid all the way back to Betty Reedy's front door. He raised his fist and banged.

"Wh-who's there?" A curtain fluttered in the window beside the door. "Nick?" Then the door flung open and Ms. Betty stood there, wringing her hands. "What's wrong? Why are you back so soon?"

"It's not safe for you to stay by yourself. You need to come with us." Nick hooked her arm and tried to walk her through the door.

The old woman dug her feet into the welcome mat. "Where are we going?"

"To camp out at the police station until this is all settled. Come on."

"What if Charles or Chris returns?" Ms. Reedy pulled her arm out of Nick's grasp. "I need to be here."

"Leave a note." Nick reached out to grab her arm again, but she dodged him.

"I can't go without my medications and a change of clothing. Wait here."

The longer Ms. Reedy took, the more frustrated Nick became. He stood on the stoop, staring into the darkness. A lone security light shone half a block away, casting a cone of light around its base.

"Can you help me with this cat carrier? I can't leave Cookie here to fend for herself."

"Ms. Reedy, leave the cat. We can have someone come check on it tomorrow."

"Oh no, I couldn't leave her. Not with what happened to Reuben's home."

Nick wanted to tell the woman to stay with her damned cat, but one look at her distress and he couldn't. To her, the cat was family and, like everyone in this godforsaken frozen land, she wouldn't leave family behind in a dangerous situation. No manner of arguing would change the woman's mind.

With one backward glance at the car, Nick strode through the hallway into the living room where Ms.

Betty had loaded her whale of a cat in a carrier half the size it needed. He bit down on his tongue and hefted the crate. "Let's go." The cat hissed and spat at him.

"Cookie isn't used to being in her crate. She gets grumpy."

With the carrier in one hand, Nick scooped up Ms. Reedy's suitcase and marched out into the snow.

Ms. Betty skipped to keep up, a worried frown denting her forehead.

When Nick reached the car, he jerked the back door open and dumped the suitcase and the carrier into the backseat.

That's when he noticed the front seat was empty.

CHAPTER 15

As she emerged on the street behind Ms. Betty's house, Mary fumbled with the zipper on her coat. Her decision to leave Nick's rental car had been a hard one.

No sooner had he entered Betty's house Mary had received a text message from her father's cell phone. A flutter of excitement soon became a lump of dread, settling deep in her belly.

Bring the package to Santa's house by midnight. Come alone or

YOUR FATHER DIES

Mary read the message twice, her hands shaking. She didn't have a package. But she had a good idea who did.

She'd glanced at Ms. Betty's house, hesitant to wait for Nick and Ms. Betty. She couldn't let Nick leave her at the police station while someone else attempted the package delivery. It was too risky. Whoever had her father expected her to deliver the package. She couldn't stand the thought of being held hostage by well-intentioned officers of the law, while her father was in danger.

Images of Bob Feegan's limp body lying in the snow surfaced, causing her body to quake. With every step, she peered into the inky shadows. With every moan of the wind or snapping twig, she jumped and spun in a circle, searching for its source, imagining some killer dogging her footsteps.

The note her father left made more sense now that she'd been by to see Ms. Reedy.

The Shop Around the Corner was a story about a woman receiving mail at a post office box. Chris had been sent to collect a package her father had expected to be delivered at his Fairbanks post office box. Find Chris and she'd find the package. She had to get to Chris and the package. Her father's life depended on it.

If Chris were in trouble, he would have headed back to North Pole. But where would he hide?

When Chris's parents abandoned him to head south, Chris had managed to stay in the trailer his parents had rented for the three years they'd lived in North Pole. He'd managed to survive for the first four months because it was still summer, the temperatures hadn't dipped into the teens and lower. Thankfully, Mary's father had caught on to his plight before the freezing temperatures of winter set in with a vengeance.

As far as Mary knew, the trailer was in such bad shape, it had never been rented out again. The property owner pretty much abandoned the home. Could Chris have gone there to hide out until he could rendezvous with Santa?

Mary's footsteps quickened, the moon and stars lighting her way through the streets and backyards. Ten blocks didn't sound like much, but clear skies meant no clouds to hold in any of the residual daytime heat. The thermometer would plummet below negative twenty. A light breeze kicked up, penetrating her jacket.

By the time she reached the edge of the lot where the lone trailer sat, her fingers burned with the cold, and she questioned her sanity at running away from someone as solid and safe as Nick. So what if the agent had enough secrets to last a lifetime? He knew his stuff. Knew how to combat a killer. If a maniac wanted to eliminate everyone vaguely associated with her father, he'd have an easy target in Mary.

Her steps slowed and her body shook violently. She'd check Chris's old home and then hustle back to someplace warm. Maybe back to Nick. The thought of being safe and warm inside the police station wasn't sounding so bad after clumping through snowdrifts.

The trailer stood like a dark, hulking monster at

the end of a deserted road. Spruce trees studded the yard like silent sentries. The branches were flocked in four inches of fluffy white. Snow lay a foot deep on the roof and piled waist-high in drifts around the base. Virgin snow, untouched by human feet.

Across the street from the trailer, Mary hunkered down near the trunk of a tree, hoping her light blue jacket and snowpants blended with the snow, tinged blue by moonlight. She scanned the empty road and the shadows beneath nearby trees. Nothing moved.

Keeping to the tree line as best she could, she maneuvered to the edge of the road, then raced across to the back of the trailer.

Her heart fluttered and she sucked in a gasp.

The snow at the rear entrance had been trampled. Someone had been here recently. But how recently?

A twig snapped and a shadow moved beneath the trees headed away from her.

Mary didn't think, just raced after the shadow. Was it Chris? Hope welled, propelling her forward.

The retreating figure ducked behind a dark structure deep in the woods.

Halfway between the trailer and what looked like an old shed, Mary returned to her senses. What was she doing? She didn't know who that was out there. It could be the killer, leading her farther away so that no one would hear her cries for help.

Fear brought her to a stumbling halt. She'd spun

in the opposite direction and took her first step back the way she came when a voice called out.

"Mary?"

"Chris?" Mary turned back toward the crumbling shed. "Chris? Is that you?"

The young man eased from behind the rotting boards, his head turning right, then left before he stepped out into the moonlight. "Yeah, it's me."

"What are you doing out here?" She hurried toward him and wrapped him in her arms. "We've been so worried."

He pulled away, his brow furrowed. "I'm worried about Santa."

"Me, too," she said. "How did you get back from Fairbanks?"

"I hitched a ride with the beer truck."

"Why didn't you wait for Ms. Betty?"

"I couldn't. Someone was following me."

"Why?"

"Because of this." Chris reached inside his jacket and pulled out a large envelope.

The package.

Mary took the item from him. Aware that delivering this package could be the only way to keep her father alive.

Her hands shook as she lifted it to the light of the moon. All that was written on the outside were the numbers she'd seen on her father's note. The numbers were the P.O. box number to a box in Fairbanks. "Did this arrive today?"

"Yes. Your father left a note and a key in my room at Mr. Feegan's."

"Did the note say The Shop Around the Corner?"

"Yes, it did. I recognized it as that crazy game he'd play when he'd want me to find a surprise."

"And you'd seen that movie?"

"Yeah." Chris shrugged. "Your dad and I watched it just the other night before all this happened. It wasn't bad for an old black-and-white. Anyway, when I got the note, I ran down to the North Pole post office, but the numbers on the boxes didn't go that high, so I figured he meant for me to go to Fairbanks."

Chris shivered and pulled his collar up around his ears. "Once I found the box and retrieved the package, I slipped through one of the back doors, like I used to slip in and out of the grocery store back when I had to steal for food." He took a deep breath and let it out. "I circled back around and watched from a distance. A man waited by the door for a while, watching everyone entering and leaving. After a while, he went inside. When he came out, he stared around like he was looking for someone. I think that someone was me."

"Oh, Chris." Mary hugged him close.

The young man pushed her away. "I can handle

myself. Since Ms. Betty had dropped me off, I figured he'd seen that and would be watching for her, so I decided to find my own way back to North Pole. That's when I caught a ride in the back of the beer delivery truck." Chris grinned. "A guy could get into a lot of trouble in the back of a beer truck."

"I'm glad you didn't."

"When I got back to town, I heard about Mr. Feegan." Chris's eyes glistened. "He'd been so good to me, letting me stay with him and all." The young man rubbed his coat sleeve over his eyes.

Mary patted his shoulder. "Mr. Feegan was a good man."

"I couldn't go there, that's why I'm here. I hoped your dad would call me on my cell phone and let me know what to do with that."

The tune to "Here Comes Santa Claus" sounded from Chris's jacket pocket. He stuffed his gloved hand in and pulled out a cell phone, staring down at the number on the display. "It's Santa."

Mary froze. Had the message she'd received been a lie? Could it be her father wasn't being held hostage?

Chris received the call and pressed the phone to his ear. "Hello." The young man listened, his eyes widening. "What did you say?" He jammed the phone to Mary's ear.

She wrapped her fingers around it and listened.

"If you want to see Santa alive," an ominous voice said, "bring the package to Santa's house by midnight. Enter through the back door. Just you. No one else. If more than one person arrives or if any of the information in the package gets out, I'll slit the old man's throat. Understood?"

Mary gulped and answered in her best Chris impersonation, "Yes."

The caller hung up.

Mary's hands shook so badly she almost dropped the phone when she handed it back to Chris. "I got a similar text message just a little while ago." She held out her cell phone, showing him the text. "He's got my dad. I have to go there. Now." She glanced down at the package, disgust curling her lips. "What could be so important in this that someone would kill a nice old man?"

"Looked like a manuscript to me. I read parts of it while I was waiting." Chris gave her a weak smile. "It's something about weapons smuggling during the Bosnia peacekeeping mission."

"Oh my God. I wonder if it names who was responsible." Mary looked around at the surrounding woods. "Is there someplace I can go to read through this?"

"You don't have much time. Midnight will be here all too soon, and you have to get across town to Santa's house."

"I have to know. Do you happen to have a flashlight?"

"Yeah, come inside the trailer, I have a flashlight in there."

Mary followed him back to the trailer and climbed up the rickety steps. Once inside, she dropped to the floor and shone a flashlight down on the loose pages of a manuscript that had somehow changed her life forever.

NOISE BOMBARDED him when Nick stepped through the doors of the police station. Chief Landham stood in the middle of Silas Grentch, Jasmine Claus, Silas's hired cameraman and half a dozen of what Nick guessed to be the concerned residents of North Pole, everyone talking at once.

Officer Trey Baskin climbed onto a chair, placed two fingers in his mouth and blew a piercing whistle that had everyone silent in seconds. "That's better. Let the Chief talk."

"Thanks, Trey." He turned to Jasmine Claus. "We haven't heard from Santa since he disappeared. We've followed every lead, questioned all his friends and I'm sorry to say, we found nothing. We're doing the best we can."

Silas shoved his way through to the chief, dragging the cameraman behind him. "Chief, do you think Santa could actually be running from the law and doesn't *want* to be found?" He held the microphone in front of the police chief.

Landham shoved the mike away. "Turn that damned thing off, Silas. There is no evidence to suggest Santa is in any trouble with the law."

"That's right. My husband is a good man. It's the people in this police department that are a bunch of fools," Jasmine Claus cut in. "I had to hire a private investigator to find my husband since your department obviously can't."

A man behind her cleared his throat. "Mrs. Claus, I haven't found him yet."

Jasmine drew up on her high heels, topping maybe five feet to the man's six feet. "Which reminds me...you're fired." She swiveled back to the chief. "I'm headed to Fairbanks to hire another private investigator. I expect you to call me immediately if you hear anything about my husband's whereabouts."

The chief nodded, his lips tightening. "Yes, ma'am."

Mrs. Claus stormed out of the chief's office, followed by the jobless P.I., arguing over his bill.

Nick couldn't help believing they deserved each other, he pushed his way through the mob, determined to report Mary as missing.

"What are you doing about Bob Feegan's murder, Chief?" a citizen yelled above the growing noise.

"We have the Alaska State Troopers examining the crime scene and collecting evidence."

"Do you have any suspects in mind?" Silas asked, shoving the mike at the chief.

Landham glared at Silas. "If you don't get that thing out of my face..."

"Could Santa have killed Bob Feegan, Chief?" Silas persisted.

"We don't know who killed Bob Feegan." Landham nodded to Officer Baskin. "Will you get these people out?"

From his perch on top of the chair, Trey whistled again to get the crowd's attention. "If you want us to catch the killer, leave and let us do our jobs."

One by one, people vacated the office, worried frowns on their faces.

The chief spotted Nick and waved him forward. "Nick, I'm glad you stopped in. I wanted to ask you a few more questions about what happened at Feegan's earlier."

"I'd be happy to answer any and all questions, but I have a more pressing need."

"What is it?"

"Mary Christmas and Chris Moss are missing."

The chief closed his eyes and ran a hand through his graying hair, standing it on end. "When?"

With Ms. Reedy's help, Nick filled him in.

The chief stood and shook Nick's hand. "I'll put extra men on patrol. If you hear anything..."

"I'll let you know." Nick left Ms. Reedy and her cat with the chief and spent the next hour patrolling North Pole, searching in vain for Santa and his daughter, the sense of impending doom weighing heavily on him.

When driving around brought nothing to the surface, he returned to his room and paced the floor, casting glances through the open doorway into the hall where Mary's door remained closed. He'd already jimmied the lock and checked inside. As far as he could tell, she hadn't been back since she'd disappeared.

Where the hell had she gone? He'd checked her room before dropping Ms. Betty off at the police station. He'd called Jimmy Janovich to see if Mary had been crazy enough to find her way out to her father's friend's house.

The older man nearly bit his head off over the phone, refusing to tell him anything. "How do I know you're not the nut case trying to kill Santa? I heard what happened to Bobby Feegan. If you were the one who done it, you'll pay."

"Sir, I'm concerned about Mary. She's disappeared and I'm afraid someone might hurt her if we don't find her soon."

"If I knew where she was, do you think I'd tell you? I don't know you from Adam. I'm hanging up and calling the police. You hear me? I'm calling the police." The line clicked and Janovich promptly dialed the police to report the call. Nick knew because he received a call on his cell shortly after from Chief Landham's phone confirming.

A call to Royce revealed no new information on Charles Mercer or his unit. He tried Kat, but she wasn't answering her cell.

Nick's frustration mounted with each passing minute. He called Kat for the third time in as many minutes.

When Kat answered, she sounded out of breath. "Yeah."

"We've got trouble."

"You're telling me," she wheezed.

Nick's pulse spiked. "Why? What's happening there?"

"I just ran six blocks," She paused to suck in a noisy breath.

"Why?"

"You wanted me to follow Gordon Thomas, didn't you?"

Nick frowned. "Not on foot."

"He slipped past his own security staff and out the back door of the hotel. Since I was inside the hotel at the time, I didn't happen to be in a car."

"Where'd he go?"

"The senator climbed into a car by himself and took off." She took another deep breath and blew it out in his ear. "Instead of running around the other side of the hotel to get in my car, I cut through some streets and ran after him. Dumb mistake, but I wanted to know which direction he headed, I knew I'd lose him if I went all the way back to my car before following him."

"Did you lose him?"

"I followed him until he hit Highway 2 headed east. It appears he's headed your way. I didn't get the opportunity to tell him about what's going on in North Pole. Maybe he's heard and is on his way to check it out for himself."

"Without his gaggle of bodyguards for protection?" Nick scratched his chin. "Doesn't sound right. But I'll get the police chief involved. He can pull him in and brief him on the local happenings." Nick gripped the phone tighter. "Right now, I need you here. ASAP."

The sound of a car door slamming passed through Nick's receiver before Kat asked, "More trouble?"

"Royce called. He thinks Cobra is involved."

"The hired assassin?"

The knot in Nick's gut tightened. "That's the one."

"Damn."

He inhaled and eased the air from his lungs. "And now Mary's missing."

"I thought you two had become Siamese twins joined at the hip."

Nick ran a hand through his hair and paced across the hall to her door and back. "I told her I was going to lock her up at the police station until this was all over."

"And she took off." Kat chuckled. "She's got spunk. I know I wouldn't put up with a threat like that if it were *my* father. That was reckless on your part."

"Tell me about it." Nick still wanted her locked in the jail to keep her safe. Nothing had changed on that front. His main regret was telling Mary his plans. He shouldn't have told her. He should have just done it. The thought of Mary at the mercy of Cobra and the image of what the murderer had done to his victims chilled the back of Nick's neck.

"You better find her before he does." The sound of an engine revving filled Nick's headset. "I'll be there in less than twenty minutes. We'll search together."

Nick ended the call. He couldn't wait until Kat got there. He had to find Mary.

He slipped into his snowsuit, gloves and boots, grabbed his keys and headed out into the darkness. If he had to, he'd comb the entire town and outlying homes. The petite blonde had slipped well under his skin and then slipped through his fingers. He didn't feel right stepping out into the cold Alaska night without her by his side, with her running commentary on North Pole, Santa and the people who meant so much to her. She'd immersed him in her life and the town, making him feel a part of their extended family.

As soon as Nick stepped out the door of the B and B, the wind hit him full in the face, turning the moisture in his breath to fine crystals. The weather reporter had warned of another winter storm blowing in from the west. He hoped he found Mary in time. If the killer didn't get to her first, the weather could.

CHAPTER 16

As MIDNIGHT APPROACHED, the wind picked up, slinging fine grains of snow like grains of sand from a sandblaster. Mary huddled on the leeward side of a tall spruce, facing the back of the little gingerbread house—the place she'd called home until two years ago. A single light shone from the kitchen. Every other room lay in darkness. Cold penetrated through the thick layers of her snowsuit, through Mary's sweater and skin and right down to her bones. Her body shook. Her mind was as numb as her fingers and toes.

This was it. She'd left Chris with strict instructions to contact Nick at exactly midnight. If Nick found out what she was going to do any sooner, he'd try to interfere with her plans to trade the manuscript for her father's life.

After spending the past hour and a half reading by

flashlight, Mary had guessed this "trade" might be a one-way trip for her and her father. But she had to try.

Frank Richards' manuscript was nothing more than a confession. Richards had been diagnosed with terminal cancer, and he had a lot to get off his chest before he passed. He'd poured his heart onto the pages, pulling from his memory and the journal he'd kept hidden since his tour to Bosnia.

As a young, aimless twenty-year-old, with no idea of which direction he wanted to go in life, he'd been on a downward spiral, hanging out with the wrong people. Caught with a pound of marijuana in his pockets on the streets of Brooklyn, he'd been hauled before a judge who gave him the choice of going to jail or going into the Army.

He chose the Army.

His first deployment was with the 1st Armored Division to Bosnia as part of NATOs peacekeeping forces. With the hostility still in the country, multinational forces all around and himself angry at the world, Richards didn't have to look far to find a source for drugs. He also didn't have to look far to find ways to make fast cash to buy the drugs. One night on guard duty, he'd stumbled across a little illegal trading going on between his squad leader and a young Bosnian woman, Jasminka who did laundry for the GIs in camp.

The outwardly meek laundress led the negotiations, her understanding of the English language excellent, her knowledge of weapons even more impressive.

Desperate for drugs, Richards promised to help with the arms deals for a cut.

Mary's heart had thudded against her ribs the more she read. "My God, Richards was a traitor."

"Yeah." Chris had read the pages, his ever-cheerful face growing graver by the minute. "Americans selling weapons to the enemy." Mary grimaced. "Seems like we never learn, do we?"

The weapons trading went according to plan for several weeks, until American soldiers uncovered a Bosnian Serbs camp with a cache of American weapons. Military investigators swarmed into the area.

Richards and his squad leader got scared. They decided to cut their losses.

The squad leader sent more than half of the squad out on a bogus mission to check out a potential enemy camp a couple of miles away. Richards led them to ensure that they were well out of the way for what his leader had in mind.

After the recon mission left, the squad leader gathered the remainder of his men, informed them that the Bosnian Serbs had infiltrated the village, pushing the villagers out into the forests. They were to go in and shoot anything that moved and burn the village to keep the Serbs from coming back. He had the soldiers so pumped up and scared that by the time they entered the village, they were fully engaged and ready to kill any and all of the enemy.

Not until they'd torched half the huts did the soldiers realize the villagers hadn't left at all. Women and children screamed in fear, as fire consumed them in their homes.

Mary had pressed a hand to her mouth, tears welling in her eyes. "They killed children."

Men of the village came out fighting with the only weapons they owned, spears and knives. The squad leader mowed them down, using an AK-47 he'd staged near the village. Then he personally targeted the hut of his contact, Jasminka.

Mary stared at her home, reliving the horror of what she'd read. Had her father been one of the soldiers in the village or on the recon mission? Had he headed for Alaska like everyone else, to leave the world and his past sins behind?

Sorrow swelled like a tumor in Mary's throat, choking off her air. Bosnia had been a terrible war where unspeakable atrocities occurred. Had the man who spent the last thirty years playing Santa committed some of those atrocities? Was his role as Santa atonement for his sins?

Mary hoped she'd have the opportunity to ask her father about what really happened. For now, someone wanted this manuscript badly enough to kill for it. But who? Richards didn't name the squad leader, preferring to make him impersonal in the position he played on the squad. A leader who'd gone wrong. The information could be traced through military records if someone wanted to dig hard enough. Maybe that was it. His squad leader wanted the manuscript kept quiet. Of the men in the picture she'd found in her father's footlocker, which one was the squad leader? Now wasn't the time to check. She hadn't risked going back to the B and B in case Nick lay in wait to stop her from doing what she had to.

She illuminated the digital display on her watch. Midnight.

Showtime.

Clutching the envelope to her chest, Mary straightened, cast another glance around the snow-covered clearing and hurried toward the rear entrance. Her heart hammered and her shallow breaths puffed steam into the air.

She entered the kitchen through the unlocked back door. A single light shone over the sink. Fear pinched her lungs as she crept across the tiled floor, forcing herself to concentrate on all the good memories of this very room, when she was surrounded by her mother and father and all the love they'd shared.

Her father couldn't have been one of the soldiers who killed the women and children of that village. He didn't have it in him.

The door to the basement stood ajar, a light shining up from the depths.

"Hello?" Under her breath she cursed, angry that her voice shook.

"Down here. Now!"

Mary jumped and stifled a scream.

"And close the door behind you." The disembodied voice rapped out the words.

She hesitated at the top of the steps. If she descended into the basement and closed the door, no one would hear what happened down there. No one would know if she and her father were being threatened or killed until too late.

Her gut told her to stall. "How do I know you'll live up to your end of the bargain?"

"You don't. But if you want to see your father alive, you'll get down here."

How long would it take Nick to get from the B and B to Christmas Towne? Would he come storming through the front door of the house or sneak in through the basement? *Stall, Mary, stall.* "How do I know he's even down there?"

The sound of something ripping echoed up the staircase. "Say something to your daughter," the voice demanded.

When there was no response forthcoming, a thump was followed by a moaning grunt.

"Don't, Mary! Run for the police! Now!"

Mary pressed a hand to her mouth to keep from crying out. She knew her father's voice. He was in the basement and he needed her.

"Run, Mary!" her father shouted. "Get the hell out of here. Do you hear me? Go!"

Another sickening thump and her father's words died.

"Daddy?" She'd been concentrating so hard on sounds emitted from the basement, she didn't know someone else was in the kitchen with her until a hand touched her back.

Relief welled in her chest. Nick had come early. When she turned, she stopped short of flinging herself in his arms. Standing before her was not the tall, broad-shouldered man she'd expected to ride to her rescue.

Her stepmother stood in front of her, a finger pressed to her lips. "Don't scream."

What the hell? "Jasmine?" Mary whispered, teetering on the edge of the step.

"On the count of three I shoot Santa and then I'm coming after you," the man in the basement shouted.

"Give me the manuscript and I'll take it down." Jasmine held out her hand for the envelope.

Mary frowned at the woman. "I can't. I have to trade it for my father's life."

Jasmine nodded. "I know but let me. Your father would want you to be safe."

"Thanks, but I can't let you do it. That's my father down there."

"That's my husband and I won't let anything stand in the way of our happiness." She held out her hand

and lifted a gun with the other, pointing it straight at Mary's chest. "Give me the manuscript."

Shock glued Mary's feet to the floor. The way she saw it, she had three choices. One, to take her life in her hands and try to disarm and beat the snot out of the woman who'd driven a wedge between her and her father. If she went with this option, she might stir up enough noise and trouble that both she and her father would end up with matching sets of bullet holes.

Two, she could hand over the manuscript and shove the woman down the steps and let her take a bullet from the bad guy in the basement.

"Don't try anything stupid. I know how to use this gun."

Mary stared straight into Jasmine's eyes, ready to implement plan three. "I'm coming down." If Jasmine wanted to shoot her, she'd have to get in line with her father's captor in the basement. She turned her back on Mrs. Claus and took the first step down. She clutched the wooden handrail and held her breath, waiting for a loud bang and the impact of a bullet that would send her tumbling down the steps.

The impact didn't come and she reached the basement floor intact.

Her eyes took a moment to adjust to the limited lighting and then she saw her father sitting in the middle of the basement on an old wooden chair. His hands were tied behind his back, and his feet were tied to the chair. A strip of gray duct tape covered his mouth and thick white mustache. His head drooped forward, his chin touching his chest and his eyes closed.

Mary ran forward, dropping to her knees in front of her father, the manuscript flopping to the stone floor. "Daddy?" She reached out and pulled the tape from his mouth.

His head tipped backward, his eyes blinking open. Then he fell forward, his shaggy white hair covering his forehead and eyes. The only things keeping him from toppling to the floor were the ropes binding him to the chair.

Booted feet came to a halt next to Mary and a hand reached out. "I'll take that." Mary's gaze climbed up the white snowsuit to the face of the man she had seen in the restaurant her first morning with Nick in North Pole. The man's dark eyes stared at her, as cold and empty as the time he'd glanced across at her in the diner. His mouth, set in a heartless sneer, and he held a gun equipped with a silencer.

"Who are you?" Mary asked.

"Some call me Cobra."

Mary studied the man, over six feet tall, muscular, probably in his mid-thirties. "Why do you care so much about this manuscript? You're not old enough to have been involved in the Bosnian War."

"I don't give a rat's ass about the package or the

war, but I'm getting paid to collect a package and dispose of anyone who knows about it."

"By whom?" Mary shifted until her knee leaned onto the envelope.

Cobra pointed the pistol at her forehead. "Hand it over."

"No, don't, Mary. Give it to me." On silent feet, Jasmine moved in behind the man, pointing her gun at his back.

His jaw twitched, his lips pulling back in a snarl. "I told you to come alone." The man jabbed his pistol against Mary's temple.

Mary winced as pain shot through her head and fear crowded her belly. "I didn't invite her, she just showed up. I never wanted her here." If this madman shot her, who would get her father out of this alive? Jasmine? Fat chance.

"Give me the manuscript," Jasmine demanded.

"Touch it and I'll shoot the girl."

Jasmine snorted. "Go ahead. It'll save me a bullet."

The man shifted his gun to Santa.

"No!" Jasmine and Mary shouted simultaneously.

Mary launched herself at Cobra's hand.

Cobra squeezed the trigger, the shot muffled by the silencer. The bullet pinged into the concrete-block wall, knocking chips of masonry onto the floor.

Another shot rang out, the sound deafening in the close confines of the basement.

Cobra staggered backward, clutching his chest with his empty hand. When he stared down at the hand stained with his own blood, his eyes narrowed. Then he tossed his head back and roared. Lifting his pistol, he aimed at Jasmine.

Without flinching, she pulled the trigger again.

The stranger's pistol dropped to the floor. He fell to his knees and then pitched forward, landing flat on his face.

Mary struggled to her feet and stood between her father and Jasmine. "I won't let you hurt my father."

Jasmine shook her head. "Stupid girl. Charles is the whole reason I wanted that manuscript."

She stalked forward and lifted the package from the floor without taking her gaze or aim from Mary. "I love your father. I've spent a lifetime searching for him and now that I have him, I won't let anything get in the way of our happiness." Her lips pressed into a tense line as she held two fingers to Santa's neck for several long moments.

Finally, a smile of relief crossed her face. "Oh, thank goodness. His pulse is strong." Her lips pressed into a thin line. "If he wasn't already dead, I'd kill that bastard again for hurting my Charles."

A fanatical gleam filled Jasmine's eyes. "I've worked hard to get to where I am, to find your father and make him remember what we had. And he remembered me." She slapped her palm against her chest, her words harsh and desperate. "Even after thirty years, he remembered me."

"You were there, weren't you?" Mary asked. "In the village that was burned down in Bosnia?"

"Yes. That's where I fell in love with him." She stroked Santa's face. "He was so young and handsome, and he fell in love with me." She bent to kiss his temple. "And I loved him more than anything. More than life. More than money."

A horrible thought crossed Mary's mind and she staggered backward. "You're Jasminka, aren't you?"

"No, I'm *Jasmine Claus*." The smaller woman straightened. "Mrs. Claus."

"You'll never be Mrs. Claus to me. My mother was the only Mrs. Claus." Mary's shoulders pulled back and she stood over Jasmine, ignoring the gun pointed at her chest. "You're the woman from the memoirs."

"What do you know about what happened? You weren't there." She glanced at the manuscript in her hands, her eyes widening, then narrowing into dark slits. "You read it, didn't you?"

"I did. You were the woman who was the go-between in the arms deals, weren't you, Jasminka?"

"I don't have any idea what you're talking about. And neither will your father."

"He doesn't know, does he?" Her father's head still hung to his chest. Had his eyes twitched? Was he awake but faking unconsciousness? "He doesn't know that you were the traitor in the village. That's why you wanted the manuscript."

"Oh, sweet, devious Jasminka. A leopard can never change her spots, can she?" A well-dressed gentleman descended the stairs into the basement carrying yet another pistol.

Mary's hopes rose. Maybe he wasn't Nick, but he looked like a reasonable man, here to rescue her and her father from the crazy woman with the gun.

"Gordon. I wondered when you'd get here." Jasmine smiled up at the man and Mary's hopes crashed.

They knew each other.

Mary stared harder at the man in the dim basement lighting. She'd seen that face recently in the news. "Gordon Thomas? Senator Thomas?"

The man answered with a regal nod. "Is Jasminka giving you problems? I must say I'm surprised to see her here."

"You assumed I was dead?" She snorted. "Not a chance. I had more spies in your own squad than you knew about."

He nodded. "I should have known. Where have you been hiding for the past thirty years?"

"Here and there. I had to leave my village in a hurry. Someone tried to kill me along with everyone else who lived there." Jasmine's eyelids narrowed into thin slits. "I hid then, but I have no intention of hiding now."

"I can't say that I'm surprised to find you here." Gordon nodded toward Santa. "You always had a thing for Mercer. I'm more surprised at how long you took to find him."

"Now that I have, I'm not letting you or anyone else get in my way. He's mine." Jasmine moved to stand in front of Santa, much as Mary had done earlier. "I've always loved him, an emotion you could never understand. All you understood was greed and lust. Charlie loved me, not for what I could do for him, but because of who I was."

"A lying, cheating traitor to your own people?" The senator laughed. "Aren't you afraid Charlie will learn the truth about you?"

Truth? Mary suppressed her own hysterical laughter. She had nothing to laugh at. One man lay dead, her father needed medical attention, and two of the four living occupants of the basement held guns. How long did it take Chris to tell Nick the bizarre story? Would he ever get there? If Mary had learned one thing about Nick, he acted first, asked questions later.

Which probably meant Chris was having trouble finding Nick. He could be anywhere in North Pole. Chris was on foot in freezing temperatures. Hopefully the teen had the good sense to go to the police if he couldn't find Nick immediately.

"You're the one to talk." Jasmine held the package against her chest and her gun aimed at the senator.

"Aren't you afraid the world will learn the truth about you? You killed innocent people and members of your own squad to cover up your treachery."

Gordon's gaze shifted from Jasmine to Mary and back to Jasmine. "I don't know what you're talking about."

"I watched from the edge of the forest. I saw you fire on your own men with that AK-47 you had staged in my village. I may have sold weapons to the enemy, but I never pulled the trigger on my own people."

She spat on the floor at Gordon's feet. "You are the traitor. You should be thankful I will destroy this." She nodded at the package in her arms. "What would happen to your precious campaign if your part in the arms sales and murder of your soldiers got out, if this memoir gets published? The great war hero isn't such a hero after all, is he? Is that why you hired the assassin to collect the manuscript and kill everyone who knew anything about what really happened?"

Mary gasped.

"He murdered women and children. He came to kill me and thought he had." Jasmine smirked. "I escaped, unlike others of my people who were not so fortunate."

"She's lying, of course. She's an expert at it." Gordon's grip turned white on the gun. Had Jasmine hit a nerve with the senator? Possibly the truth? How could a man running for president get away with the atrocities listed in Richards' memoirs?

Mary inched a step away from the two. "But you saved Taylor Rayburn. You were a war hero."

Jasmine laughed. "He probably didn't think the man would live. And when he did survive, he'd suffered brain damage. He lost his ability to talk in that attack, along with his memory of his entire tour. He couldn't tell the truth of what happened." Jasmine smiled. "Gordon saves a soldier he set out to kill, becomes a hero and all is forgotten about weapons sales to the enemy. Now look at him, running for president. Don't worry, your secret's safe with me. All I want is to live the rest of my life with Charles."

"I'm supposed to trust you?" Gordon shook his head. He bent to retrieve Cobra's fallen weapon. When he straightened, he aimed the nose of the silencer at Jasmine. "This story dies here."

Mary threw herself over her father's body and squeezed her eyes shut. Whatever happened, would happen.

"Oh no, you d—" Jasmine's weapon blasted out a round.

The sound reverberated off Mary's eardrums. Out of the corner of her eye, she saw Gordon duck to the right. Jasmine's bullet completely missed him. The basement grew silent, the residual echoes receding at once. A soft thud broke the silence.

Jasmine dropped to the floor at Mary's feet, her

chest covered in a red stain, her eyes open, staring into nothingness.

Bracing herself, Mary turned to face Gordon Thomas. Was she next?

Thomas lifted the manuscript from the floor, pulled out a lighter and set the paper on fire. Smoke curled from the corner of the envelope upward. "Richards was a fool." He tossed the envelope into a pile of old clothing.

"No!" Mary lunged for the burning package. She had to stop the fire before it spread to the pile of old newspapers beside the box of clothing. Her father lay unconscious, unable to help himself, and she didn't have the strength to carry him up the stairs.

Gordon blocked her path. "Like I said, the truth dies here." Then with a powerful, double fisted swing, he hit her hard enough to send her flying backward. She landed on her back, her head connecting with the stone floor in a bone-crunching thump.

CHAPTER 17

NICK PULLED up in front of the police station, disheartened and hovering on desperation. After driving every little street, he hadn't come any closer to finding Mary or her father. The longer she remained missing, the stronger the possibility he wouldn't find her. Or wouldn't find her alive. Not with a trigger-happy Cobra on the loose.

"Damn it!" He slammed his palm against the steering wheel and then jumped when someone pounded against the driver's side window.

With his hand already on his SIG Sauer, he stopped short of pulling it from the holster. Beating on the window of his rental car was Chris Moss.

Nick slung the door open and jumped out.

"Mr. St. Claire, I've been looking all over for you. I was just about to go to the police when you drove up."

Nick grabbed the boy's shoulders. "Where's Mary?"

"That's just it. She sent me to get you. She has the package and is trading it for her father as we speak."

A cold wash of fear pierced Nick straight through the heart. The fool woman didn't know who she was up against. Cobra didn't negotiate. He killed. "Where?"

"At Santa's house."

As Nick dove into the driver's seat, he shouted through the open door, "Get the police over there. Now!" Before he even shut his door, he shifted in reverse, spinning out of the icy parking lot onto Santa Claus Lane.

Please, God, let him be in time to save Mary. She'd managed to crawl under his skin, and he wanted more than anything to get to know her better. He had only begun to scratch the surface of Mary's magic and that of year-round Christmas Towne. If something happened to Mary, he'd lose all chances of capturing the magic for himself. And for once in his life, he wanted to experience the enchantment of Christmas, a time of year up until now, he'd avoided.

For the first time in his life, Nick prayed.

When Nick reached the cottage, he slammed on his brakes and the car skidded to a halt against a mound of icy snow left by the snowplows.

He leaped from the car and ran for the front door.

It was locked. If he picked the lock, he'd waste valuable time and risk alerting the assassin to his presence. Nick abandoned the front door and dove around the side of the cottage.

Adrenaline pumped through Nick's veins, powering his limbs into action. Every second counted. He raced for the back door and found it locked, the dead bolt as strong as on the front of the house. Windows were positioned high on the sides of the house, too high to make climbing in easy.

The tunnel.

Nick ran for the back of Christmas Towne and dug into the snow once again piled against the back door. When he found the elf statue, he reached inside the cavity for the key. His heart skipped several beats when he didn't find it.

Dropping to his knees, he shucked his gloves and sifted through snow bare-handed, his search nearing frantic. Cobra wasn't known for dragging out an execution. He wouldn't hesitate to pull the trigger, an equal-opportunity assassin, he didn't spare a second thought if his target happened to be a woman.

Nick's freezing fingers touched on icy metal, and he pulled the key from the snow, a wash of relief quickly shoved aside. He inserted the key in the door handle and flung the door open. Without the alarm combination, he had only seconds to get to Mary.

He raced through the aisles of boxes and bins. When he reached the basement door, alarm signals blared to life, blasting his eardrums, red and white lights strobed at the inside corners of the building. Nick only hoped whoever was inside Mary's house couldn't hear the cacophony emanating from the Christmas Towne store.

Nick scrambled down the steps, closing the door behind him to douse the noise from above. In the basement, the alarm wasn't quite as loud. He hurried across the floor to the closet in the far corner and flung the mop and bucket out of the way.

Something didn't smell right. An acrid scent overpowered the musky, moldy smell of damp basement. Nick slid behind the water heater and pushed open the wooden door. Smoke filtered through the tunnel into the closet, burning his eyes.

"Mary!" Nick pulled his turtleneck collar up over his mouth and nose, ducked low and raced to the end of the tunnel. He still had to get through Mary's cubby into the basement. If smoke already stung his eyes and throat, what would the basement be like on the other side of that hidden doorway?

His pace quickened. Mary needed him, he couldn't just give up and go back.

When he reached the cubby, he curled his shoulder in and threw himself through the secret door. Unsure what or who he'd find, he hit the floor on his side and rolled.

Smoke hit him, burning his eyes and lungs. Crouching low, he shined his flashlight into the haze, unable to make out much. If he could get to the door leading up into the house, he might have a chance to get to Mary. Flames licked up a timber beam, racing for the floor joists that held the upper story aloft.

He didn't have much time before fire consumed the house and even less time before he succumbed to smoke inhalation.

Nick blinked smoke-induced tears from his eyes and set off across the floor. Halfway to the staircase, he ran into something. He shone his light down at a body, sitting in a chair. A white-haired, bearded man.

Santa!

Nick pulled a knife from his boot, cut the bonds holding the man to the chair and eased him to the floor. Could Mary be down here as well?

Now crawling on his hands and knees, Nick felt around the floor, until he came upon a woman's body. Blood soaked her clothing and Nick held his breath as he shone the light into her face.

Jasmine Claus's blank eyes stared up into the light, the pupils unresponsive. Nick didn't have to check for a pulse. The woman was dead.

Smoke filtered through his turtleneck collar, but he pulled it aside and yelled, "Mary!"

Coughing sounded from a few feet away. "I'm here."

Nick scurried across to her and pulled her into his arms. "We have to get you out of here." He tugged her collar up over her mouth and nose and, hooking an arm beneath hers, dragged her back the way he'd come.

When they passed Santa's inert form, Mary dug in her heels. "I'm not leaving without my father."

"I can't help you both out at the same time. Let me get you out, and then I'll come back."

Mary pushed away from Nick, tears trickling down her soot-covered face. She reached down and grabbed one of her father's arms and dragged him a few inches across the floor.

Nick handed the flashlight to Mary. "Hold this." He lifted her father from the floor and slung him over his shoulder in a fireman's carry and ran for the cubby, the smoke so thick that he hit the wall first and then had to feel his way along it to the portrait of George Washington.

Mary pulled the secret door open.

"You first," Nick commanded.

Mary dove through and reached back as Nick dumped her father through the opening.

He fell like deadweight onto Mary knocking her to the floor.

Nick clambered over the two, closing the door behind them, effectively blocking some of the smoke from entering the room.

"We don't have much time. The tunnel is too narrow for me to carry your father out." Nick said. "Go and find help."

Mary burst into a coughing fit, her eyes tearing. "I can't leave you two here."

Nick grasped her face between his hands and made her look at him. "You have to. We don't stand a chance if you don't. I promise I'll be working my hardest to get your father out of here, but I'll need help getting him up from the basement."

"But I can't lose you both." She grabbed his hand and leaned her face into it, pressing a kiss to his palm.

"Don't worry. I plan on sticking around. I want to get to know a certain woman named Mary Christmas a little better. I might even ask her out on a real date when this all settles down." He smiled, pulling her close so that he could press his lips to hers. "Now take the flashlight and run as fast as you can."

Mary staggered backward, then turned and raced down the tunnel.

Nick's gaze followed her until the light disappeared around the water heater. Left in the dark, he coughed and struggled to his feet.

That Santa Claus hadn't woken up through all of this had him concerned, but he couldn't waste valuable time worrying at this point. He had to get the man out of danger.

Nick hooked his arms under the man's shoulders and dragged him toward the tunnel. The door to the cubby wouldn't last long once the fire found its way across the basement. Already the smoke thickened in the tunnel, making Nick's lungs struggle to provide oxygen to the rest of his body. If he didn't get out quickly, it wouldn't matter.

THE BACK of Mary's head throbbed and her lungs burned, but she didn't dare stop to catch her breath or she'd fall into another coughing fit and never make it out. Her feet stumbled twice on the basement steps leading into the storage room of the Christmas Towne store. Alarms blasted her ears and lights blinked off and on.

Mary ran out into the front of the store. Through the double set of glass doors, she could see police cars, fire engines and emergency vehicles skidding to a stop in the street out front. Too exhausted to think, she ran to open the store doors, making it through the first set, but she bounced off the outer doors kept locked when the store was closed. The doors could only be unlocked using a key. Mary sobbed and ran back into the store.

Nick and her father didn't have time for her to find a key. Mary grabbed a wooden reindeer modeled into a rocking horse, ran back to the outer doors and slammed the toy into the double-paned glass. One pane cracked and splintered. On the second swing, the second pane shattered and Mary almost fell through.

A fireman must have heard the glass break because he turned toward the truck and grabbed an ax. Then he skidded across the snow and ice toward her.

Mary leaned toward the jagged hole. "I need help. There are people trapped in the basement!" Her voice came out in a croak, barely loud enough to carry over the store's alarm. "Help!"

With his ax, the fireman hooked the door and pulled hard. The door jerked loose of the locks and flung wide. The fireman rushed inside. "Where are they?"

"In the basement. You have to hurry." Mary fought free of the fireman's grip and ran back the way she'd come, weaving through the aisles and Christmas decorations to the rear of the store. When she reached the stairs to the basement, smoke filtered up.

"I'll take it from here." The man pushed past her, intent on going it alone.

"You can't. You won't know where to go." Before he could stop her, Mary slipped around him and leaped down the steps two at a time, the fireman clumping down behind her, hurrying to keep up.

More smoke billowed from the back of the basement where the tunnel connected the two buildings.

"Oh God, please don't let me be too late," Mary sobbed. She ducked low and ran for the closet at the back of the basement. "They're through here!" Mary pressed against the wall and slipped through the opening.

The fireman yelled, "Mary!" Decked out in all his gear, he couldn't squeeze past the water heater.

The smoke was worse than when she'd left the tunnel and she couldn't see anything, even with the flashlight. "Nick! Where are you, damn it! Don't you die on me! It's a lousy way to get out of a real date." Tears streamed down her face as she waited for the fireman to slip out of his gear and squeeze through the opening.

As soon as he was through, Mary inched down the tunnel, coughing and gagging, the smoke so thick she couldn't see two feet in front of her.

"Get out, Mary! I'll find them." The fireman grabbed her arm and yanked her back.

"I want to help."

He pushed her back toward the closet. "You'll help more by bringing the others down here."

"Mary?" Nick's voice called out from the haze, scratchy and choking. A coughing fit burst from the darkness and Nick's back came into view, as he dragged her father by the arms through the tunnel. "Do as the fireman says."

"Nick!" Mary stepped forward, ignoring the smoke, the burning in her eyes and lungs. Nick was alive and he had her father.

Nick turned toward her, his sooty forehead creased in a frown. "Go, damn it!"

Mary backed out of the tunnel, slipping around the water heater to stand in the basement of the store. The fireman came out first and between him and Nick, they wrestled her father through and laid him out on the floor.

Mary ran up the steps to the storage room and was met by Chris leading several medical technicians carrying a backboard. "Oh, thank God."

They pushed her aside and descended into the basement. Mary leaned against a wall. Her strength gone and no adrenaline left to stiffen her legs, she sank to the floor and let her face fall into her hands. Sobs racked her body and she burst into a coughing fit. The coughing turned to wheezing.

"Mary?" Chris squatted next to her, his young face creased in a frown. "Are you all right?"

Unable to speak, she shook her head. Gray clouds crept into the sides of her vision. Gray clouds that had nothing to do with smoke.

"We need a medic here!" Chris's voice came to her from a long way away. The alarms were mere beeps of noise as if muffled by giant pillows.

Pillows sounded good. She needed to rest her eyes. They stung from the smoke. Her eyelids drifted closed.

CHAPTER 18

MARY'S EYES fluttered open when emergency medical technicians hoisted her onto a stretcher, strapped an oxygen mask to her face and wheeled her out into the cold night air.

Every rescue vehicle in North Pole had to be there.

Silas Grentch hovered near another stretcher being loaded into an ambulance. "Is he awake? Can we get a statement from Santa?"

An EMT held his arm out to block Silas. "No, sir, please get back so we can do our jobs."

Mary half sat up, but the medic attending her pressed a hand to her shoulder. "Please lie back."

"Get him out of here," she said, her voice sounding like a hoarse bullfrog.

The medic laughed, his breath raising a cloud of

steam in the chill air. "You must be feeling better if you're ready to tear into old Silas."

Mary wanted nothing more than to pass out and let the world go on without her for a while, but she wanted Silas away from her father more. "Is my dad going to be all right?"

"He appears to have a concussion and suffering from smoke inhalation, but his vitals are strong."

Not enough assurance for Mary.

Once they loaded her father into the ambulance and closed the door, Silas turned his attention to her and hurried across the snow-covered parking lot. "Mary Christmas, with the destruction of the store, the death of Mrs. Claus and your father being out of commission, will this mean the end of Christmas Towne store and year-round Christmas in North Pole?"

"Christmas Towne is smoke-damaged, not destroyed," she said.

"How could a man who has just lost his wife possibly come back to rescue Christmas this late in the season?"

Mary pulled the oxygen mask from her face. "Christmas will happen as always. My father will recover and so will the Christmas Towne store and year-round Christmas in North Pole."

"If you're tired of all the hassle of the store, I know someone who would like to buy it, as is, smoke-damaged and all." He waved toward a man standing on the fringes of the excitement. "Nelson, come over here, I want you to meet someone."

The EMT tried to shove Silas out of the way, but the older man wouldn't budge.

The man Silas had motioned over hurried forward and held out his hand to Mary. "Hi, name's Nelson Bailey. I just want to tell you how sad I am that your family was attacked so viciously."

"I don't care who you are." Mary refused to take the man's hand. "My father isn't selling and if the choice is up to me, neither will I."

Norton gave her a gentle smile and dropped his hand. "I fully understand how you feel. And I wouldn't dream of offering. It would be an insult to you, your father and everyone who cares about Christmas Towne and what you've built in this community through your work. It's an honor and a pleasure to make your acquaintance." He sketched a slight bow and backed away.

Silas's face puckered into a distressed frown that almost made Mary laugh. "But I thought you wanted to buy Christmas Towne." He turned to Mary. "Mary, this would be best for you and your father. Sell the store. If not to Nelson, then to me. I'll pay you top dollar."

Mary held out her hand. "Give me the microphone, Silas. I have something to say to the people of Alaska."

Silas hesitated.

"Give it," Mary demanded, a cough racking her lungs.

The older man handed her the microphone.

Mary waved the cameraman closer. "For the record, Santa will be fine, he isn't selling Christmas Towne, Operation Santa will go according to schedule and Christmas will happen as it does every year. Merry Christmas, everyone." Then she forced a smile. Once the cameraman lowered the camera, Mary threw the microphone as hard as she could. It landed with a soft whoosh in a snowdrift. A loud round of applause rose from the people gathered around to witness the spectacle.

Satisfied she'd set the record straight, Mary collapsed back against the stretcher and proceeded to cough so hard she thought she might hack up a lung. The EMT pulled the mask over her face and the coughing eased. As he wheeled Mary toward the second waiting ambulance, she had only one thought left in her exhausted brain. Where was Nick?

NICK STAGGERED THROUGH THE SHATTERED, gaping front door of Christmas Towne in time to hear Mary's speech and the applause of onlookers. When rescue workers pushed her stretcher toward a waiting ambulance, Nick gathered his last bit of energy and hurried toward her. He had to know she was all right.

Long, blond hair matted with soot lay tangled against the clean white sheets. Her dirty face stared up at him, perhaps the most beautiful sight he'd seen, ever.

"Move it, buddy." The EMT tried to push past Nick. "She needs medical attention."

"No, wait." Mary pulled the mask off her face and smiled up at Nick. "You made it."

"I had incentive." He lifted her hand in his and squeezed.

Her eyelids swooped down and he could swear that beneath the smudges of ash, her cheeks reddened. "And what was that?"

"What do you think?"

She sucked in a breath and let it out in a cough. "I'm too tired to guess, just tell me."

He lifted her smoke-smudged hand and pressed a kiss to her palm. "You, Mary Christmas. You were my incentive."

"Oh." Her eyes widened. "Does that mean you're going to ask me out on that real date you mentioned?"

"Absolutely."

"Could you hurry it up, then?" The rescue worker stamped his feet in the snow.

"Well, will you go out with me?" Nick stared down at Mary. "Even though I'm a man who has more secrets than he has hairs on his arms? I promise, I'm not married, nor have I ever been."

A slow smile spread across her face. "I guess I can risk it, just this once. For some foolish reason, I can't stop trusting you. Oh, and one other thing..." Her brows drew together.

Nick's heartbeat kicked up a notch. Would she tell him she only wanted the one date, then for him to get the hell out of her life? He'd do as she asked, but he'd rather she didn't ask him to do that.

"Someone needs to catch up with Gordon Thomas. He murdered Jasmine Claus and tried to kill Reuben Tyler when he was a soldier in his unit. Oh, and if you check the other man's body, you'll find Jasmine's bullet in it." Her voice cracked and she coughed, pulling the mask back over her face.

"Interesting. I'd like to hear the rest of the story."

"You will," she wheezed, "if you stick around."

While the ambulance driver opened the rear of the ambulance, Nick held Mary's hand, delaying her departure for just a moment longer. "I'll see you later."

"Promise?" She held tighter.

"Promise."

The door closed, Nick's last image of Mary was that of a medic inserting an IV into her arm.

If he didn't have more work to do, Nick would have ridden with her to the hospital. He straightened, sucking in a deep breath that sent him into a coughing fit.

"You need to be in that ambulance." Kat appeared

at his side, her jacket covered in snow as though she'd been in a scuffle.

"You missed the excitement." Nick coughed, glanced at her and back to the ambulance pulling away.

"Had a little of my own to contend with." She brushed at the snow clinging to her short dark hair. "Found our senator slipping through the streets on foot. When I stopped to ask him why he was on foot instead of in his car, he took off."

"And being the suspicious agent you are, you pursued." Nick laughed, the image of Kat, at least six inches shorter, if not more, than Gordon Thomas, chasing him across the snow on foot. "Did you catch him?"

"I always get my man, St. Claire."

"Where's he now?"

"In the back of an Alaska State Trooper's car on his way to the Fairbanks Jail."

"What did he charge him with?"

"Murder." Kat crossed her arms over her chest and stared at the scene around her. "I think I scared him a little. He spilled his guts on a number of issues."

"Just to you?"

"No, he was more than willing to share with the trooper, by the time I was through with him." She nodded toward the gingerbread cottage, scorched with smoke. "It really makes me mad when someone messes with a fellow Alaskan."

"Remind me not to make you mad." Nick's lips twisted to hide a smile. "I might be confessing to sins I haven't committed."

"Yeah. And don't forget Mary Christmas is a fellow Alaskan." Kat's brows rose in a challenging gesture.

Nick rocked back on his heels and let a long gap fill with the noise of firemen reeling in their hoses, the fire effectively quenched.

Crime scene investigators entered the house with cameras and rubber gloves.

Nick and Kat waited out of the way until firemen brought up not one but two stretchers, clean white sheets draped over the faces of the victims.

Kat's cell phone rang.

While Kat hung back to answer, Nick moved forward.

Trey Baskin pulled back the sheet and checked the identity of the first one. Even from the distance and beneath the layer of soot, Jasmine Claus's diminutive body could be easily identified.

With his special investigator badge that SOS had designed for just such occasions back before they'd quit as a government agency, Nick was able to slip by the police personnel to join Trey.

"Hey, Nick. Glad you made it out of there. A few more minutes and you'd have been a goner." Trey nodded at the man lying on the stretcher, with a gunshot wound to the chest. "I haven't a clue who this guy is."

"Call in the FBI. This man went by the code name Cobra."

"Cobra, huh?" Trey's eyes widened. "Cobra? The hit man for hire? Damn, I've read about him. What the hell's he doing in Alaska?"

Nick's mouth twisted into a wry smile. "I suspect the price was right."

"Holy crap. And he was after Santa? Isn't that taking hatred of the holiday a bit far?"

A state trooper called to Trey, leaving Nick standing in the snow. Medics loaded the two stretchers into the back of another ambulance, both bound for the state medical examiner's office.

As she closed the distance between them, Kat slid her cell phone into her pocket. "That was Royce, he wants to know when you're headed back to Texas."

Nick stared up into the sky. The clouds cleared, exposing a million stars like jewels adorning the heavens. "I was thinking of staying here for a while."

"A long while or for an extended weekend?"

"I'd like to play it by ear, but if things work out, I might ask for a transfer."

"Oh? I'm sure we could find room for another agent in the Alaska office of the SOS. Considering there are only two in it now."

"Sounds like a plan." Nick inhaled the crisp clean Alaskan air. "You know, this place grows on you."

Kat crossed her arms over her chest, a smile playing around her full lips. "The place or the people?"

Nick didn't answer. "If you could stick around to answer questions, I'd like to get to the hospital." He didn't wait for her response, instead he strode toward his rental car. He needed to get to the hospital and have the staff check him for smoke inhalation. If he hurried, he could catch Mary before they gave her a sleeping sedative.

Now that the danger had passed, he was looking forward to an extended vacation and the chance to get to know North Pole, Santa and Mary Christmas a little better. And not in that order.

He was willing to start believing in Santa for the first time in his life. Knowing how stubborn Mary was, Nick wondered if he'd have any trouble convincing her that he'd had a change of heart.

EPILOGUE

Nick adjusted the white beard over his chin and hefted the heavy velvet bag full of toys over his shoulder. The plane had landed and it was time for his big entrance. For a man who'd been shot at, stabbed a couple of times and nearly killed by smoke inhalation, he was more nervous about facing a bunch of little kids than any of that other life-or-death stuff.

A small hand curled around his. "You'll be fine. But maybe you should trade your cowboy hat for the right one."

Mary snatched his cowboy hat from his head and in its place plopped the red velour hat trimmed in white with the snowy white ball on the tip. She smiled up at him. Her red dress fringed with white faux fur made her cheeks glow a rosy red. Her long blond hair had been sprayed silver and piled neatly on top of her head. She looked the part of Mrs. Claus.

"I don't know about this." Nick didn't feel the part of Santa, having never believed in the man up until a couple of weeks ago.

Now with the real Santa still recovering from his injuries, being tended to by an ever-optimistic Ms. Reedy, Nick had been "volunteered" to play Santa on the annual Operation Santa flights.

"You promised Dad. If he had been up to it, don't you think he'd have done it?"

"He's had more practice," Nick grumbled.

Santa had more than just his injuries to recover from. Having temporarily lost his home to smoke damage, he'd had to come to grips with the loss of his new wife and the lies she'd lived thirty years ago. He'd read through Frank Richards' memoirs from start to end, his jolly face aging more with each page. But he'd pushed through anyway. When he'd finished, he'd set it aside and sank into deep depression.

If not for the town of North Pole coming to visit and their efforts to cheer him, he might never have recovered. But North Pole wanted their jolly Santa back and they wouldn't leave him alone until he returned.

"Now, don't be nervous," Mary said. "You'll do just fine as Santa. Remember, you're doing your part like everyone else."

Nick had been amazed at how everyone in North Pole pitched in to help Santa get back on his feet.

Chris moved in with Ms. Betty after Bob Feegan's death and they were getting along great, cleaning up and refurbishing the store and Santa's house. Lenn was managing on his own at the diner while Ms. Betty worked the store. Uncle Jimmy had even come in to take over the toy-making demonstrations, once the store reopened.

Mary straightened Nick's beard and smiled. "I bet Dad's champing at the bit, wishing he was here."

"That would make two of us." Nick chuckled. "I'll bet he's driving Uncle Jimmy nuts." He silently marveled at how he talked as if he fit into her wacky extended family, calling them by names like Uncle Jimmy and Dad, as if he belonged. They'd all welcomed him with open arms after he'd pulled Santa from the fire.

"I'm sure he's driving everyone nuts. I should never have given him that cell phone." She stopped fussing with his beard and hat and clutched the front of his suit, a playful grin lighting her face. "Has anyone ever told you that you look good enough to eat even stuffed in a red suit four times too big for you?"

Nick chuckled. "Never."

"Well, you do." Her smile faded and she stared up into his eyes. "Thanks for sticking around."

"I wouldn't have missed it." And he meant it.

Despite the herd of butterflies attacking his stomach, his pulse quickened. He never thought he'd admit it, and still might not, but he was excited to play the part of the jolly old elf. Kids lined up along the runway, waving and calling out for Santa.

The back of the C-130 airplane lowered at the same time Nick and Mary moved to the top of the ramp descending from the aircraft. A cheer rose into the crisp, frigid air.

Still standing in the shadows of the opening, Mary reached up and captured Nick's face in her hands. "I'm sure glad you stuck around."

"I'm glad you're glad, considering you're going to be seeing a lot more of me."

"You mean our first date was everything you dreamed of?" She pressed a kiss to his lips, savoring the feel of his body against hers, even through the extra stuffing they'd had to add to the Santa suit.

"No, I don't think our date was everything I'd dreamed of."

Her face fell. "No?"

"I have a lot more dreams where that came from."

"Oh yeah?" Her kiss deepened, their tongues intertwining until Nick thought he would explode. He set her away from him and adjusted the pillows around him.

Seeing her draped in a saggy red dress, her hair colored gray and lines painted onto her face, he could imagine her old and the thought didn't put a single dent in his attraction to her.

Mary's beauty lay in her ability to love her family and extended family. She cared about her community and the children of Alaska and children all around the world who still believed in Santa. And she believed in him, former orphan Nick St. Claire, despite being bound by duty to keep his secrets.

Nick knew from shortly after running into her in the airport that first night that he was a goner. It took him a while to understand why. He loved her, her father and all their quirks, and he loved being a part of Christmas. So, he'd missed this when he was growing up, he could help other children know the excitement and joy of Christmas and a visit from Santa Claus.

Mary hooked her arm through his and gave him a nudge toward the ramp and dozens of happy-faced children.

Life didn't get much better than this.

"You're on, Santa."

Continue reading more of Stealth Operations Specialists
Stealth Operations Specialists Series
Saint Nick (#1)
Rogue (#2)
Crusher (#3)

ELLE JAMES

Draco (#4)

ATHENS AFFAIR

BROTHERHOOD PROTECTORS
INTERNATIONAL BOOK #1

New York Times & USA Today
Bestselling Author

ELLE JAMES

CHAPTER 1

HIRING on with the Jordanian camera crew as their interpreter hadn't been all that difficult. With Jasmine Nassar's ability to speak Arabic in a Jordanian dialect and also speak American English fluently, she'd convinced the Jordanian camera crew she had the experience they needed to handle the job. However, the resume she'd created, listing all the films she'd worked on, had probably lent more weight to their decision.

Not that she'd actually worked on any movie sets. Her ability to "be" anything she needed to be, to fit into any character or role, was a talent she exploited whenever needed since she'd been "released" from the Israeli Sayeret Matkal three years earlier.

Her lip curled. Released was the term her commanding officer had used. *Forced out* of the special forces unit was closer to the truth. All because of an affair she'd had with an American while she'd been on holiday in Greece. Because of that week in Athens, her entire life had upended, throwing her into survival mode for herself and one other—her entire reason for being. The reason she was in Jordan about to steal the ancient copper scroll.

The Americans arrived on schedule for the afternoon's shoot at the Jordan Museum in Amman, Jordan. The beautiful film star Sadie McClain appeared with her entourage of makeup specialists, hairstylists, costume coordinators, and a heavy contingent of bodyguards, including her husband, former Navy SEAL Hank Patterson.

Sadie was in Jordan to film an action-adventure movie. All eyes would be on the beautiful blonde, giving Jasmine the distraction she'd need to achieve her goal.

Much like the movie heroine's role, Jasmine was there to retrieve a priceless antique. Only where Sadie was pretending to steal a third-century BC map, Jasmine was there to take the one and only copper scroll ever discovered. The piece dated back to the first century AD, and someone with more money than morals wanted it badly enough he'd engaged Jasmine to attain it for him.

Up until the point in her life when she'd been driven out of her military career, she'd played by the rules, following the ethical and moral codes demanded by her people and her place in the military. Since the day she'd been let go with a dishonorable discharge, she'd done whatever it took to survive.

She'd been a mercenary, bodyguard, private investigator and weapons instructor for civilians wanting to know how to use the guns they'd purchased illegally to protect themselves from terrorist factions like Hamas.

Somewhere along the way, she must have caught the eye of her current puppet master. He'd done his homework and discovered her Achilles heel, then taken that weakness in hand and used it to make her do whatever he wanted her to do.

And she'd do it because he had her by the balls. He held over her head the one thing that would make her do anything, even kill.

Her contact had timed her efforts with the filming of the latest Sadie McClain blockbuster. The museum was closed to the public that afternoon but was filled with actors, makeup artists, cameramen, directors and sound engineers.

The American director had insisted on an interpreter, though Jasmine could have told him it was redundant as nearly half the population of Jordan spoke English. Part of the deal they'd struck with the Jordanian government had been to employ a certain percentage of Jordanian citizens during the production of the movie. An interpreter was a minor concession to the staffing and wouldn't interfere with the rest of the film crew.

Plus, one inconsequential interpreter wouldn't be noticed or missed when she slipped out with the scroll in hand.

For the first hour, she moved around the museum with the film crew, reaffirming the exits, chokepoints and, of course, the location of her target. She'd visited the museum days before as a tourist, slowly strolling through, taking her time to examine everything about the building that she could access, inside and out.

The scroll was kept in a climate-controlled room away from the main hallways and exhibits. Since the facility was closed to the public, there wouldn't be anyone in the room.

While the crew set up for a scene with Sadie McClain, Jasmine slipped into the room to study the display cases once more.

The copper scroll had been cut into multiple pieces. Each piece had its own display case with a glass top, and each was locked. She'd brought a small file in the crossbody satchel she carried, along with a diamond-tipped glass cutter in the event the locks proved difficult. Cutting glass was the last resort. It would take too much time and could make too much noise if the glass shattered.

She'd honed her skills in picking locks and safe-cracking as a child, one of the many skills her mother had taught her. She'd insisted Jasmine be able to survive should anything ever happen to her parents.

Her mother had been orphaned as a small child in the streets of Athens. To survive, she'd learned to steal food and money, or valuables that could be sold for cash or traded for food.

From picking pockets and swiping food from stores and restaurants, she'd worked her way up to stealing jewelry, priceless antiques and works of art from the rich all around the Mediterranean. She'd used her beauty and ability to quickly learn new languages to her advantage, infiltrating elite societal circles to divest the rich and famous of some of their wealth.

She'd gone from a starving, barefoot child, wearing rags in the streets of Athens, to a beautiful young woman, wearing designer clothes and shoes and moving among the who's who of the elite.

Her life had been what she'd made of it until she'd met Jasmine's father, a sexy, Israeli Sayeret Matkal soldier, at an Israeli state dinner attended by wealthy politicians, businessmen and their wives. She'd just stolen a diamond bracelet from the Israeli prime minister's wife.

The special forces soldier outfitted in his formal uniform had caught her with the diamond bracelet in her pocket and made her give it back as if the woman had dropped it accidentally.

Rather than turn her in for the theft, he'd kept her

close throughout the evening, dancing with her and pretending she was just another guest.

Her mother had fallen for the handsome soldier and agreed to meet him the next day for coffee. Less than a month later, they'd married.

For love, her mother had walked away from her life as a thief to be a wife and mother. But she'd never forgotten the hard lessons she'd learned on the streets. She'd insisted her daughter learn skills that could mean the difference between independence and dying of starvation or being reliant on someone who didn't give a damn about her health or happiness.

Her mother had taught her what school hadn't, from languages, dialects and staying abreast of the news to learning skills like picking locks, safe cracking, picking pockets and hacking into databases for information. She'd learned skills most parents didn't teach their children or warned their children to avoid.

Jasmine had earned her physical capabilities from her father. As an only child, she'd been the son her father never had. As an elite Sayeret Matkal, her father had kept his body in top condition. Jasmine had worked out at home with him and matched his running pace, determined to keep up with the father she loved so fiercely.

He'd taught her how to use a variety of weapons and the art of defending herself when she had no weapons at all. Because of her dedication to conditioning, her hand-to-hand combat skills and her ability to speak multiple languages, when she'd joined the Israeli military, she'd been accepted into Sayeret Matkal training soon after.

After the Athens affair and her subsequent release from the elite forces, she'd continued her training.

Now, due to circumstances out of her immediate control, she was on the verge of stealing from a museum the priceless copper scroll the Jordanians were so proud of.

Her jaw hardened. If she had to steal every last item in the museum, she would—anything to get Eli back alive.

She pulled the file from her satchel, glanced toward the room's entrance and then bent to stick the file into the little keyed lock. She fiddled with the lock until she tripped the mechanism, and the lock clicked open.

Jasmine tested the case top by lifting it several inches and then easing it back down. One down, several more to go. She'd work them a few at a time. When she had all the locks disengaged, she'd take the scroll and walk out of the museum or leave with the Jordanian film crew.

She cringed at the thought of waiting for the crew to head home. They could be there well into the night, filming take after take until they perfected the sequences.

No, she'd head out as soon as she could. She had a deadline she would not miss—could not miss—if she wanted to see Eli again.

Jasmine jimmied the locks on a few more of the displays and then returned to where the crew was staging the next scene with Sadie McClain.

In the shadow of a statue, one of Sadie's bodyguards shifted, his eyes narrowing. He wore a baseball cap, making it difficult to see his face.

Something about the way he held himself, the line of his jaw and the dark stubble on his chin struck a chord of memory in Jasmine. A shiver of awareness washed over her. She hurried past him without making eye contact.

When she looked back, the space where he'd been standing was empty.

Jasmine shook off a feeling of déjà vu and stood near the Jordanian camera crew, interpreting when needed but basically remaining quiet and out of the way.

With the preparations for the big scene complete, the camera crews stood ready for the director to shout *action*.

All other personnel were to move out of the line of sight of the cameras. This gave Jasmine the opportunity to slip back into the room with the copper scroll. When she heard the director shout, *"Action,"* Jasmine went to work quickly and efficiently, lifting the tops off the glass cases one at a time, wrapping each piece of the copper scroll in a soft swatch of fabric she'd brought in her satchel, handling them carefully so as not to break the fragile copper.

Jasmine placed each piece inside a box she'd designed specifically for transporting the delicate scroll. Once all the pieces were stored, she closed the box and slid it into her satchel.

Taking the extra time, she returned all the tops of the glass cases to their original positions so they wouldn't draw attention until a museum employee just happened to notice the cases were empty. That should buy her time to get the items out of the museum and out of Jordan before anyone became suspicious.

With her satchel tucked against her side, Jasmine hurried out of the room. At that moment, the director yelled, "Cut!" He motioned to the film crews and gave orders to the American and Jordanian cameramen.

Some of the Jordanians looked around for their interpreter.

Ready to get the hell out of the museum, Jasmine had no choice but to approach the cameramen and provide the necessary translation for the director. All the while, her hand rested on her satchel, anxiety mounting. The longer she stayed in the museum, the greater the chance of someone discovering the copper scroll was missing.

Short of racing out of the building and drawing

attention to herself, she remained, forcing a calm expression on her face when inside she was ready to scream. A life depended on her getting out of the museum and delivering the scroll—Eli's life.

Ace Hammerson—Hammer back in his Navy days—thought he recognized the interpreter as soon as she'd stepped through the museum doors with the Jordanian camera crew. The more he studied her, the more he was convinced it was her.

Jasmine.

The woman with whom he'd spent an amazing week in Athens. A week he could never forget.

Had it really been four years?

Granted, she looked different from the last time he'd seen her. She'd changed. Her dark hair peeked out from beneath the black scarf she wore over her head and draped around her shoulders. Her curves were hidden beneath a long black tunic and black trousers. Her face was a little thinner, but those full, rosy lips and her eyes gave her away. There was no mistaking the moss green irises that had captivated him from the first time he'd met her at an outdoor café in the Monastiraki district of Athens.

He'd come to Antica Café on a recommendation from a buddy who'd been there a year earlier. The place had been packed, with no empty tables left. Tired and hungry after the twenty-hour journey from San Diego to Athens, he'd just wanted to eat, find his hotel and crash.

Rather than look for a less crowded café, he'd looked for an empty seat. A beautiful woman sat in a far corner, a book in her hand, enjoying a cup of expresso. Ace had approached, hoping she wouldn't blow him off, and asked if she spoke English.

She'd looked up at him with those amazing green eyes and smiled. In that moment, he'd felt a stirring combination of lust, longing and... strangely...homecoming wash over him. It could have been exhaustion, but more than hunger made him want to join this woman at her table.

She spoke English with a charming accent he couldn't place as either Greek or Arabic. When he'd asked if he could share her table, she'd tilted her head and stared at him with slightly narrowed eyes before finally agreeing with a relaxed smile.

That had been the beginning of the most incredible week of his life. His only regret was that he'd had to go back to work after that week. Before he'd had time to look her up, based on the phone number she'd given him, he'd deployed for several months to Afghanistan, where the mission had been so secret, they'd gone incommunicado to avoid any leaks.

By the time he'd returned to his home base, her number had been disconnected.

He hadn't known where to begin looking for her. In all their conversations, she'd barely revealed much about her life other than both her parents were dead, having been killed in a Hamas strike in Israel.

Because of her reference to her parents being killed in a Hamas strike, he'd assumed she was from Israel. She'd talked about her mother having been from Greece and her father from Israel. Like him, her father had been on vacation in Athens when he'd met her.

Ace had searched for her online, hoping to find out something about her whereabouts, but failed miserably. On his next vacation, he'd gone back to Greece, to the same restaurant where they'd met, hoping by some strange coincidence he'd find her there. He'd walked the same paths they'd walked through the city, looking for her. He'd stayed in the same hotel where they'd stayed, even insisting on the same room.

She hadn't been there. He'd gone to Tel Aviv and talked with some acquaintances he'd met during joint training exercises with the Israeli military. They hadn't heard of her.

As many people as there were in Israel, Ace hadn't expected to find her just by asking around. But he'd hoped that the same magic that had brought them together the first time would help him find her again. After a year, he'd admitted defeat and tried to forget her.

That had never happened. Every woman he'd dated after Jasmine had never sparked in him the fire and desire he'd felt with the woman he'd met in Athens.

Now, here he was, freshly out of the military, working with Hank Patterson and his team of Brotherhood Protectors in Amman, Jordan. Nowhere near Athens and four years after that fated affair, she walked back into his life.

New to the Brotherhood Protectors, Ace had agreed to accompany Hank and members of his team to Jordan to provide security for the film crew and actors who were friends of Hank's wife, Sadie McClain, on her latest movie set. He'd be an extra, there to observe one of the team's assignments.

They didn't always provide security for film crews, but since significant unrest existed in the countries surrounding the relatively stable Jordan, the film producers and studio had budgeted for a staff of security specialists.

Hank had worked with the studio and cut them a deal to ensure his people provided security for his wife and the crew there to make movie magic. Brotherhood Protectors were the most qualified to provide the safety net they might need if fighting spilled over the borders from countries surrounding Jordan.

Though he'd been excited and curious about the mechanics of making a movie, Ace's attention had shifted the moment Jasmine entered the museum.

His gaze followed her as she moved among the Jordanian film crew, standing between Americans and Jordanians, interpreting instructions when needed.

As the camera crew set up, Jasmine left them to wander around the museum, looking at ancient artifacts on display. At one point, she disappeared into a side room and remained gone for several minutes.

Ace started to follow when Hank approached him. "It's amazing, isn't it?"

Ace nodded. "Yes, sir."

Hank grinned. "I never imagined the amount of people it takes to produce a film until I accompanied Sadie on set for the first time."

Though Ace would rather focus his attention on Jasmine's movements, he gave his new boss all his attention. "I never realized there was so much involved."

"Right? It takes an incredible amount of coordination to set up a gig like this, from securing a location to getting permission, in this case, from the government to film here, to transporting all the equipment. Not to mention hiring people to do all aspects, including lighting, sound, video, makeup and costumes."

Ace's gaze remained on the door through which Jasmine had disappeared. "And that's just the filming," he commented, mentally counting the seconds Jasmine was out of his sight.

Then, she emerged from the room and rejoined her camera crew.

Ace let go of the breath he'd been holding.

Hank continued the conversation Ace had lost track of. "After the filming, there's the editing, music, marketing and more." The former Navy SEAL shook his head, his lips forming a wry smile. "I have so much more respect for all those names that scroll across the screen in the movie theater when they show the credits." He chuckled. "I always wondered, and now I know, what a key grip is."

Jasmine worked with the cameramen once more, then stepped back into the shadows.

Once the cameramen were in place, the lighting guy gave a thumbs-up. The director nodded, spoke with Sadie and then stepped back.

"They're about to start filming," Hank said.

When the director raised a hand, everyone grew quiet.

The director looked around at the placement of the cameras, Sadie and the lighting, then nodded.

Ace felt as though everyone took a collective breath, waiting for it...

"Action!" the director called out.

Ace's attention was divided between Jasmine, the actors, the cameramen and the supporting staff.

The beautiful, blond actress, Sadie McClain, did not command his attention like Jasmine.

Sure, Sadie was gorgeous, dressed in khaki slacks that hugged her hips, boots up to her knees and a flowing white blouse tucked into the narrow waistband of her trousers.

Her mane of golden hair had been styled into a natural wind-swept look with loose waves falling to her shoulders. She worked her way through the museum corridor, pretending to be a patron until she arrived at a golden statue encased in a glass box.

As Sadie studied the statue, her character assessing her chances of stealing it, Jasmine slipped out of the main museum corridor into the side room again.

What was she doing in there?

Ace wanted to follow her, but to do so, he'd have to pick his way through the camera crews and lighting people. He didn't want to get in the way while the cameras were rolling. God forbid he should trip over a cable, make a noise or cast a shadow and make them have to start all over again.

So, he stood as still as a rock, all his attention on that room, counting the seconds until Jasmine came out or the director called, "Cut!"

Finally, Jasmine emerged from the room.

At the same time, the director yelled, "Cut!"

The crossbody satchel she'd worn pushed behind her now rested against the front of her hip; her hand balanced on it. Her head turned toward the museum entrance and back to the organized chaos of camera crews shifting positions and responding to the director's suggestions. An American cameraman approached the Jordanian crew and spoke in English.

Members of the Jordanian camera crew frowned, looking lost. One of them spotted Jasmine and waved her over.

Jasmine's brow furrowed. Her gaze darted toward the museum entrance once more before she strode across the floor to join the cameramen. She listened to the American cameraman and translated what he was saying for the Jordanians, who, in turn, grinned, nodded, and went to work adjusting angles.

Jasmine stepped back into the shadows.

Ace nodded to Hank. "Excuse me. I want to check on something."

Hank's eyes narrowed as his gaze swept through the people milling about. "Anything to be concerned about?"

Was there anything to be concerned about? Ace's gut told him something was off, but he didn't see a need to alarm Hank until he had a better idea of what. "No, I just want to look at some of the displays."

"Are you a history buff?" Hank asked.

"A little. I'm always amazed at artifacts that were created centuries much earlier than our country's inception."

Hank nodded. "Yeah, some of the items in this museum date back hundreds of years before Christ."

He gave Ace a chin lift. "Explore while you can. It looks like they're getting ready for another take."

His gaze remained on Jasmine as Ace strode across the smooth stone floors to the room Jasmine had visited twice in less than an hour.

The room was climate-controlled, with soft lighting and several display cases positioned at its center. At a brief glance, nothing appeared out of place, but as Ace moved closer to the display cases, he frowned. They appeared...

Empty.

His pulse leaped as he read the information plaque beside the row of cases.

COPPER SCROLL. 1ST CENTURY AD.

He circled the cases and found that they all had keyed locks. He didn't dare lift the tops off the cases. If he did, he'd leave his fingerprints all over the glass and possibly be accused of stealing what had been inside.

His stomach knotted. Jasmine had been in here. Had she come to steal the copper scroll? Did she have it stashed in that satchel she'd carried around all afternoon?

Ace spun on his heels and left the room. His gaze went to the last place he'd seen Jasmine. She wasn't there.

His pulse slammed into hyperdrive as he scanned the vast corridor where the film crew worked.

She was nowhere to be seen.

Ace strode toward the museum's entrance. As he neared the massive doors, someone opened the door and slipped through it.

That someone was Jasmine.

What the hell was she up to? If she'd stolen the scroll, he had to get it back. If he didn't, the museum would hold Hank's team responsible for the theft, especially considering they were the security team.

The copper scroll was a national treasure. If he didn't get it back, it could cause an international incident as well as delay film production.

Ace slipped out of the museum and paused to locate the thief.

Dark hair flashed as Jasmine rounded the corner of a building across the street from the museum.

Ace had to wait for a delivery truck to pass in front of him before he could cross the road. As he waited, two large men dressed in black entered the side street, heading in the same direction as Jasmine.

Once the delivery truck passed, Ace crossed the street and broke into a jog, hurrying toward the street Jasmine had turned onto.

As Ace reached the corner of the building, he heard a woman shout, "No!"

He turned onto the street.

A block away, the two men in black had Jasmine by her arms. She fought like a wildcat, kicking, twisting, and struggling while holding onto the satchel looped over her neck and shoulder. One man ripped the scarf from her head and reached for the satchel's strap.

"Hey!" Ace yelled, racing toward the men.

Jasmine used the distraction to twist and kick the man on her right in the groin. When he doubled over, she brought her knee up, slamming it into his face.

The injured man released her arm.

Jasmine turned to the other man, but not soon enough. He backhanded her on the side of her face hard enough to send her flying.

As she fell backward, the man grabbed the satchel and yanked, pulling it over her head as she fell hard against the wall of a building.

Clutching the satchel like a football, the man ran. His partner staggered to his feet and followed.

Ace would have gone after them but was more concerned about Jasmine.

The men ran to the end of the street. A car pulled up, they dove in, and, in seconds, they were gone.

Jasmine lay against the wall, her eyes closed, a red mark on her cheek where the man had hit her.

Anger burned in Ace's gut. He wanted to go after the men and beat the shit out of them. But he couldn't leave this injured woman lying in the street.

He knelt beside her and touched her shoulder. "Jasmine."

Jasmine moaned, blinked her eyes open and stared up into his face, her brow furrowing. "Ace?

What—" She glanced around, her frown deepening. "Where am I?" She met his gaze again. "Is it really you?"

His lips turned up on the corners. "Yes, it's me. You're in Jordan." His brow dipped. "You were attacked."

She pinched the bridge of her nose. "What happened?"

"Two men attacked you," he said.

"Two men..." She shook her head slowly. "Jordan..." Then her eyes widened, and she looked around frantically. "My satchel! Where is my satchel?"

"The men who hurt you took it."

She struggled to get to her feet. "Where did they go? I have to get it back." As she stood, she swayed.

Ace slipped an arm around her narrow waist. "They're gone."

"No!" She raked a hand through her hair. "I need that satchel." Jasmine pushed away from Ace and started running back the way they'd come, then stopped and looked over her shoulder. "Which way did they go?"

He tipped his head in the direction the men had gone.

When Jasmine turned in that direction, Ace stepped in front of her and gripped her arms. "They're gone. You won't catch up to them now."

"Why didn't you stop them? They stole my satchel!" She tried to shake off his grip on her arms.

His lips pressed together, and his grip tightened. "What was in the satchel, Jasmine?"

"Something important. I have to get it back. Please, let go of me."

"Was the copper scroll in your bag?" he asked quietly so only she could hear his words.

Her gaze locked with his. For a moment, she hesitated, as if deciding whether or not to trust him. Then she nodded. "I had to take it. If I don't get it back, someone I care about will die."

Thank you for reading SAINT NICK. If you enjoyed reading the first chapter of ATHENS AFFAIR please click HERE to read the rest of the book and get all the books in the ***Brotherhood Protectors International Series***

Athens Affair (#1)
Belgian Betrayal (#2)
Croatia Collateral (#3)
Dublin Debacle (#4)
Edinburgh Escape (#5)
France Face-Off (#6)

ABOUT THE AUTHOR

ELLE JAMES also writing as MYLA JACKSON is a *New York Times* and *USA Today* Bestselling author of books including cowboys, intrigues and paranormal adventures that keep her readers on the edges of their seats. When she's not at her computer, she's traveling, snow skiing, boating, or riding her ATV, dreaming up new stories. Learn more about Elle James at www.ellejames.com

Website | Facebook | Twitter | GoodReads | Newsletter | BookBub | Amazon

Or visit her alter ego Myla Jackson at
mylajackson.com
Website | Facebook | Twitter | Newsletter

Follow Me!
www.ellejames.com
ellejamesauthor@gmail.com

ALSO BY ELLE JAMES

Stealth Operations Specialists Series

Saint Nick (#1)

Rogue (#2)

Crusher (#3)

Draco (#4)

A Killer Series

Chilled (#1)

Scorched (#2)

Erased (#3)

Brotherhood Protectors International

Athens Affair (#1)

Belgian Betrayal (#2)

Croatia Collateral (#3)

Dublin Debacle (#4)

Edinburgh Escape (#5)

France Face-Off (#6)

Brotherhood Protectors Hawaii

Kalea's Hero (#1)

Leilani's Hero (#2)

Kiana's Hero (#3)

Casey's Hero (#4)

Maliea's Hero (#5)

Emi's Hero (#6)

Sachie's Hero (#7)

Kimo's Hero (#8)

Alana's Hero (#9)

Bayou Brotherhood Protectors

Remy (#1)

Gerard (#2)

Lucas (#3)

Beau (#4)

Rafael (#5)

Valentin (#6)

Landry (#7)

Simon (#8)

Maurice (#9)

Jacques (#10)

Everglades Overwatch Series
coauthored with Jen Talty

Secrets in Calusa Cove

Pirates in Calusa Cove

Murder in Calusa Cove

Betrayal in Calusa Cove

Raven's Cliff Series
with Kris Norris

Raven's Watch (#1)

Raven's Claw (#2)

Raven's Nest (#3)

Raven's Curse (#4)

Brotherhood Protectors Yellowstone

Saving Kyla (#1)

Saving Chelsea (#2)

Saving Amanda (#3)

Saving Liliana (#4)

Saving Breely (#5)

Saving Savvie (#6)

Saving Jenna (#7)

Saving Peyton (#8)

Saving Londyn (#9)

Brotherhood Protectors Colorado

SEAL Salvation (#1)

Rocky Mountain Rescue (#2)

Ranger Redemption (#3)

Tactical Takeover (#4)

Colorado Conspiracy (#5)

Rocky Mountain Madness (#6)

Free Fall (#7)

Colorado Cold Case (#8)

Fool's Folly (#9)

Colorado Free Rein (#10)

Rocky Mountain Venom (#11)

High Country Hero (#12)

Brotherhood Protectors

Montana SEAL (#1)

Bride Protector SEAL (#2)

Montana D-Force (#3)

Cowboy D-Force (#4)

Montana Ranger (#5)

Montana Dog Soldier (#6)

Montana SEAL Daddy (#7)

Montana Ranger's Wedding Vow (#8)

Montana SEAL Undercover Daddy (#9)

Cape Cod SEAL Rescue (#10)

Montana SEAL Friendly Fire (#11)

Montana SEAL's Mail-Order Bride (#12)

SEAL Justice (#13)

Ranger Creed (#14)

Delta Force Rescue (#15)

Dog Days of Christmas (#16)

Montana Rescue (#17)

Montana Ranger Returns (#18)

Brotherhood Protectors Boxed Set 1

Brotherhood Protectors Boxed Set 2

Brotherhood Protectors Boxed Set 3

Brotherhood Protectors Boxed Set 4

Brotherhood Protectors Boxed Set 5

Brotherhood Protectors Boxed Set 6

Iron Horse Legacy

Soldier's Duty (#1)

Ranger's Baby (#2)

Marine's Promise (#3)

SEAL's Vow (#4)

Warrior's Resolve (#5)

Drake (#6)

Grimm (#7)

Murdock (#8)

Utah (#9)

Judge (#10)

Delta Force Strong

Ivy's Delta (Delta Force 3 Crossover)

Breaking Silence (#1)

Breaking Rules (#2)

Breaking Away (#3)

Breaking Free (#4)

Breaking Hearts (#5)

Breaking Ties (#6)

Breaking Point (#7)

Breaking Dawn (#8)

Breaking Promises (#9)

Hearts & Heroes Series

Wyatt's War (#1)

Mack's Witness (#2)

Ronin's Return (#3)

Sam's Surrender (#4)

Hellfire Series

Hellfire, Texas (#1)

Justice Burning (#2)

Smoldering Desire (#3)

Hellfire in High Heels (#4)

Playing With Fire (#5)

Up in Flames (#6)

Total Meltdown (#7)

Take No Prisoners Series

SEAL's Honor (#1)

SEAL'S Desire (#2)

SEAL's Embrace (#3)
SEAL's Obsession (#4)
SEAL's Proposal (#5)
SEAL's Seduction (#6)
SEAL'S Defiance (#7)
SEAL's Deception (#8)
SEAL's Deliverance (#9)
SEAL's Ultimate Challenge (#10)

Cajun Magic Mystery Series

Voodoo on the Bayou (#1)
Voodoo for Two (#2)
Deja Voodoo (#3)

Texas Billionaire Club

Tarzan & Janine (#1)
Something To Talk About (#2)
Who's Your Daddy (#3)
Love & War (#4)

Billionaire Online Dating Service

The Billionaire Husband Test (#1)
The Billionaire Cinderella Test (#2)
The Billionaire Bride Test (#3)
The Billionaire Daddy Test (#4)
The Billionaire Matchmaker Test (#5)

The Billionaire Glitch Date (#6)

The Outriders

Homicide at Whiskey Gulch (#1)

Hideout at Whiskey Gulch (#2)

Held Hostage at Whiskey Gulch (#3)

Setup at Whiskey Gulch (#4)

Missing Witness at Whiskey Gulch (#5)

Cowboy Justice at Whiskey Gulch (#6)

Boys Behaving Badly Anthologies

Rogues (#1)

Blue Collar (#2)

Pirates (#3)

Stranded (#4)

First Responder (#5)

Cowboys (#6)

Silver Soldiers (#7)

Secret Identities (#8)

Warrior's Conquest

Enslaved by the Viking Short Story

Conquests

Smokin' Hot Firemen

Protecting the Colton Bride

Protecting the Colton Bride & Colton's Cowboy Code

Heir to Murder

Secret Service Rescue

High Octane Heroes

Haunted

Engaged with the Boss

Cowboy Brigade

An Unexpected Clue

Under Suspicion, With Child

Texas-Size Secrets

Made in the USA
Columbia, SC
31 December 2025